CASUAL CRUELTIES

ALISON IRVING

BLOODHOUND
— BOOKS —

First published in 2023 by Bloodhound Books.

www.bloodhoundbooks.com

Print ISBN: 978-1-5040-8961-6

To Mum and Dad.

CHAPTER ONE

I woke the morning after my 28th wedding anniversary with the vaguest feeling of disquiet. After opening one eye, I recognised the shape of my husband James lying beside me, the sound of his somewhat laboured breathing seeping into my consciousness.

What is he doing there? I wondered uneasily. *Why isn't he in his own room as usual?*

Gradually I pieced together the memory of last night. A celebratory dinner out in Belfast and the inevitable outcome of too much alcohol.

I rolled onto my back as I mulled over the events that had led us to spending well over half our lives together. We met in first year at university, followed by a short engagement and a small wedding a few weeks after graduation, before the slow descent together into mid-life.

James was the clichéd tall, dark and handsome, standing well over six foot with black hair and striking blue eyes.

I have never felt pretty with my red hair, freckles and sticking out ears that I thankfully had pinned back when I was eight. There has always been a part of me that can't understand why someone as attractive as James would choose someone so ordinary as me.

I decided to get up and make myself a cup of coffee, so gingerly placed one foot after the other on the carpet, silently creeping out of the room, taking care to avoid the creaky floorboard by the door. One quick display of passion was enough; no need to celebrate all over again this morning.

While I waited for the kettle to boil, I perused our neat back garden, pondering again about the chances of talking James into buying a garden room, which would be perfect in the far corner. He refused to contemplate it, dismissing it as a waste of money. Two chaffinches swung on the bird feeder and a row of sparrows lined up on the fence patiently waiting their turn. The bird feeder had been a source of friction since I'd spotted a rat helping itself to the nuts in the spring. Despite that, James took great pleasure in the birds' antics, so it remained.

As much pleasure as I would get if he presented me with a bunch of flowers.

He used to buy me flowers for the smallest reason.

Now I didn't even get an orchid for our orchid anniversary.

After stirring milk into my instant coffee, I crept into my crafting room. As usual the room was in total chaos and with a sigh of pleasure, I closed the door and booted up my ancient laptop. Whereas James insisted I keep the rest of the house neat and tidy, my room was indicative of my mental state; messy, half-forgotten projects littering the tabletops and thick with dust.

No one else was allowed in except to offer me a cup of coffee. No one else wanted in because it resembled a bombsite. I'm pretty sure I'd once read that a messy room was a sign of a creative genius but I may be wrong. Anyway, once I shut the door I could either play *Candy Crush* in peace, make some pretty beaded jewellery to sell on Etsy or just listen to music that I chose. Normally James decided what was to be played throughout the house on the sound system.

I scrolled through the *Daily Mail Online* and heard noises from upstairs, meaning my peace was about to be shattered. Sure enough, after thumping about for a while and using the upstairs loo, he appeared at my door clad head to toe in Lycra. As well as becoming a twitcher, he had become a MAMIL. Middle-aged men in Lycra seem to be everywhere nowadays and they wear it irrespective of size or shape. I longed to have even half of their self-confidence.

'Missed you when I woke, Laura,' he said, sweeping his longish hair off his forehead. Although the black was now sprinkled with grey, he still had a full head of hair of which he was excessively proud, and a couple of years ago he had therefore decided to grow it longer. I much prefer the feel of a short back and sides.

'Sorry darling,' I lied smoothly. 'Going cycling?'

'Yes, the club wants to try out a new route over the Antrim Hills, maybe even up the coast as far as Cushendun. We could be away till around three.'

'Say hello to them all for me.' I smiled, thinking of the day stretching ahead of me. I could do anything I wanted without having anyone making demands.

'What's for dinner and what time is it at?'

'Beef and ale stew at around half past six'.

'Lovely, see you later.' He gave me a quick kiss on the cheek.

Once he had left, after coming in and out the front door half a dozen times as he remembered things he had forgotten, the sound of cleats click-clacking on the taupe-grey hall tiles, I left the mayhem of my crafting room and settled back on the charcoal sofa in our pristine living room.

I started watching YouTube videos and somehow ended up engrossed in *The Best Flash Mob Wedding Proposals* and *The Most Emotional Reunions Ever*. As I lay on the sofa still in my pyjamas at half past eleven on a Sunday morning, crying while watching American soldiers surprising their mothers, I wondered what was wrong with me. Half my precious day to myself had become a sob-fest.

Sunday was my favourite day of the week, the day when our only child Robbie, who was at university in Scotland, would ring for a chat. He was completely averse to FaceTime so apart from a quick text each evening to confirm he was alive, Sunday was the only day I got to speak to him.

He was in his final year. Three years since I felt my heart was ripped out of my body as we left him in halls and drove from Stirling to Cairnryan to get the boat home.

Three years I'd been pretending that I loved the new-found freedom of having only James and me to think about; the fridge never emptied of food by the time I got home from work, the wash basket in the bathroom not spilling over from his bedroom floordrobe being deposited into it in a tangled heap.

Apparently Gordon Ramsay, that tough sweary chef, had been so distraught when his son went to university that he wore his underpants. I'd never resorted to that but empathised greatly with the sentiment.

Sick of feeling maudlin, I turned my music up full blast and danced to OneRepublic's 'I Lived', my go-to song when my mood is low. Considering my dancing had once been described by James 'like Baby before Patrick Swayze's dance lessons,' I'm pretty self-conscious when I dance but now alone, I forgot my worries as I listened to the music and jumped about the living room. Out of breath but already less morose, I went for a shower.

Being Sunday, it was time for my HRT patch change and therefore time to loofah my poor skin to within an inch of its life. As much as I can credit HRT for keeping me saner, the horrible black residue the innocuous-looking patch leaves on my skin drives me mad. I'd tried the HRT gel but kept forgetting to apply it twice a day. At least the patch only needs changing twice a week.

I dried myself off, then critically examined myself in the

mirror. Not a pretty sight if truth be told. How can you feel attractive while your waistline is expanding, your chin is sprouting and your boobs are heading south? Hastily I dressed in a navy-and-white-striped top and jeans and immediately felt more positive about myself. Clothes definitely hide a multitude of middle-aged sins.

Downstairs I made another cup of coffee, cut a slice of shop-bought chocolate cake, resumed my position on the sofa and switched on the television.

My guilty pleasure when I've got the house to myself is watching re-runs of *Sex and the City*. Oh, how I love the fashion, the friendship, the second-hand excitement of watching those thirty-something women living their best lives. Living vicariously through their love affairs, city dwelling and designer dressing, I've watched it over and over again. From Carrie's selfishness, Samantha's pushing of the boundaries, Charlotte's desperate search for love to Miranda's really bad hair. As a fellow redhead it always frustrates me that Miranda dresses the worst, has a really dire haircut and before Steve, gets the most unattractive men.

'At least you've got an attractive man,' I tell myself. 'And a really good haircut.'

One thing I'd never appreciated before was that redheads don't go grey in the same way as brunettes. All though the Covid lockdowns when the hairdressers were shut and my friends were spraying their roots, wearing scarves or embracing the grey and going *au naturel*, I just had to deal with a longer bob. No grey roots. It took fifty years for me to realise being ginger has one advantage.

Of course, the disadvantage is that you spend all your time when it's sunny reapplying sun-cream, wearing long clothing and looking for the shade. On one trip to Barcelona with the Book Club girls, there's a photo of my four friends in strappy sun-tops and sandals, standing out in the midday sun with huge smiles. If you look really hard, I'm hiding in the shade of the building wearing a sunhat the size of a golfing umbrella. I always laugh it off saying you'd need to play *Where's Wally* to see me when it's sunny. If you laugh at yourself first, you give people less ammunition to hurt you.

Just as I watched Carrie demanding of sweet Aidan 'You have to forgive me' for cheating with Big, I caught sight of James cycling up the driveway.

Three o'clock already. With a sigh I switched off the television and watched as he dismounted. Taking a proper look outside, I noticed it was a truly beautiful autumn day with a clear blue sky and I'm sure there would be that crisp, smoky smell as neighbours raked up the leaves and made bonfires of them. From the sofa, I saw James stop to admire our Japanese Acer flaming red against the sky.

He really loves that tree.

CHAPTER TWO

B y the time James came indoors after washing, stroking and putting his bike away safely in the shed, I was already chopping vegetables and prepping dinner.

'Good ride?' I asked, as he appeared at the kitchen door.

'Yes, but I'm exhausted,' he replied, casually dropping his hat, gloves, damp jersey, water bottle, half-eaten flapjack and sunglasses on the table. 'I'm going to have a shower and then watch some television. I think I'll light the fire when I come down.'

He disappeared, leaving the detritus of his cycle on the kitchen table.

'I'll just clear that away, will I?' I muttered under my breath, instantly irritated with him. When my child went off to university it was like I got another one in his place.

The best way to relieve the annoyance I felt simply at his presence today was to listen to music, so I commanded Alexa to play eighties music as I furiously chopped and sliced. I'm not one of those cooks who looks in the cupboard and conjures up a delicious spread from scratch, I have to slavishly follow a recipe even if I've made it ten times before.

I may not be the best cook around but I enjoy trying new recipes and even have a file full of them that I've torn out of magazines. Although I do have a tendency to leave out some ingredients when I've no idea what they are. I mean, how often do you cook with xanthan gum, shelled edamame beans or enoki?

My cooking has significantly improved since the early days when I didn't think to check a chicken while it cooked, and it ended up burned to a crisp. Or the time I forgot to add broccoli to the tuna and broccoli bake.

Although I'm a reasonably good cook now, James is a glory chef, insisting on always cooking for guests and receiving great compliments. It's not uncommon for me to be told, 'You're so lucky being married to a man who can cook,' which agitates me enormously.

By the time the casserole was in the oven, I heard the crackling of the fire and the muted sounds of some sport or other being played on the television in the living room.

I had no interest in watching sport, so opted instead to wrap up warm and go for a walk before shouting that I'd be back in about half an hour and to please give the casserole a stir.

I pulled on my padded green coat and warm woolly hat before wandering towards the pond nestled within the small woodland at the edge of my village. The smoky smell of bonfires lingered in the air and I felt myself relax as I strolled past grazing sheep and listened to the birds chirp in the trees.

Sundays are the day I miss Robbie the most, maybe because Sundays were always family time with no work or school, a leisurely dinner and some easy television we all watched together. Sitting down on the wooden bench at the edge of the pond under my favourite tree, watching the russet, red and gold leaves drop onto the surface of the water, I inhaled deeply.

Then I tried once again to master mindfulness, except as ever after about ten seconds my mind wandered. The seat was uncomfortable, my nose was running and the baaing of the sheep in the field beside the pond was annoying.

Giving up, I fished my phone out of my pocket.

I had missed half a dozen messages from my friends and as always, found myself laughing at the silly chat. I've always been someone who needs friends as I quickly get bored of my own company and female friends are essential to my well-being. When we moved to Castlebrook village around fifteen years ago, I set up a book club in order to meet people. I'd invited two friendly mums from school and a couple of chatty neighbours. We started out as virtual strangers but now the five of us are a solid group that have come through all sorts together; cancer, bereavement, empty nests.

Over the years the Book Club got nicknamed the Wine Club and Robbie even likes to call us the Wino Club with a roll of his eyes. It's still a source of great hilarity that I brought a notebook with me to the first Book Club meeting so we could score the recommended book out of ten. I honestly can't remember the last book we read as a club, but I do remember the last weekend break we had together.

In November 2019, just before Covid struck, we had treated ourselves to a long weekend in an expensive spa in deepest County Waterford. The weather was gorgeous, the treatments luxurious and the food incredible. Thankfully it's not the kind of spa where all you get to drink is green smoothies, so we had a raucous two days lazing around and laughing at the fact that although it was acceptable to wear your dressing gown down to breakfast, we really didn't need to see hairy blokes wearing very little while we were eating.

I was really looking forward to our planned weekend away to London in the spring.

A short time later, I noticed it was already getting dark, so made my way back to the house. I let myself in through the back door before I slipped off my shoes and replaced them with my comfy slippers. As expected, the casserole had not been stirred since I went out. Crossly I wondered what it would be like to not have to make a proper dinner every day; to not be questioned daily as to what was for dinner; to have someone who offered to cook on some ordinary nights, instead of just when we were having friends over.

No point in dwelling on it, I thought, putting the potatoes on to boil. *He's not going to change now.*

We sat together at the kitchen table a little later and I surreptitiously watched my husband eating dinner while he watched *Countryfile*. I took in his lingering summer tan, his collar-length hair gently curling against his neck and his long slim fingers with precisely trimmed nails. I smiled at him, thinking there were worse ways to spend a Sunday evening.

'Are you looking forward to the dinner dance next Friday night?' I asked.

'Yes, it should be a good night,' he replied. 'We've not been back to the Melville Hotel since the last time, when Will made an eejit of himself stealing the microphone from the lead singer during 'American Pie'.'

We laughed together, remembering the night that had started so formally ending with the spontaneous stunt by my friend Claire's husband that nearly resulted in him being escorted from the building.

Then James said, 'Very nice, though it needed more seasoning,' as he pushed his plate away.

Mentally I rolled my eyes as James was always quick to criticise and slow to compliment. He looked at me sharply. Sometimes when I think something has been just inside my head, I realise too late that I've actually said or done it. Thankfully he got distracted by a riveting report from John Craven and the moment passed.

Once we had finished eating and the dishes were done, it was time to ring Robbie. He and his flatmates always do what they call Sunday Fun-day, when they pick a different country, cook themselves a meal and drink that country's beer. He's come a long way from first year when he sent me a photo of a banana sitting on the empty cardboard from a six-pack of beer and told me that was his Sunday dinner.

It's fair to say my heart was singing as he filled me in on the bones of his life in Stirling. Yes, he was still going to the gym regularly, yes he'd bought himself an Oodie as the weather was already freezing, and yes his flatmate was recovering well after he'd broken his collarbone playing football.

What I desperately wanted to say was, 'When will you be back for Christmas? Have you decided if you're going to look for graduate jobs in Northern Ireland? I love you. I miss you. I want you home.' But of course, I said none of that. It's a mother's role to only give advice when it's asked for, to ask a maximum of three questions per phone call and to pretend that daily life as a couple rather than a family is the best thing ever.

After our phone call James resumed his position in front of the fire, quickly falling asleep and I pottered about in the kitchen.

I'd done my degree in history followed by a PGCE but I found teaching was quite stressful. Although I felt passionately about my subject, I couldn't enthuse teenagers in the way a really great teacher can, so once Robbie was born James had encouraged me to be a stay-at-home mum. I'd had two miscarriages after we had our son and one of my greatest sorrows is that we couldn't have another child. I know that I'm overprotective, that I spend many unnecessary hours catastrophising myriad ways Robbie could come to harm, and if I could, I would have him living with me forever.

As he grew up and needed me less, I decided to become a classroom assistant and found my niche. I currently work in a large school in Belfast helping a teenager with ASD. Much less exacting than teaching, it gives structure to my week and a chance to mix with other people.

Since Covid, James, who is a journalist with a local paper, has been working from home which he adores and which I don't. To be honest I long for him to go back into the office so when I come in from work, I have some time to myself. Instead, the minute I walk through the door I'm greeted with, 'Why are you late tonight?' Or 'What's for dinner and what time's it at?' One of these days I'm going to shout back, 'Takeaway and half past seven!' to shake things up a bit.

I made sandwiches for tomorrow's lunch, before going through into the living room. The fire was nearly out, just wisps of smoke left and no flame. Gritting my teeth with frustration, I glared at the slumbering form of my husband. Although not a snorer, he had issues with his sinuses and had a tendency to snort and sniff repeatedly, even when sleeping. It's one of those little peeves that gets on my nerves nowadays.

It was only a quarter to eight, too early to go to bed, but if I turned on the television then I'd no doubt be forced to watch something I didn't want to. I could always go into the snug, the small sitting room off the kitchen, but then I'd get accused of ignoring him.

Instead, I chose to run myself a bath, so I went upstairs and poured two caps of my favourite bubble bath into the tub. I read the back of the bottle while waiting for the bath to fill:

Softening. Soothing. Calming. De-stress in a bottle.

Good, as it was either that or a large glass of Pinot Gris. I vaguely remembered the time when an evening in front of the fire snuggled together on the sofa, and watching a film we had chosen, was the routine not the exception.

When had spending time together gone from being essential to a chore? When did all the small aggravations become insurmountable?

Afraid of the answer, I lit a couple of candles, played some soothing music and soaked in the bath while reading my latest psychological thriller.

There's nothing quite like a good book to stop the mind dwelling on questions you didn't really want to know the answer to.

CHAPTER THREE

The following Friday night was the long-awaited dinner dance.

After being diagnosed with breast cancer in her forties, my friend Annie had given up her job in financial services for a big firm, saying her health was not worth the stress. So now she works for much less money and much greater job satisfaction for a cancer charity.

Her charity held an annual dinner dance to raise funds, and tonight would be the first one post-Covid. I was practically fizzing with the anticipation of getting dressed up, and had even booked to get my hair and make-up done after work.

I've been going to the same hairdresser for about ten years as she knows exactly how to cut my rather thin hair to hide my forehead, which is so big Robbie once told me I had a five-head not a forehead.

Oh, how he and his father laughed, and of course I laughed too. An eight-year-old really didn't have a clue how self-conscious I was about it, but my husband should have known better.

I'm slightly obsessed about it now and before anyone takes a photo of me, I'll always shout out, 'How's my fringe?' I've lost count of the number of photos I've deleted because my fringe is misbehaving. Probably every woman has an Achilles heel and maybe all around the world there are women shouting out, 'How's my double chin?' or 'How's my nose?' before deleting a hundred photos until they are happy with one.

I'd bought a lovely black dress in the Coast sale during lockdown. Like the rest of the world, I'd resorted to online shopping then in the hope we would all socialise together again sometime. I'm also proud to say I'd never resorted to baking banana bread or doing Joe Wicks workouts during the lockdowns either. I took the moral high ground and unlike everyone else, decided against exercise during lockdown because I'm a leader not a follower. Actually, I'm too lazy. And yes, I did watch his workouts, usually while eating another biscuit. Just to see what all the hype was about.

By the time I got home I felt good about myself. It's amazing how the thrill of getting dressed up and going out with friends can put a spring in your step.

My beautiful dress was hanging on the wardrobe door and I admired it as I changed into my heavy-duty shapewear. The dress had a lace bodice and a long, pleated skirt with a diamanté brooch at the front. The genius of it was that it was empire line so it hid the fact I was a stone heavier than when I bought it. I slipped it over my head just as James called up the stairs that it was time to go over to Vicky and Tom's for pre-dinner drinks.

I stepped out onto the landing and glided down the stairs, taking care not to step on the hem of my dress with my stilettos. I'd contemplated wearing my trainers as they are now acceptable with anything, but decided that for once, it would be glamour over comfort.

James stood at the bottom, impatiently holding my coat.

I hesitated momentarily before I asked, 'Do I look all right?'

'Your not-so-little black dress looks fine,' he replied as he opened the door and disappeared outside.

My insides twisted with disappointment. I know I have put on weight, and I know it's not all menopause-related either, but if anyone is supposed to have your back through life's ups and downs, it's your husband of twenty-eight years.

I blinked frantically to hold back easy tears, grateful it was dark as we silently crossed the street to our friends' house. I wanted to go back home, take off my dress, put on my jeans and sit in front of the television eating chocolate.

As we reached Vicky and Tom's door, we were joined by Kate and David who live beside them.

'Wow, who is that stunner?' said David, leaning forward to kiss my cheek.

'Love your dress, Laura,' said Kate, who looked gorgeous in a slinky cobalt-blue dress and possibly the highest silver sandals I'd ever seen. 'It really suits you.'

Appreciative of my kind friends' compliments, my smile was genuine.

We went through to Vicky and Tom's kitchen and I saw that Annie and Matt had already arrived; leaving just Claire and Will. As we hugged, complimenting each other on our dresses and how dapper the men looked in their dinner suits, I could barely look at James I was still so hurt. Then I heard him remark to all my friends on how lovely they looked, and my hurt churned within me. I had been envisioning this night for many months, so I decided I would not let him ruin it for me. Instead, I straightened my shoulders and drew myself up to my full five foot nine inches plus two-inch heels.

Claire and Will soon arrived, and as we stood around chatting, I gradually relaxed.

These were my friends, the girls I am closest to, the ones I can tell anything to without judgement. We had no secrets.

Except I couldn't tell them I wasn't sure I liked my husband very much anymore.

Vicky's oldest daughter Alex had designated herself as official photographer and with lots of laughing and jostling for position, we posed for a group photo in their conservatory. They had decorated it with fairy lights and balloons, adding to the party atmosphere.

James edged over to me and I heard a hushed, 'You do look nice you know,' in my ear. I gave his hand a squeeze and he smiled back at me. Despite how upset he had made me feel a short time ago, I felt a little better.

We all climbed into our minibus and the drive through Belfast to the Melville Hotel passed in no time. Arriving at the drinks reception, the men relieved us of our coats, and we took our champagne to the ladies' room.

I observed my friends in the mirror as I reapplied my lipstick. Annie with her bouncing chestnut curls was wearing an emerald-green one-shoulder dress and was pouting for a selfie with petite and curvy Kate. Vicky with her chocolate-brown eyes and long brunette hair turned heads wherever she went, although she appeared to be completely oblivious. She, like Claire, was wearing red and I could tell by the furtive glances Claire was giving her that she was kicking herself for not sussing out what colour of dresses we had chosen beforehand.

The trouble with being friends with someone who is a total knockout is that you have to give yourself a serious talking to or else you can have a severe case of the green-eyed monster.

'Come on, team!' Vicky ushered us out of the bathroom and towards a pale-pink balloon arch. 'Let's get a Book Club photo.' She strode over to the bar and commanded her husband Tom to be our photographer.

'How's my fringe?' I called out, as Claire simultaneously shouted out 'How's my nose?' and Vicky blurted out, 'I have to stand at the end so I don't look like a giant in the middle.'

We burst into giggles as we posed for our photos. Tom refused to let us scrutinise the photos, said we all looked amazing and forwarded a couple to the WhatsApp group. Of course, once we saw them, we spent ten minutes criticising ourselves and complimenting each other.

'For goodness' sake, I look like I have one eye bigger than the other,' moaned Annie.

'When did my stomach start sticking out further than my boobs?' asked Kate, sucking herself in.

'Wish I hadn't worn red like Mrs Northern Ireland,' said Claire. 'I look like her shorter, fatter sister.'

Vicky had let it slip at the end of a Book Club evening that she'd once won a beauty contest as a teenager. She tried to laugh it off that it was 'Miss Glenshane Pass' or something, but it was one beauty contest more than the rest of us had won. As well as being gorgeous, she was a GP and had won multiple triathlons before having her daughters. It was just as well that when she sang, she sounded like a cat being strangled and was the nicest person you could meet, or I would have felt obliged to hate her.

We heard a call for all guests to please find their seats and we paired up with our husbands to go into the function room. Our table was right beside the dance floor with a prime view of the band.

'Let's have a toast to health and friendship,' said Matt, taking Annie's hand.

We dutifully raised our glasses and recited, 'To health and friendship.'

'And to our beautiful wives,' James suggested obsequiously.

He can be a complete prat at times.

After the meal, the dancing started and it didn't take long for the dance floor to fill up. When the band played Abba's 'Dancing Queen' even the men joined us. One of the great things about middle age is that you gradually stop caring what other people think about you. I mean, to most of the population we aren't worth a second glance anyway, so I danced unselfconsciously for once.

The night flew by quickly, filled with laughter and dancing.

By midnight my feet were pinching, my shapewear was chafing and my eyes were closing. I was ready to go home. The table around me was empty and although some diehards were still on the dance floor, most of the men had congregated around the bar.

I realised that I hadn't seen Kate for a while and wondered where she was. I went in search of her and met her as she exited the ladies' loos. She waved when she saw me, staggering a little in her high heels. She had lipstick smeared on her teeth and her eyes looked a little glazed.

'You are the best friend ever. I don't know what I'd do without you,' she slurred as she sat down heavily on the floor. Her blue dress rode up above her knees as she laboriously worked to open the buckle of each sandal. Eventually she gave up on the left one before swinging the other around a bit wildly by the strap. I was totally at a loss what to do. She was clearly more than just a bit worse for wear, she was completely stocious.

I couldn't understand it as she'd had no more to drink than the rest of us. Then I took a closer look at her right leg and there on her thigh was a hip flask secured with a garter. I'd heard stories of the girls at school formals sneaking hip flasks under their dresses but why on earth would my friend feel the need to? It's not like she would be the only one drinking alcohol here and no one would judge her for having one glass too many on a night out like this. Hurriedly I pulled her dress down to hide it and took the sandal from her before she put her eye out.

'Why don't we go and get some water?'

Stubbornly she shook her head. 'No way! I need something stronger than water. You have no idea what I've been putting up with recently.'

Afraid someone else would hear her, I tried my best to placate her while desperately scanning around for David.

'You are so lucky that Robbie is in Stirling,' she continued, 'and it's just you two lovebirds at home. Try having a house full of teenagers who despise you. All I ever hear is doors slamming or else being told I'm an idiot because I can't remember things.'

To my horror, she started to cry. Big fat tears ran down her cheeks and she reached for the hip flask, but before she could quite get it manoeuvred from under the garter, thankfully David appeared.

His face tense, he squatted down and took her hand. 'Kate, look at me,' he said gently. Silently she raised her eyes. 'Let's get you up from here.'

Obediently she took his hand and he helped her up. I handed him the sandal as he wrapped a protective arm around her.

'Could you get her a glass of water please?' he asked me as he steered her towards the quiet reception area, away from any prying eyes. Nodding, I went over to the bar, got the water and followed them out.

Kate had stopped crying and was sitting on a leather sofa with her head on David's shoulder. He was gently rubbing her back as I handed her the water.

'Thank you,' he mouthed to me and I took the opportunity to leave them together.

Unsure what had just happened, I went back to our table where most of our friends were now chatting. I took a seat on a free chair beside Will.

'Where's Claire?' I asked, as he drained his pint of Guinness.

'No idea,' he replied, 'I thought she was with you somewhere. Have you seen David or Tom? They were with us at the bar but disappeared a while ago.'

Before I could answer, Claire reappeared with Annie, whose cheeks were flushed with happiness. 'Thanks so much for coming and supporting us. Time to call it a day? I think the minibus is waiting.'

We went out to the foyer, got our coats and all headed outside. David held Kate's hand and she appeared much less upset. The men had obviously finished the evening with 'a wee dram' so they needed guiding to the waiting taxi. After we took our seats, James leaned over me and went to give me a sloppy, wet kiss. I tried not to flinch at the stench of whiskey on his breath, turned my head just in time and he kissed my cheek instead.

'Give me a kiss,' he demanded petulantly and rather than cause a scene, I did. Placing a hand on top of my thigh he rubbed it suggestively.

You have two hopes of that tonight, I thought irritated, *Bob Hope and no hope.* I let him knead my leg like a lump of dough, and gazed out of the window as the minibus sped through the city. The orange streetlights shone bright, reflecting on the still waters of Belfast Lough. As we drove on towards Castlebrook, James thankfully dozed off. Annie was sitting across from me with Matt asleep on her shoulder.

'Had a good night?' she asked.

I nodded and I realised I really had, despite a rocky start and Kate's concerning behaviour.

I'd worry about that another day.

CHAPTER FOUR

Next morning James woke with a stonking headache and I was surprised when he asked me if I'd enjoyed my one-to-one with Will while Claire was elsewhere. I couldn't even remember having a chat with Will, but James was adamant I had looked very intimate with him for a long stretch of the evening.

'You embarrassed me the way you were fawning over him. I'm sure Will was mortified.'

I apologised profusely even though I wasn't sure what I was apologising for, as I was a bit preoccupied about whether to ask Kate about her sneaky hip flask and subsequent tearful admission. She probably didn't even remember it and if she did, she would be contrite. I knew after I reached menopause that hang-xiety is a very real thing and she would be wrecked with worry about what she had confessed. Therefore I felt the best way to deal with it was not to bring it up unless she mentioned it first.

'I'm going to visit Mum and Dad. Do you want to come with me?' I asked James as I prepared us a lunch of celeriac and leek soup.

'No thanks,' he retorted curtly. 'I'm planning on staying here and pottering about once this headache has cleared a bit. Do you have to visit them today? I thought we could spend the afternoon together.'

'I haven't seen them in ages, and I've told them I would. Do you fancy cooking dinner tonight as I might be a bit late back?'

He looked at me like I'd asked him to boil his own arm for dinner, so I quickly replied that I'd leave a lasagne out of the freezer and not to worry.

My parents live in a smallholding around half an hour from us, and although both in their early eighties, they continue to work hard caring for their menagerie of animals.

James has never seemed to particularly care for my large family, although he never openly ridiculed them. They say actions speak louder than words, and as he usually tried to avoid them, it was patently obvious to me what he thought of them.

On the drive to my parents' house, I recalled the first time James had introduced me to his parents, Donald and Heather. They live in a gated enclave in an affluent area in Belfast, and I was a little awestruck as we drove up their monoblock driveway, before laying eyes on their enormous mock Tudor detached home.

Nevertheless they were perfectly pleasant to me as I was handed an aperitif, and they asked about my course, my family and my aspirations.

I also remembered James's younger sister Olivia looked at me as if I had two heads when I said my family lived in the country. I could practically read her mind as she sipped her drink. *Country bumpkin.* It was clear that she considered me much less suitable for her big brother than his previous girlfriend Hermione.

James's father Donald was a retired orthopaedic surgeon and his mother Heather had been a theatre sister when they met. After having James, she had given up work and now involved herself with various charities and played tennis regularly. When they learned I was returning to work after Robbie went to grammar school, she took me aside and told me I was lucky James allowed me to go back to work after having his child. For once I saw beyond the glamorous blonde hair, chic clothes and perfectly applied make-up, and instead recognised a woman who had deferred unquestionably to her husband throughout her married life. It was then I had warmed to her, realising that their façade of a perfect marriage was perhaps slightly less shiny that I had assumed.

Mum and Dad's house sits on a hillside in the heart of Northern Ireland, just a couple of miles from Lough Neagh. It is pristinely kept and they love to spend time in their extensive garden that has a vegetable plot, apple orchard and several large cherry blossom trees. A few years ago they even got a beehive, and regularly give me some of their delicious honey.

My mum is a traditional Irish mother who shows her love by overfeeding us. I had no sooner arrived than the kettle was switched on, and she produced an enormous plate of cheese, homegrown tomatoes and homemade wheaten bread.

Dad was sitting in front of the television watching a live feed of a local livestock market. During Covid farmers were not allowed to attend the animal markets in person, Mum had learned how to put it on the television through Facebook. I was very impressed with her technical savvy, although less impressed when Dad got a bit overexcited by a ewe selling for ten pounds more than he had expected. He soon disappeared back out to his beloved garden and Mum settled down on their old sofa for a chat.

Their little Westie Paddy had jumped up onto my lap, and was dozing contentedly as I sat at the kitchen table.

'You're looking tired, Laura,' Mum said. 'How's Robbie?' She knew how much I worried about him and missed him.

'I'm a bit tired because it was a late one last night at the dinner dance. Robbie's great, not too much longer till he will be home for Christmas.'

Mum concentrated on buttering some wheaten as she asked, 'And how's James?'

'He's fine. Working hard as usual.'

'Have you decided where to go on holiday next summer yet?'

'We're going to Dubrovnik,' I answered mildly.

'I thought you really wanted to go to Sorrento?' She finally looked up at me, her pale-blue eyes steady.

Studiously avoiding eye contact, I instead watched Dad out of the window as he staked up a plant that had blown over. 'James thought Dubrovnik would be nicer. You know how hot the south of Italy gets in the summer. He's worried that I'd find it too hot and Dubrovnik looks lovely. We'll do a daytrip to Bosnia to see the Kravice Waterfalls and maybe even a trip to Montenegro.' I stopped chittering.

'You've wanted to visit Herculaneum and Pompeii for years! You were really looking forward to it.' Mum wasn't buying my half-hearted enthusing about Croatia.

'Well maybe next time,' I mumbled.

'James can't always make all the decisions,' she reminded me gently. 'Your opinion is as valid as his.'

I looked at her and absorbed her goodness. She has raised all six of us with an abundance of love and rarely gives advice unless I ask for it. When I started going out with boys, she advised me to 'Keep your legs crossed not your fingers' and then before we married, she advised me to iron creases into James's shirts so he'd never expect me to do it again.

The only other piece of advice she'd given me was to have my own savings account, what she termed my 'running away from home account'. She and Dad had opened an account for me before I went to university, and although there wasn't a huge amount in it, I regularly tried to put something aside for a rainy day. I'm not sure why, but I have never told James about it. It was my 'just in case' safety net.

Swiftly I tried to reassure her that James did not always have the final say and that when I really wanted something, I got it. However, denying myself things I really wanted was a fundamental part of my life. Appearing to concede the point, for the rest of my visit we discussed my many siblings and their families.

On the drive home, I brooded about what Mum had said and, more importantly, what she had omitted.

When we first married, James had been careful to always visit my parents with me and took enormous pains to buy them rather ostentatious gifts. Gradually he visited less, never suggested inviting them over for lunch and left it up to me to buy their presents. I presumed Mum thought he was a bit overbearing, and although she had never expressed it, I don't think she particularly liked the man he had become.

Rather than return straight home, I took a detour along my favourite stretch of coast. Parking my red Mini facing the Irish Sea, I grabbed my jacket from the back seat. Zipping it up outside the car, I wished I had thought to bring a pair of gloves and a hat with me, as it was a wild autumn day with a brisk sea breeze.

I love the sea. Well, I love being by the sea, I don't like being on it or in it. I have no idea why anyone would choose to go wild swimming. Even if my anxiety levels were sky high, I would never see the attraction of stripping off to just get cold and wet. Although I have considered buying myself a dry robe to pose about in, as they are a bit of a status symbol now.

I walked slowly along the coastal path as the waves relentlessly chased each other over the black rocks and sandy beach, which was strewn with damp seaweed. Breathing in the salty air, I felt a calmness that I've never achieved with yoga or mindfulness. The coastline of Northern Ireland is spectacularly beautiful in a fierce, untamed way. Jagged cliffs overshadow a sea that is usually an angry grey or like today, a benign steel blue. There are long stretches of golden beaches with crashing waves to entice hardy surfers and body boarders. And of course, the wild swimmers.

Today there was a family playing on the beach, dad, mum and small boy of about four years old. He was digging a hole with a red plastic spade at the water's edge, laughing delightedly as the water rushed in to fill it. His curly black hair reminded me of Robbie at that age and I instantly felt nostalgic for the past, when my only worry about Robbie was that he cried each morning going to school. I watched the dad patiently help his son to dig a trench while the mum took photos on her phone. Such simple pleasures, I couldn't help smiling at the happy family unit.

My phone buzzed and I checked it to see a text from James.

> Teeny, what time will you be home? I'm getting hungry.

A couple of years ago when my memory had become so bad that I feared I had the onset of dementia, I had forgotten our postcode when I was countersigning an official document for a colleague. I resorted to ringing James because it was as if my mind was completely blank. I tried to laugh it off that night by saying my tiny brain had obviously lost even more brain cells and was now teeny-tiny. Since then, James calls me Teeny from time to time.

He finds it hilarious. I don't.

I messaged back to let him know that I would be home in half an hour and if he was hungry to put the oven on and warm up the lasagne. He didn't bother responding. I'm sure he just does things like that to wind me up.

As I retraced my steps towards the car, I noticed the little boy had fallen over as a big wave had taken his feet from under him. His dad rushed to help.

That's the role of family, I thought as I started the car. *Always there for each other, lifting each other up when they fall.*

Even families that have frayed a little at the seams.

James and I made promises to each other that bitterly cold day so many years ago.

'For better, for worse… to love and to cherish until death do us part.'

Although when you're a naïve twenty-four-year-old, *for worse* seems like something that only happens to other people. For years I'd been flummoxed when I heard of marriages that had faltered then fallen after many years together, but now I was beginning to understand. It is rarely a sudden ending at least for one partner. Maybe they had been avoiding the inevitable for years while children bridged the chasm between them. Or conceivably they had only ever thought they loved each other.

Perhaps one day the scales fell from her eyes, she realised that life was full of possibilities and that no one was forcing her to stay.

It seemed to me the triple whammy of James working from home, menopause and empty nest had led us to the precarious position we were in now. James's world had shrunk. Whereas before he would have been out in the office all day, sometimes working there late into the evening or going out for drinks with colleagues, working from home had given him an opportunity to be in the house all the time.

Every single day. Waiting for me. Watching my every move. Sometimes it is claustrophobic to say the least. I now think of WFH as *what fresh hell* rather than *working from home.*

Each time I tentatively considered what it would mean for us to no longer be together, my mind scrabbled around for something else to focus on, as my heart raced and my breath became ragged. Having been a couple since I was eighteen, the fear of being single was terrifying. I had never lived on my own, never had to worry about finances, had relied on James completely to make all the important decisions.

But was I afraid of being alone or afraid of being without James?

I refused to dwell on that persistent little earworm as I arrived home and put the oven on.

Best to just put it to one side and focus on the good.

CHAPTER FIVE

As November ticked on, James informed me he had purchased tickets for a jazz concert in Belfast. To say I detest jazz is putting it mildly. The discordant noise sounds to me as though the musicians have swapped instruments and been on the wine since lunch. To make matters worse, he also bought tickets for his parents as an early Christmas gift. The only part of the evening I was looking forward to was dinner at a new Asian tapas restaurant.

The night before the concert the Book Club met for the first time since the dinner dance. We take it in turns to host at each of our houses and this month it was Claire's turn. She and Will live a few miles out of the village and we usually ask one of our husbands to do taxi for us.

Surprisingly Kate had offered to drive, informing us that her thirteen-year-old daughter Sophie needed to be taken early to netball practice in the morning. It seemed the incident with the hip flask was a one-off and I was relieved it wouldn't need any further worrying about.

The five of us settled into Claire's living room, blethering animatedly in the way that old friends do. We chuckled as we recalled the dinner dance, chatted about our plans for a Christmas night out and how much those of us with children at university were looking forward to them returning for the holidays.

I mentioned that James had got the tickets for the jazz concert.

'But you hate jazz!' exclaimed Annie. 'Why on earth would he insist on you sitting through that?'

'No idea.' I shrugged. 'Maybe he thinks it will convert me.' In reality, he had informed me that he was embarrassed by my lack of interest in what he termed 'cultured activities' and it was time I learned to appreciate 'the finer things in life'. It seemed that it didn't take much for me to be an embarrassment these days.

'Think of it as one of your fifty before fifty,' suggested Annie.

They all laughed. I had decided that rather than worry about my milestone birthday a couple of years ago, I would embrace fifty things I'd never tried before. Except after number thirty I'd run out of interesting things to do. Even then, I'm not sure that reading the first twenty pages of *Anna Karenina* counts as a bucket-list item you'd want to share on Facebook. The most exciting thing I'd done was to snorkel with sharks at the London Aquarium and I'd felt so nauseous afterwards that I couldn't even enjoy the glass of champagne James had booked for us at the top of the Shard.

'Fifty before fifty-five.' I grinned. 'The next time I see fifty it will be on a door.'

'Speaking of such things, I think I may finally be hitting the menopause,' said Claire. 'I've been having the most overwhelming hot flushes even though it's November.'

'Well, you are nearly fifty,' answered Vicky smiling at her. 'It's about time too.'

'Not sure how you know if you are, though.' Claire looked a bit puzzled, fine lines appearing between her perfectly manicured brows.

Before Vicky the doctor could reply, I jumped in. 'Well, it's like playing dot to dot,' I answered. 'You get one odd symptom, then another, then another. Like I had sore, swollen fingers, making it impossible for me to wear my rings, so the GP sent me for a hand X-ray. Then I developed tinnitus so they sent me for a brain scan. Then the anxiety was so bad I remember freaking out at the autobank and walked off, leaving one hundred pounds sticking out of it for the next person. One day the penny dropped, I joined the dots and realised that I could be menopausal.'

'What happened then?' asked Claire, refilling my glass of Pinot Gris, which had mysteriously emptied.

'I rang the GP, said I thought I could be menopausal, and she asked when my last period was. I said 2003 after I had Robbie and the miscarriages. I've had a Mirena coil since then.'

The girls giggled as I joked about how the GP had taken my bloods and when she rang the next day to confirm I was menopausal, my reply was, 'My husband will be happy.' I meant that he would be happy now there was a reason for my mood swings and raging anxiety rather than me going a bit mad. The GP didn't really get the joke and seemed a bit perplexed. Within three weeks of HRT, my hands no longer hurt, and I could wear my rings again. Unfortunately, the tinnitus remained and I now played a white-noise machine at night to help mask the buzzing in my head. James swore he couldn't sleep with the sound, so I'd gladly moved into the spare room.

'It sounds like I need to have a chat with the GP,' mumbled Claire.

'Or you could swim half naked in the Irish Sea and eat raw garlic like some of us.' I winked at Kate who said she would never take HRT as menopause was natural and we should embrace it rather than fight it. Therefore she dutifully froze every Sunday morning while wild swimming at Ballygally Beach, and her breath reeked of garlic while she was at it. I'd much rather stick chemicals on me.

'Did James notice an improvement in your anxiety?' asked Annie, tucking her legs up on the sofa beneath her.

'Well, he did go through an annoying phase of telling me I needed to stick another patch on when I got irritated with him, but thankfully he's stopped that.' Laughing off what had been hurtful at the time, I swiftly changed the subject to our planned Christmas party night at the fabulous Belfast Gaol.

The night passed quickly, although we were a bit taken aback when Kate suggested at only half past ten that we should go home. Normally we stay out until around midnight, but it seemed a bit mean to make her stay late when she was being good enough to drive, so without fuss, we returned to the village. Part of me was relieved that James was already in his own bed when I got in.

That's the beauty of separate rooms, no expectation of a quickie when all you want to do is sleep. My libido was in my boots.

The following night I dressed in a lovely new royal blue shirt dress that I had treated myself to. What my friends don't know is that I buy most of my clothes from charity shops, or when the prices are slashed in a sale. I'm careful to only buy good brands that are in great condition, and my friends are none the wiser. James was wearing a new Tommy Hilfiger jacket that I was certain he hadn't bought in a charity shop, but of course I didn't say anything, just told him how handsome he looked. He drove us both into Belfast in my Mini before parking close to the venue.

When we arrived at the restaurant, Donald and Heather were

already waiting on us. Heather looked gorgeous in a smart olive-green dress with matching jacket.

Donald pecked me on the cheek, said I was looking lovely and then spoiled it by saying, 'Heather could never get away with a dress like that, she's too short and plump.'

Heather blushed, laughed off his comment and told me how well I looked. I was horrified at his crassness, as this was not the first time he had made an underhand comment about his wife. But this was the first time I appreciated how mean he could be, and how Heather automatically covered for it by being the perfect lady.

I glanced at James to see his reaction, but he was too busy greeting his father to compliment his mother. Suddenly I understood that James was simply a product of his upbringing. In many ways, he was no different to Donald; it was just that he was sly enough to save his condescending remarks for behind closed doors.

Silently seething, I took my place beside my husband. Donald commanded the table, pontificating about something he had been watching on an obscure Sky channel, with James hanging off his every word. Every now and then I would try and interject to ask Heather her opinion, but I was basically ignored by both James and his father. Heather simply sipped her tonic water, nodding mutely.

When the wine arrived, Donald swirled it around the glass, tasted it and told the waiter it was fine. He'd ordered without asking anyone else what they preferred. Typical for him.

'Did you get a taxi here?' I finally got an opportunity to ask Heather, when Donald excused himself to go to the bathroom.

'Oh no,' she answered, 'Donald doesn't like getting taxis so I'm driving.'

'That's a shame,' I said carefully, 'you could have had a glass of wine with dinner.'

'I've always driven when we're out late, dear. Are you getting a taxi home?'

'James doesn't like getting a taxi, so I'm driving.' This was true, as the only taxi he never complained about was the minibus taxi when we were going out with all our friends.

She looked at me kindly, with a wry smile. 'Like father, like son.' Her reply was murmured, but loud enough for me to hear. I had really warmed to this woman over the years. She may have been a traditional wife who believed that her husband was boss, but underneath her cool, calm exterior I knew she was compassionate and understanding. I'm just sorry it took me so long to figure that out.

Throughout the meal, Donald would direct the odd question to me but otherwise continued to dominate the conversation. James appeared completely happy with this, and as always when I'm forced to spend any length of time with my father-in-law, my agitation grew. I've discovered that after fifty my tolerance plummeted while my irritation sky-rocketed.

Then Donald surprised me by asking, 'Have you booked Dubrovnik yet?'

James replied, 'Not yet but we plan to soon.'

'I told you it is a much better place to visit than the south of Italy. You need to get it booked soon and go to that restaurant I told you about.'

My head shot up. James had discussed our holiday plans with his father? And now we were going to Dubrovnik rather than my choice of Italy? Although furious with them both, I held my tongue, because that was a row for later.

Instead I made my excuses, found the ladies' toilets and exhaled hard a couple of times while looking at my reflection in a full-length mirror on the end wall. Tired blue-grey eyes stared back at me, my pale face in need of summer sunshine. Or a shot of happiness. Just a few more hours of Donald's company, and I could retreat into the solace of my own bedroom.

Thankfully the meal was soon over, and we walked to the Waterfront Hall for the concert. Like Baldrick, I had devised a cunning plan to guarantee that I wouldn't have to listen to the jazz. It involved sitting beside Donald who was sure to fall asleep quickly, and a pair of AirPods.

I led the way into the row, Donald swaggered in beside me followed by Heather and finally James. Excellent. The first step of my plan had worked. Not long after the band came on stage and struck up a 'tune', I swiftly stuck my AirPods in my ears ensuring they were covered by my hair. I concealed my phone at my side as I pressed play. George Ezra singing 'Paradise' came flooding through, drowning out most of the cacophony from the stage.

When the concert was over, Heather nudged Donald awake as I furtively removed my AirPods, popping them back into my handbag.

'Did you enjoy that?' asked Heather.

'Very good indeed.' For once I didn't even have to lie.

We said our goodbyes outside the venue and returned to the car park.

'We're going to Dubrovnik rather than Italy on your dad's say-so?' I demanded angrily, the minute we were out of earshot.

'Calm down, Laura, and stop making a scene. Everyone is staring at us. You are upsetting me. We are going to Dubrovnik because Italy is too full of tourists.' His face was distorted with fury that I would dare to question him.

'Oh right, so we won't be tourists. We'll be visitors in Dubrovnik?' I hissed back.

'Exactly.' We faced each other behind the car, a metre apart but metaphorical miles separated us.

'Rubbish! You only want to go to Dubrovnik because you're afraid to say no to your father.'

'For goodness' sake, Laura,' he snapped tersely. 'I'm sick to death of this conversation. Dad is widely travelled and has been to both; if he says Dubrovnik is a better destination than the south of Italy, he knows what he's talking about. Stop screeching at me like a washer woman and drive me home.'

Subdued, I got behind the wheel and drove home. Once I'd pulled into the driveway, I summoned my courage before saying quietly, 'The next time we go out in Belfast with your parents, you will be driving me home or I will bloody well not be going.'

I suppressed a small smile as James's mouth dropped open. I rarely swore as he thought women who swore were cheap, but I really wanted to stress my point.

Maybe it was time for the worm to turn.

CHAPTER SIX

Upon waking the next day, I lay alone in bed listening for James to get up. As it was a dry Sunday morning, I expected he would go out on his bike with his cycling club. Sure enough I soon heard him clump around his bedroom and heavily make his way downstairs. If he was in a good mood, I could expect a cup of coffee in bed. If not, he'd go straight out on the bike without disturbing me, and I wouldn't see him again until late afternoon.

He did not return upstairs which meant he was in a foul temper with me.

Excellent, I thought, *that means I will do exactly as I please today and sod him.*

The thought of a day without him and his bad form, filled me with intense pleasure. I go could anywhere, do anything I wanted, knowing that he wouldn't be back to check up on me for hours.

I would go for a walk along the beach, then make myself some lunch and get out of the house for the afternoon. And I defiantly vowed that I wouldn't be making dinner for him tonight.

When we first got married and I was a desperate-to-please

new bride, I would from time to time do something trivial that James became angry about. In those days our arguments were vicious and volatile, and part of the fun was making up in bed later.

Throughout the years James's temper increased while mine depleted. Now he liked to prolong the disagreement, while I tormented myself with the potential repercussions. It had been many years since we had resolved our differences in bed. Sometimes it would be days before he dished out his retribution.

And today would play out exactly like all those other times. He would arrive back from his bike ride and I had no idea what his mood would be like. There was a chance he would be all sweetness and light. Equally he could simply ignore me. The uncertainty was always the hardest part.

One thing I was certain of: I was weary of his father dictating our choices. Donald spoke, James acquiesced immediately. I vowed to spend as little time as I could in my father-in-law's company from now on.

It was a bleak sort of day, and dark clouds stretched as far as the eye could see as I wandered along my favourite stretch of beach, listening to my music. No family playing in the sand today, just me with some screeching seagulls for company. I thought about the night before and my outrage with James's decision about our holiday. Once upon a time we would have discussed it and then together selected the best place to visit. It was more usual now that he would make all the decisions, expecting me to unquestioningly agree with him. It was as if my opinion no longer mattered and when I tried to give it, he would get ferociously angry with me. Usually it was easier to let him be in charge, rather than to have yet another fight that I would inevitably lose.

Invigorated by my walk, I nipped home, had a bowl of butternut squash and sweet potato soup and decided to go shopping in Belfast. It was almost the end of November and the shops would be displaying their Christmas wares to entice shoppers into parting with their cash. The continental Christmas market held annually in the centre of Belfast would also be open, so I planned to browse the stalls and get myself something to eat there.

I adore Christmas, the planning, the anticipation, choosing presents. It is also an opportunity to overindulge in food, drink and parties. Needless to say, James did no planning, no buying of gifts and generally had a miserable outlook about it all. This had never especially bothered me, because Christmas has always given me such pleasure. If he got no enjoyment out of family time and gift giving, I considered it his loss.

Surprised that I got parked easily in one of the busy multi-storey car parks, I strolled off in the direction of the market which was already jammed with shoppers. The wooden huts nestled together in the grounds of the imposing city hall, trimmed with bright lights and Wizzard's 'I Wish It Could Be Christmas Everyday' was playing full blast. The stalls were selling food, drinks, trinkets and delicate Christmas ornaments. I got a beautiful angel decoration for our tree and for Dad a fleece-lined winter hat. The place was thronged with groups of friends and couples holding hands. To eat there were crêpes, hot dogs made with the longest frankfurters I'd ever seen and cartons of seafood paella. I resolved to come back later for a venison burger.

Leaving the market behind, I wandered along to Victoria Square with its high-end shops, restaurants and iconic glass dome. I was standing outside Phase Eight studying a forest-green jersey dress that would be perfect for Christmas Day, when I heard my name being called. I swung around and came face to face with an old colleague, Lisa. She was wrapped in a faux fur jacket and clutched a Michael Kors handbag. Her face had the surprised look of someone who had overindulged in fillers and Botox.

'Long time no see!' She air-kissed me. 'How's the world of work?'

'All good, how's retirement?' I asked her, unable to take my eyes off her huge diamond engagement ring. I couldn't take my eyes off it because she is an effusive hand-talker, and I was afraid she would take my eye out with it if I wasn't careful.

'I highly recommend it. Best thing I ever did. We've been making up for all the enforced staycations over the past two years and I do Pilates three times a week. Then there's lunches with friends, shopping...'

She droned on and on and I remembered why I was relieved to see the back of her when she retired, and why I had made no effort to keep in touch. She flicked her perfectly highlighted shoulder-length hair, held back by a pair of Oakley sunglasses despite the lack of winter sun.

Eventually I noticed she had finally stopped talking, and was giving me a look as artificial as her jacket. 'Still having issues,' her voice dropped a notch, 'with the menopause?'

'Not at all, nothing a little HRT couldn't sort.' I tried hard not to adopt my resting bitch face. Her insincerity was testing my limited patience.

'I never had to take those chemicals. I took a little black cohosh, walked five miles a day and was through it in a few months.' The look she gave me was pity mixed with superiority.

'Lucky you,' I said, bade her an abrupt goodbye, and left her standing on her own with a startled expression. Well, as startled as someone who had overdone the tweakments could manage.

Sometimes I've found that a woman who has sailed through pregnancy, birth or menopause can be less than empathetic to someone who has had a difficult time. I'm probably jealous as I struggled so much with each of them. Why are some women a slave to their hormones while others escape relatively unscathed?

Women like Lisa are energy vampires; they leave you exhausted and drained while they feed off the attention they garner. My way of dealing with energy vampires now is to focus on making myself feel better and don't waste time on them. Life really is too short to spend it with people who make you feel bad about your life, your job, your home or yourself.

Deciding I could make myself feel even better by spritzing myself with a Jo Malone perfume in House of Fraser, I enjoyed some scent time before turning towards the market for food.

I felt my mobile vibrate in my bag as I was returning to the market. Taking it out, I read a text from James. Half expecting it to be *What's for dinner and what time's it at?* I was amazed instead to read,

> Teeny, I'm making spaghetti Bolognese for dinner, it will be ready about half six.

Incredulous, I stopped walking, nearly causing a collision with a man behind me. Profusely apologetic, I stepped out of the way before reading the message again. Yes, it really did say that James was making dinner. Wonders would never cease. I texted back that I would see him soon and headed for the car park.

At home, I found James standing in the kitchen wearing his Grumpy Old Git apron that Robbie had bought him for his last birthday. Part of my brain registered that there were somehow four saucepans, three ladles and two chopping boards scattered around the worktops. The other part of my brain was on tenterhooks, waiting for him to speak.

'I'm sorry about Dad,' he said immediately. 'I shouldn't have spoken to him about our holiday until we had agreed it. He can be a bit overbearing about things sometimes.'

Wrongfooted by this surprise admission, I was unsure how to reply. James did this from time to time, leaving me completely uncertain about how to respond. I hesitated, waiting for him to continue.

He amazed me further by saying, 'I do think that the south of

Italy in July will be too hot for you to enjoy it properly, so maybe we could consider it over Easter the following year?'

One thing I had always loved about James was his understanding of my fear about burning in the sun. He had rarely complained about our holidays to accommodate this over the years, and for that I would be eternally grateful. No beach holidays for us, although I'm sure he and Robbie would have loved them.

Kissing him on the lips, I apologised for my blaze of bad temper, that Dubrovnik would be lovely and we should book it as soon as possible.

He took me in his arms, before replying over the top of my head, 'We need to have a chat though. You don't seem very happy recently. You're so touchy if I don't agree with everything you say, and you're always finding fault with me. This holiday is just one more thing that you're unhappy about and I wonder if you need to see the doctor again about a higher dose of HRT.'

He released me abruptly, before stepping back to gauge my response.

So many things flashed through my head; frustration with his behaviour, questioning my feelings for him, his constant presence in the house. I was also fed up with his continued insistence that I should see the doctor again. Afraid that if I started talking I wouldn't be able to stop, I couldn't face the potential repercussions. Not until I had got things clearer in my own mind.

'I'm sorry, I've just been allowing things to get me down when I shouldn't and I'm sorry if I've been a bit on edge. I'll try harder not to upset you. Shall I pour us a glass of wine?'

James nodded and turned back to the hob.

We'd survived another blip.

CHAPTER SEVEN

The next couple of weeks flew past, filled with meals out, shopping for presents and the usual end of term excitement in school.

I was also busy with orders for my jewellery on Etsy and before I knew it Robbie was due home in a few days. I'd washed his bedding before dusting and hoovering his room, though I knew that approximately five minutes after he arrived home it would be covered in clothes, shoes and all the paraphernalia he brings back with him. Sometimes he doesn't even unpack his bag properly, just lives out of it for the duration of his stay like some perpetual backpacker.

James and I muddled along together and thankfully I wouldn't have to see his parents again until Christmas Day. I am an expert at burying my head in the sand and remained ostrich-like in my refusal to address my marriage concerns. Whenever I lay sleepless in the middle of the night, I deployed a new tactic to help myself drift off, resolutely avoiding the glaringly obvious cause of my insomnia. Now I listed every menopause symptom beginning with each letter of the alphabet.

Usually I got stuck at Q and trying to think of one generally caused me to fall back to sleep. I had once chosen *quietly losing my mind* but as that should have been *loudly losing my mind* I had to rule it out.

The first weekend in December, as was our custom, we brought the tree down from the attic and I played *Now That's What I Call Christmas* as I decorated it. For many years James and I had had our annual fight about real tree versus fake.

We used to go with Kate, David and the kids to a local Christmas tree farm so we could choose our favourite. Every single year James would request we get an artificial one, as we would still be finding pine needles lurking in February. Every single year I dug my heels in and refused, insisting on a real one. Eventually as Robbie got older and the novelty of trudging through the pine forest waned, I succumbed to James's demands. No pine needles and no scent, only flakes of the faux snow adorning the fake tree dropping onto the wooden floorboards. To compensate for the lack of fir tree smell, I lit candles and the festive aroma of cinnamon, orange and cloves infused the air, as I gently unwrapped each ornament.

When Robbie was old enough, I had started the tradition of letting him choose a new tree decoration each December. Now we had the story of his growing up, from squashy soft Santas to his final teenage selection of a prickly fox. Sadly, I knew at that point he had outgrown this custom. Instead, I purchased Christmas tree decorations on our travels each year. As I revealed each treasure, it evoked memories from our holidays over the past few years. From an NYPD policeman holding a candy cane from my one and only trip to New York, to a beautiful, painted glass ball from Vienna.

After I unwrapped the final decoration, a hideous Grinch from Robbie's selection, I called to James to put the star on top of the tree as was our ritual. He came in complaining that I could reach it myself, and that he was watching rugby on the television.

For goodness' sake, I thought, *why can't you just put the bloody thing on top of the tree without a whingeing session. Stop ruining the atmosphere.*

Reluctantly he shoved the star on the tree, before leaving the room without a backward glance, or waiting for the lights to go on.

Unperturbed by him, I switched them on myself, and sat in the semi dark listening to cheesy Christmas music while admiring my tree. I loved how the lights twinkled, the baubles glistening bright. Enjoying the calm, I convinced myself that no matter how much James annoyed me this Christmas, I would try and let it wash over me. Robbie would only be home for a short time and I didn't want to sour it.

The reason for James's grumpiness was that I was going out with the Book Club on our Christmas party night tonight. He never overtly complained when I was going out without him, but it was obvious by his short temper and general crankiness that he wasn't happy. I dreaded his fury and tried my best to keep the peace as I feared his jaw tightening and his eyes becoming chips of ice. Even so, I knew I had to remain strong about one festive night out without him and tolerate his dark mood as best I could.

Originally, we would bring the husbands along too, but for the past few years we'd booked a fancy meal in Belfast and usually ended up dancing on some tiny dance floor along with other middle-aged women who are such an embarrassment to their teenagers. This year we had booked a table at the Gaol and had organised a taxi there from the village. The five of us were giddy with the excitement of getting dolled up in our party dresses and high heels with the expectation of a great night's fun. For so much of the year we middle-aged women are undervalued and overlooked but tonight we shone bright.

As we clamoured out of the taxi, I surveyed the austere and bleak edifice of the Victorian-era prison which is now a top visitor attraction. The black basalt-rock walls rose high above me and behind the blank windows, births, deaths and marriages had taken place along with other unspeakable acts. Although now a welcoming events venue, I knew without doubt that I would never be brave enough to attend one of their paranormal evenings. Even the thought of it made the hairs on the back of my neck stand up.

Tonight, we were offered glasses of bubbly on arrival and I was enthralled with the sparkling lights, giant Christmas tree and garlands of holly and ivy. It all looked so inviting and exciting, everyone dressed in sequins or satin, wobbling on stilettos, bursting with anticipation. We found our table with its tiny snow-covered trees, silver baubles and crackers, which we pulled and read out our terrible jokes before putting on our paper crowns.

We munched our way through the delicious meal, and as we chattered together, I would occasionally sneak a glance at Kate, but it seemed that she was having no more wine than the rest of us. In fact she looked lovelier than ever with her black hair in a neat chignon.

I noticed that Claire appeared to have a glow about her, her blonde hair newly cut in a sharp chin-length bob. She was wearing a slinky silver minidress that complimented her long legs. My friends were truly lovely both inside and out and I thanked my lucky stars that I had such a great support network who also knew how to enjoy themselves.

While waiting for our desserts Annie said, 'Right then, time for peaks and pits.' It was time for our annual summary of our year's highs and lows, a tradition that usually evoked much hilarity.

'You first, Vicky,' she commanded, pointing at my friend, who was looking even more beautiful tonight in a plunging V-necked black dress.

Vicky wrinkled her brow as she considered. 'Peak first: Flora passing her driving test, so no more taxiing her around. Pit would have to be that new colleague at work. She really is the pits.' Vicky had spent most of the year complaining to us about the new receptionist in the GP practice. This woman spent more time trying to get out of work than actually working. She sounded like a complete nightmare and we all groaned in sympathy.

'Claire next,' Vicky continued, turning to her right.

Claire took a few minutes to decide what her peak was. Apparently, it was the spa day she spent with her mum at the Averie Hotel in November, and the pit was her boss Imelda at the estate agents. 'She never has a positive word to say about anyone. Did I tell you she thinks I am "bad with my nerves"? I'm only bad with my nerves when I'm struggling not to shout out "witch", "bollocks" or "arse" when she talks to me.'

We all laughed. 'Bad with your nerves' is the old-fashioned expression that demeaned women of a certain age who had anxiety issues.

'Anyway, Laura, it's your turn next.'

Swirling the white wine in my glass, I thought hard. Peak was easy enough; could I bring myself to admit my pit was James? Quickly dismissing it as it would be a downer on our big night out, I simply said my peak was Robbie coming home for the summer and my pit was having Covid over my birthday in September. That was really rotten, though it was helped by several family-pack bags of crisps and lots of chocolate cake.

'Kate, it's your turn.' I motioned to my friend, who emptied her glass as she considered her options. Pushing her hair back from her face, she grinned.

'Peak was that day when I was swimming at Ballygally beside the seal. And pit was that day I was swimming at Ballygally, got stung by the jellyfish and no one offered to pee on me to make it better.'

We all giggled. I would have thought her pit was eating raw garlic but it seemed not.

Eventually it was Annie's turn. 'Pit first. Matt buying his

faster-than-a-speeding-bullet motorbike, and my peak? I got the all-clear on my mammogram. Five years cancer free!'

We whooped and cheered, hugging Annie tight. Such fantastic news! We were all so delighted and relieved for her.

'This deserves another bottle of prosecco,' declared Kate, turning to flag down one of the waiters. Our jubilation at Annie's news was contagious and even the table beside ours joined us in our celebration. Once the meal was finished the music started and before long, we were all dancing along to one of my favourites, 'Things Can Only Get Better' by D:Ream.

Maybe they will, I told myself. *Maybe this is simply a bump in the road and James and I will find our way again.* It was Christmas, the season of goodwill to all men, so it was up to me to extend that to my husband. Wanting to forget about him and our marriage for a while, I joined in the dancing and partying with enthusiasm. I'd think about everything else later.

Towards the end of the night when our energy was flagging and we were seated more than we were dancing, I found Kate alone at the table. Unsure how to bring up the subject of her drinking, I opted instead to ask her about her children.

'You mentioned at the dinner dance that you were having a hard time with the kids,' I began gently. 'Is everything okay?'

She rolled her eyes before answering, and then it all came out in a rush as if the floodgates had opened. 'Not really. It's just that every time I open my mouth to express a point of view, I'm immediately shouted at by one of the kids, sometimes before I've even had a chance to speak. It doesn't seem to matter what I say, I'm usually completely wrong. It's so exhausting and I'm worn out having to walk on eggshells around them.' She flashed me a small smile, the relief of confiding in someone clear to see.

As I squeezed her hand, I let her talk. I was used to working with teenagers in school and knew how profound and passionate they could be. While not liking their sometimes vehement opinions, I nonetheless tried to not let it get to me. However, I did not live with three of them and could guess their constant bickering and certainty they were always right would be draining. Kate eventually drew a shaky breath and gave me a hug.

'Thanks for listening, I'm sorry if I've come across as an old moan. I love my kids to bits; I just don't think I'm being a very good mum at the minute.'

'You're doing a great job; all you can do is be there for them and let them have their say. They always take things out on the ones they love the most.' I tried to reassure her but felt a bit out of my depth. Mercifully Robbie had never really given us much cause for concern. Apart from the stage when he was horrified by my existence, he seemed to have outgrown the worst of his stroppiness. Before I could say any more, Annie came over and dragged us both up for one final dance.

On the way home in the taxi, I was still wearing my silly paper crown. The blisters on my feet had blisters and I was ready for my bed, but happiness bubbled within me, for Robbie would be home in a few days.

CHAPTER EIGHT

I t wasn't long before the big day arrived. As I stood at the wet and windy Belfast docks waiting on Robbie's ferry, I felt a frisson of excitement. He would be home for a couple of weeks and my sudden maternal urge to hold him was so strong, I was rocking with barely contained delight. Only the rather nonplussed look on the face of the man beside me made my rocking stop, and I struggled to keep the inane grin off my face. After weeks of unrest at home with James, I was counting on a calmer atmosphere in the house with Robbie there.

One by one the foot passengers disembarked. I caught sight of Robbie and raised a hand of welcome. My handsome six-foot-two son had his usual rather sardonic look on his face, obviously mentally begging me not to run into his arms or cry, like I had when he arrived home that first Christmas. Then I really had lost whatever marbles were left, as I sobbed and clung to my baby.

Now I suppressed my tears of joy and simply reached for a hug. After disentangling himself, he looked at me with eyes as blue as his dad's, and asked me how I was.

'I'm great, pet, really great.' And I meant it.

When we reached the car, he deposited his bag onto the back

seat and we made for home. In person he is more talkative than on the phone, so he chatted away about how it was freezing in Stirling, but his friend Fergus from the Outer Hebrides was still wearing only a T-shirt outside, and how hard he'd been studying. I took that last snippet of information with a huge dose of salt.

James met us at the front door with a smile, for although he rarely admitted it, he did miss Robbie too. They gave each other a quick hug before Robbie disappeared upstairs. After chucking his bag in his room, he then promptly announced he was going out to meet his mates.

'What's for dinner and what time's it at?' he asked, with a backwards glance as he made to leave.

Like father, like son.

It doesn't annoy me at all when it's Robbie who's asking, as he genuinely wants to know and looks forward with anticipation to any meal he doesn't have to cook himself.

'Macaroni cheese at half six,' I answered happily. My boy was home and he could ask anything he wanted of me and I wouldn't mind.

'You don't look that pleased to see me when I come in,' grumbled James, following at my heels into the cloakroom where I deposited my coat.

'That's because the longest I go without seeing you is about eight hours not three months,' I answered sharply, wanting to shake him with frustration. I simply could not bear his poor-me act.

Is it just him or are all men envious of the mother–child relationship? Do they all need constant reassurance that their partners are devoted to them, even when they are not especially good at doling out devotion to us?

I retreated to the sanctuary of the kitchen, firmly shut the door and prepared dinner. I had bought flaked salmon to stir through the mac and cheese as I knew that was a luxury Robbie couldn't afford at university.

When he had first gone to Stirling, he had rashly spent much of his student loan before Christmas. We had a hysterical phone call from him one weekend, when he realised he had very little money left to get him to the end of the semester, but James infuriatingly refused to help him out, insisting he had to learn the hard way. Behind his back, I had dipped into my secret savings and subbed Robbie a couple of hundred pounds to see him through. He was under strict instructions not to divulge this to James, and I had reiterated it was a one-off.

If you have the money and your child is in need, do you help them out and guide them on how to manage the issue? Or do you say 'Tough cookie, it's not my problem' and leave them to struggle? Another example of how different my husband and I are. Sometimes we really are poles apart and I don't understand him at all.

After dinner the three of us sat in front of the open fire watching our favourite film, *National Lampoon's Christmas Vacation* and I felt a deep contentment for the first time in quite a while. Even James's sniffing couldn't irritate me tonight. We had a lot of socialising planned over the next couple of weeks, and I knew Robbie would want to see as much of his school friends as possible, so I savoured this time with him.

The next few days were busy with multiple glasses of mulled wine, mince pies and get-togethers with friends and family. Before I knew it, it was Christmas morning and after opening our gifts, we had our traditional pancake stack and Buck's Fizz for breakfast before church.

James thought he had excelled himself this year by getting me an air fryer. Part of me wanted to throw it at him, the other part of me was a tiny bit pleased he had remembered I'd said I would like one. I didn't mean as my Christmas present though.

It was a beautiful winter morning, crisp and cold with mist lying low in the valley, so we choose to walk through the village to church. Robbie moaned and groaned about having to go, but once I gave him my stern look, he obediently trailed along with us. The church was decorated with candles, holly and poinsettias and was packed with families, kiddies brandishing their gifts and wearing their new Christmas outfits.

I love the carols and the quiet contemplation of a Christmas morning service before having to spend the rest of the day with my in-laws. We had only once invited both sets of parents to ours for Christmas Day, but Donald had spoken to Mum and Dad as if they were lobotomised and it was an unmitigated disaster. Now we alternate.

Robbie offered to drive us to their house, partly because he was 'hanging' from the night before on the Belfast beer bike, so I would at least be able to have a couple of glasses of wine to see me through the torture. Even worse was that the Dimmocks – Olivia and her brood – would be there too.

No sooner had we arrived at Donald and Heather's, than we were met by Olivia's two badly behaved children, Tobias and Octavia, who were running about like feral animals in the front garden, chasing each other with their Disney JetPack Buzz Lightyears. Trust them to have one of the most sought-after Christmas toys.

At seven and nine they were much younger than Robbie; however, he tolerated them good-naturedly. Their oldest child Giles had outgrown running around as he was thirteen, and was sitting quietly reading a book in the window seat in the lounge. He was a lovely child, despite Olivia and father Jasper, who were both as obnoxious as each other and mind-numbingly boring.

To brighten my day, I played Snob Bingo, where you make a note each time someone says pre-selected words. Today's phrase of choice was 'holiday cottage'. I decided other winning words would be 'Range Rover' and 'nanny'. Olivia was dressed as though she were on a photo shoot for *Tatler* in a clingy sequined dress and Louboutin shoes, while her husband sported a rather tight Prada shirt, which strained over his portly figure. If he made it through the whole dinner without losing a button I'd be astounded.

We sipped our Dom Pérignon in the conservatory while Heather busied herself with finalising the Christmas lunch. Donald, James, Olivia and Jasper held court, and sure enough it wasn't long before Snob Bingo commenced.

'We just haven't had a chance to get up to the holiday cottage since half term, although it would only take an hour in the Range Rover,' announced Jasper, brushing a non-existent piece of lint from his trousers. 'Olivia and I have booked ourselves a long weekend away in the New Year to Krakow. The nanny will be minding the children as she had the audacity to take this week off.'

Snob Bingo is no fun when you get a full house within five minutes of the conversation starting, so I changed the words to 'stock market' and, for a change, 'skiing'. Allegedly Jasper had made his fortune from dabbling in the stock market, but secretly I had surmised it was from inheriting the astronomical fees his accountant father had charged rich clients. He liked to boast about their annual ski holiday and had a tendency to get inexplicably furious if things like a worldwide pandemic prevented it.

Privately I called him The Dimwit and was always worried I'd inadvertently call him it to his face one day.

Shortly after, Heather announced that lunch was served and we duly went through into their formal dining room. It was exquisitely decorated in shades of pale pink, silver and white to compliment the muted shades of their décor. Unfortunately, Octavia and Tobias didn't care for the hours of painstaking preparation that Heather had clearly spent perfecting the table settings, as they raced around the dining room snatching the crackers and pulling them all before anyone else got a chance.

Jasper ignored them completely and left it up to Olivia to try to contain her boisterous children. Robbie was seated beside me and I could see he was struggling not to laugh when Jasper dripped soup down his shirt and Olivia accidentally hit him on the face as she swung her arms around to emphasise a point. I quickly downed another glass of Donald's very best Sauvignon Blanc. It was going to be a long day.

We gradually ate our way through the meal, which really was delicious. Goose served with a variety of vegetables and three types of potato followed by a choice of either Christmas pudding or snow eggs with an almond crumb. Heather must have been preparing it for days.

After everyone had finished, we traipsed into the lounge for coffee and watched the film *Syriana,* where George Clooney and Matt Damon rather earnestly did convoluted CIA things. Heather refused my offer of help in the kitchen, so I had no option except to watch the film while desperately trying to stay awake. Thank goodness for George and Matt, who made it a bit easier.

As the sky darkened and the moon illuminated the quietening city, the day was over and we could say our goodbyes. Robbie drove us home past the fluorescent Santas and strings of coloured lights and I thought about the family I had married into. It seemed to me that Olivia was playing the role of the dutiful wife whose opinions didn't matter, a bit like Heather. Fleetingly I wondered what they thought of me.

Then I realised that it no longer mattered. What they thought of me was unimportant, and if they didn't like me, so what? One of the beauties of getting older is you stop caring as much about what people think of you and that included my extended family. I'd always been a bit of a people pleaser but I was outgrowing that flaw.

The following day we visited my parents for their Boxing Day gathering, which included all five of my siblings, their partners and a total of fourteen grandchildren. They had decorated the house with an eclectic mishmash of green and red decorations, shelves were crammed with Christmas ornaments and a giant tree was topped with a wonky angel. We were greeted by the din of twenty-six voices all talking over one another, bodies squeezed onto every available chair or stool, mismatched crockery set on two tables. I loved it and to me, this was the embodiment of love and homeliness. Mum had cooked us a massive spread which had obviously taken many hours to prepare and we all enthusiastically cleared our plates.

Once the washing up was done, we moved through into the front room to exchange our Secret Santa novelty gifts. There was good-natured squabbling, no feral children and no Snob Bingo.

These were my tribe and I wouldn't change them for anything.

CHAPTER NINE

As ever we were hosting our New Year's Eve party. My day had been spent cleaning, polishing cutlery, setting the table and making canapés. I made carrot and halloumi fritters with a coriander dip, mozzarella sticks with a chilli tomato sauce and honey mustard cocktail sausages. I'd also made a melting-middle nut roast as a meat alternative.

James was cooking his stalwart New Year's main course of stem ginger and mustard-glazed ham, which required every single saucepan, bowl and wooden spoon we owned. A large part of my day was spent washing these dishes, usually the same saucepan several times.

By evening, the house was ready for our guests and I slipped upstairs to get dressed into a black sparkly shift dress that I knew would hide a multitude of sins. Robbie was going to a party at a friend's house and wouldn't be with us to see the New Year in, so before he left we decided to take some photos of us dressed in our finery. Robbie posed with me for humorous selfies in front of the candle-and-ivy-adorned mantelpiece in the living room.

Then James strode through from the kitchen with a spatula in his hand, face flaming, eyes hard. 'Your stupid nut roast is taking up far too much room in the oven. You need to lift it out immediately for me as I have a sore arm,' he bellowed at me. 'No one's going to eat it anyway. I'm cooking for ten people in case you'd forgotten.'

He disappeared from sight and Robbie gave me a quick look of sympathy. Fighting back the tears that had sprung unbidden, I attempted a weak smile and told him I'd sort out the oven before going upstairs to put on some lipstick. Giving him a quick hug before he left, I told him to have a great night and I'd see him in the new year.

I just about made it into the kitchen without crying, obediently removed the nut roast and covered it with tin foil, as James silently stood watching me with his hands on his hips. I couldn't even bring myself to ask about his arm pain, he had upset me so much.

I retreated to the privacy of the en suite and the tears flowed. Yet again he had dismissed me with a few acerbic words. Within a few minutes I had stemmed my tears and then redid my mascara, which had run in rivulets down my cheeks. In the bathroom mirror I saw that my eyes were red rimmed, and my cheeks drained of colour. James's usual modus operandi was to acknowledge his bad form later, assume instant forgiveness, then repeat. For now, the last thing I felt like doing was to play the perfect hostess.

When I heard the doorbell chime I knew I had no option but to apply some lipstick, swallow my unhappiness and greet our guests.

From the bottom of the staircase I could hear Annie, Matt, Vicky and Tom in the kitchen so I went through to join them. They had all made an effort to dress up and as we greeted each other, Annie whispered in my ear, 'Looking lovely, my friend,' and I gave her a tremulous smile. She answered with an uncertain smile of her own, her hazel eyes concerned, mouthing, 'Are you okay?' behind James's back. Nodding brightly, I turned to kiss Tom's cheek, while thanking him for the bottle of prosecco.

As usual my friends were laden with gifts of food and drink, as although we host the party each year, it really is a team effort. Matt was opening a beer and chatting to James who was guffawing at something humorous, as though our altercation had never happened.

Right at that moment, I was as close to disliking him as I had ever been.

The doorbell rang again, and I escaped his presence to welcome our remaining guests. Soon the house was full of amiable chatter, the clink of glasses and great hilarity. Our friends made their way through to the living room, where I had left out the canapés.

James had chosen the playlist beforehand and Tina Turner blasted 'What's Love Got to Do with It' throughout the house.

What indeed? I thought to myself morosely.

James appeared at the door and announced with a flourish that dinner would be ready in a few minutes, then sidled over beside me. I felt his arm wrap around my waist and it took immense effort not to step away.

'Thanks to my sous chef for all her assistance today.' He made a great show of raising a toast to me, ever the picture of the perfect husband.

I was having difficulty rearranging my face into the vestige of a smile, as I clinked glasses with him, still unable to meet his eye.

'Sorry about earlier,' he murmured into my ear. 'Just a bit stressed about the cooking. Hope it will be okay, seems a little dry to me.'

'I'm sure it will be lovely,' I replied flatly. At least he had apologised quickly this time.

I led them all through to the dining room and James made his grand entrance with the succulent ham. Wine and conversation flowed around me as I sat at one end of the table, surveying my husband and friends. James caught my eye and winked at me. As he raised a glass in a silent toast, I swallowed down my hurt.

'Fabulous meal, James,' announced Tom. 'You're lucky to have him, Laura, I can't cook at all. The most poor Vicky gets is the occasional beans on toast.'

'I'm lucky indeed.' I bit my tongue to prevent myself blurting out that obviously the house had cleaned itself, the pots had washed themselves and the table had set itself. And that James wouldn't know one end of a nut roast from the other.

The evening wore on and I began to relax and enjoy the company. We switched on the television to watch the midnight countdown live from Edinburgh and James filled champagne glasses so we could cheer the new year in. There were kisses and hugs galore among the ten of us and when James gave me a kiss before saying, 'Another year together, Teeny, and we survived,' I nodded and pliantly kissed him back.

If our long marriage had taught me one thing, it was that you need to have the patience of a saint, otherwise you would be tempted to thump your other half most of the time.

The following morning, I woke in bed beside James, who was still fast asleep. The overindulgence of alcohol had enabled me to sleep in James's room without the need for my white noise machine. Quietly I rose and pulled on my dressing gown, before making my way downstairs to wash the glasses from last night.

While watching the sun rise, a mug of coffee in my hands, I felt a sense of renewal and optimism that this New Year, with its new hope, would mean we could fix our issues and by this time next year I would feel happier.

James made his way into the kitchen as I was scrolling through my Facebook feed filled with positive quotes, New Year's resolutions and links to slimming plans.

'How's your arm this morning?' I asked him, as he waited for the Nespresso machine to come to life. No instant coffee for him.

'It feels fine, I must have just hurt it yesterday with all the effort of cooking for so many,' he answered dismissively, completely oblivious as to how feeble that made him sound. But I just nodded before saying,

'That's good. Do you have any New Year's resolutions?'

'Nothing,' he replied. 'What about you?'

'I've decided to learn Spanish on one of those apps.' Mostly because I wanted to learn how to say 'Shut your whingeing mouth' in a language he couldn't understand. 'And I'm also going to do the Couch to 5K.'

His lip curled contemptuously. 'Aren't New Year's resolutions supposed to be achievable?'

'You're welcome to try and achieve it with me, but I will stick with it,' I shot back.

Determination to disprove him flowed through my veins. I'd actually said that as a spur-of-the-moment thing, but now I was certain I would do it. I had another resolution too that I wasn't going to share with him, as I'd weighed myself yesterday morning and had been gutted that I'd gained another half a stone. Therefore I was adamant that I was going to lose at least ten pounds before my weekend away with the girls to London in April.

But I wasn't going to share that with my husband, in case it all went horribly wrong, and he would sneer at my attempts.

I placed my cup in the dishwasher and went upstairs to see if I had anything suitable to run in. Rummaging in the back of the wardrobe, I unearthed an old pair of trainers I'd used when I was going to Pilates regularly and a super stretchy pair of leggings that would do. Filled with positive energy I downloaded the Couch to 5k app and pulled my 'running kit' on.

I was pretty sure I shouldn't run straight after a cup of coffee so passed the time examining photos of anorexic-looking models while psyching myself up to run in front of the unsuspecting public.

I think the last time I had gone for a run was PE in school and that was in 1987. Thankfully, we live at the edge of the village and I was certain there would be few people around on New Year's morning if I turned right at the end of the street towards the country.

Robbie's bedroom door was firmly closed, suggesting he wouldn't surface till much later, and James had disappeared out to his man-cave, so I quietly shut the front door behind me without being seen.

The app encouraged me to warm up with a brisk five-minute walk, followed by sixty seconds of running and ninety seconds of walking for a total of twenty minutes.

After my five-minute walk, I started to run. I felt the wind in my hair, my stride long and sure as my feet flew over the pavement. I ran and ran; this was so easy I should have done it years ago!

Just how long is sixty seconds? Surely my phone was broken? I should have heard the beep telling me to walk as no way was this only sixty seconds. Finally, after what seemed like an eternity, the beep sounded and I slowed to a walk, my chest burning, struggling to breathe as I desperately sucked air into my lungs. The app was definitely faulty for I had hardly recovered until the beep went off again, and I struggled to complete another sixty seconds, plodding at a snail's pace.

How on earth was I to keep this going for twenty minutes? I hadn't thought this through properly. In my haste to pick a route that would have as few spectators as possible, I had inadvertently chosen the hilliest route. Except I hadn't really thought it was hilly until I had to run it. How can something that seems flat in the car suddenly turn into a fifty per cent incline when you're jogging?

If James hadn't been so dismissive of me earlier, I would have given up, returned home and comforted myself with a Bounty bar.

At last the torture was over and the longest twenty minutes of my life ended. Staggering into the back garden, I flopped down on the damp grass, unable to even make it into the kitchen for a seat. I gasped for breath as I stared at the sky, watching rain clouds scurry overhead, willing my poor body to return to normal. My heart was racing, my chest was tight and my stomach queasy but as I gradually recovered, I felt something else.

Pride in my achievement.

I was going to do this not only to prove my husband wrong but for myself too.

At the end of eight weeks, I would be running without stopping for thirty minutes.

CHAPTER TEN

Before I knew it, it was time for Robbie to return to university. The tree and the decorations had been boxed up and stored in the attic. The days were short and dark as the Christmas lights were packed away for another year, and the weather roared and blew a ferocious gale to welcome the new year. I have always detested and loathed January, and since it now meant saying goodbye to Robbie, I hated it even more.

He packed all his belongings into his bag and I felt forlorn as I drove him to the ferry terminal, knowing the worst bit would be returning home to see his empty room, unnaturally tidy after the chaos of the past few weeks. As I hugged him tight and told him I loved him, I breathed in his unique smell and relished these last few moments alone with him. He gave me one final smile, threw a wave over his shoulder and walked into his future.

Having contained my tears while he was there, I let them flow on the drive home, knowing that James would consider me self-indulgent.

I couldn't face him yet, so drove on to the coast, where the Irish Sea was irate, huge waves splashing angrily over the sea wall, spraying me if I ventured too close. As I stood with the wind whipping my hair wildly around me, I howled my distress to the heavens, my cries mingling with those of the gulls.

I didn't care who saw me, after all, don't middle-aged women regularly use scream therapy to beat stress? Finally there was a break in the black clouds, and a weak winter sun broke through. I had wailed myself hoarse and returned to the car composed enough to drive home and face my husband.

James was pottering about in the shed when I arrived home, no doubt fondling one of his bikes.

'Everything okay? That seemed to take a while.' He didn't even bother to look up from the bench, where he was cleaning the spokes of his bike wheel.

'Yes, it's all fine though it will be a rough crossing today with that wind,' I answered dejectedly, ready to slip past him.

'There's hardly a breeze; he'll be all right. What's for dinner and what time's it at?'

How could he be married to me for over half my life and yet still not understand me? He has the innate inability to read my mood, so I simply said prawn curry around half six and with a sigh, retreated into the solitude of my crafting room.

I put on some happy music to lift my mood and did some planks. Delighted I'd held one for nearly twenty seconds, I rested and did another one. Rather than succumb to my longing for a large glass of Pinot to take the edge off my melancholy, I instead decided to go for a run.

It was nearly the end of week two of the C25K as I now called it and I no longer needed to lie on the ground gulping air at the end.

I had accepted that I was not going to be one of those runners who go out with a full face of make-up, gently perspire and bounce along looking like they just stepped out of a *Runners Weekly* ad. Instead, I resemble an overcooked lobster that is in danger of its head exploding. Not to be deterred, I pulled on my kit and set off. I was now running for two minutes at a time and had even downloaded a training playlist for my phone.

Twenty minutes later I slogged home and managed not to collapse on the front step. I know self-satisfaction is a sin, but I enjoyed the look that briefly crossed James's face as I went indoors. He had no faith I would continue running, especially on a stormy day like today.

After dinner I left him to do the dishes and went upstairs into Robbie's room. The duvet was untidily pulled up, discarded trainers lying haphazardly on the rug, a half-drunk glass of water sitting beside the bed.

'It won't be long until Easter,' I assured myself. 'Only a few weeks and he'll be home again before I know it.'

January slowly trudged on with its stark days punctuated by heavy frosts and a smattering of snow. Work was a good distraction from our quiet home-life, and I treated myself to regular coffees with my friends to help get through the most dismal month of the year. My weight-loss plan had got slightly derailed, as after three weeks of 'being good' I had only lost a pound. It wasn't fair. I was exercising more than ever, I'd swapped Pinot Gris for PiNo Fris at weekends, and had been feeling virtuous as I refused all the post-festive chocolates that work colleagues were trying to offload.

James went on a rare night out into Belfast with his cycling club towards the end of the month, so I had the house to myself. Feeling decidedly sorry for myself, I binged on my favourite Chinese takeaway, a curry chip. Thick gloopy curry sauce buried a full serving of chips and I was salivating as I dug in. I ate it so quickly I felt a little sick. Then guilty. How can something so delicious make you feel remorseful? And bloated and disgusted with yourself. Sometimes I think it would be so much easier to give in to the slippery slope of mid-life, eating and drinking whatever I fancied, to stop plucking my chin, stop wearing shapewear and instead invest in several pairs of elasticated trousers. Then I'd think, 'I'm not old yet, this is my Second Spring' or some such nonsense that I'd read about in my *MenoPositive* magazine.

So many phrases have been hijacked by putting 'meno' in front of them recently. Meno-belly. Meno-obsessed. Me-no chance of a quickie.

In an effort to keep myself motivated I had downloaded the MAAF – Middle-Aged and Fantastic – app. Although I like to think of it as the Mad As Absolute Feck app. It was full of helpful tips on how to get through the rollercoaster ride that is menopause, expert advice and encouraging mantras on 'living your best mid-life'.

However, I got a bit irritated with the syrupy sweet quotes after a while.

Be the bestest version of yourself, for yourself and no one else.

Only being true to me can ever really set me free.

No booze and no cakes a dull bore makes.

I may have made that last one up.

Later that evening, I decided to update one of the photos of Robbie that we have displayed in the snug. As I removed his photo from the frame, I realised there was another one underneath it. One that had been taken of me just before I got married, on a trip to northern Italy with my college friend Karen.

While in Verona we had hung out with a couple of Italians she had met back-packing in Greece the summer before. Giovanni and Matteo had taken us on the back of their scooters to a theme park and in the photo, I am wearing tiny shorts while bouncing on a trampoline. My most vivid memory of that trip was an Italian man shouting 'mozzarella and tomato' after me as I walked out of the train station in Verona. 'White and red' for my pasty skin with sunburned bits. For the rest of the trip, I had been a self-conscious twenty-three-year-old hating my paleness among the exotically tanned Italians. Now as I studied the photo I had forgotten existed, I saw myself through new eyes.

Yes, my skin was white but my slim, long legs went on forever. No need to covet a tan when you have a thirty-four-inch inside leg. Why, oh why hadn't I appreciated that when I was young? Why did it take three decades for me to see that I wasn't quite as plain as I had always thought? My red hair flowed halfway down my back and I was laughing with pleasure.

That slightly gawky girl had married a man she idolised, given birth to a son she adored and yet she didn't like herself very much.

Now I was smack bang in middle age and wished that I had worn my factor fifty with pride and shouted '*idiota viscido*' back at the slimy idiot. Mind you, if I were stepping out of the train station in Verona now, I'd be invisible to everyone under the age of thirty. Maybe growing old disgracefully was the way to go. Snickering to myself, I lovingly put the photo of my son into the frame and replaced it on the shelf.

The next day I had arranged to meet Claire for a walk followed by coffee. After power walking a brisk couple of miles through the woods, we went to a local garden centre that had the most delicious raspberry and white chocolate scones. I had worked out if I didn't eat breakfast, I could indulge in one without feeling too guilty.

Claire really was looking fantastic and I felt slightly envious. How did she get that glow in the middle of winter? She was wearing a fuchsia cashmere sweater with matching nail polish and on-trend leather-look leggings. I was in my usual jeans and striped Breton top. I'd forgotten my gloves on the walk and my hands were still blue with the cold.

'What's your secret to looking so great?' I asked, spreading butter on my scone. She radiated positive energy.

'Dove,' she replied. 'It saves me wearing foundation and gets rid of the awful winter pallor.'

'But you look amazing,' I continued. Surely it couldn't be down to a layer of Dove?

Her phone pinged and she looked at it briefly before putting it on silent. I could have sworn a soft blush brightened her cheeks further, but she didn't comment on the message and instead we discussed our work.

Then out of the blue, she asked me a surprise question. 'Laura, when was the last time you were truly happy?'

I was stumped. I didn't have the first clue so I picked the standard response.

'The day Robbie came home for Christmas.'

'And leaving Robbie out of it?'

I chewed my lip as I considered her question.

'I don't know. Why?'

She glanced out of the window at the flowering winter blooms in their terracotta pots before answering me. 'Do you ever wonder if we waste too much time fretting about things we can't change? That not every action has consequences and we should accept our lot without complaining?'

I was unsure what to say. Was she trying to let me know that she had guessed I wasn't happy or did she mean herself?

Uncertain, I simply replied, 'Sometimes.' Then stupidly I continued, 'Is this because you have a big birthday coming up?'

'That's probably it.' She shrugged and gave a small laugh.

But it must have been the wrong thing to say, because she abruptly changed the subject and instead enthused about the fiftieth birthday party she was planning in a couple of months' time. I was puzzled. Had she been trying to tell me something and I had ruined the mood? She and Will seemed like they had a lovely life, she adored her part-time job in a bustling estate agents and Will was a successful and well-paid air traffic controller. Their children Eva and Poppy were both at university in Belfast and as far as I knew caused them no real worry.

As she prattled on about balloons, DJs and party food, I looked beyond her attractive exterior. Was her picture-perfect life not as glossy as it appeared? Did she, like me, have deep buried worries and all was not as it seemed? Whatever it was, she had obviously decided not to confide in me at the minute. There was nothing I could do except nod along, although I was desperate to ask, *What is it you're keeping from me?*

At home I was relieved to find that James was still out on his bike. I ran a bath, lit my Jo Malone Lavender & Moonflower Candle – a gift from Heather – and slipped under the water. Claire's question was playing over and over in my mind, like it was on repeat.

Why doesn't my brain play ball? When I want to remember something important, I draw a blank. When I want to forget something, it stays stuck on replay for hours.

When was the last time you were truly happy?

The question was stuck in my mind because truthfully, I didn't have an answer.

CHAPTER ELEVEN

Soon the days were longer and brighter, the shops emptying of the muted winter shades of black, plum and olive and instead there was the odd pop of spring colours. It always amuses me that lightweight clothes hit the shops while we are still struggling with the bitter chill of winter. I suppose they start to stock spring clothes early as it's meant to be a reassurance that warmer days are coming.

They say that your mental state is reflected in your appearance and I had taken a long, hard look at myself in the mirror at the weekend. My eyes were dull and sad, and I was an unhealthy shade of pale. I lived in jeans and striped tops. Somehow, thinking of an alternative was beyond me. I was waking every night with the same thoughts swirling around my head, even my surefire list was unable to help me drift off.

I had found my menopause symptom beginning with Q.

Questioning my relationship.

So now I woke in the middle of the night and recited my list,

Non-existent libido

Overthinking everything

Paranoia

Questioning my relationship

I could never get past Q, not because I couldn't think of anything beginning with R, but because I was stuck questioning my marriage. Round and round it would go in my head until I was ready to scream.

If I ever made it past Q, R would definitely be *ruminating*.

On Wednesday I left work early due to parent-teacher interviews and decided to indulge myself with a wander around the city centre shops. I was now on week five of the C25K and had managed to run twenty minutes without stopping.

Unfortunately my weight-loss programme had stalled somewhat, so I secretly joined a well-known slimming club online and had lost another three pounds: only six to go until I achieved my goal.

Not wanting to invest in any new clothes in case I was able to lose a few more pounds, I instead treated myself to an anti-ageing moisturiser 'guaranteed to smooth wrinkles after just fourteen days' use'. Of course, I'm not so much of a fool to expect miracles but the packaging was so pretty and the fragrance so enticing, surely it would do something amazing?

In the next aisle I spotted nail varnishes and recalled Claire's perfectly manicured nails as I looked down at my hands. The skin was red rough with a couple of broken nails and suddenly I felt ancient. I used to love painting my nails. In fact, one summer Mum accused me of sniffing nail-polish remover as there was always the smell of it in my bedroom. There's little as ageing as dry, scaly hands so I invested in a scrub, reparative hand cream and some neutral gel polish.

Then I got a bit carried away and looked at the make-up counters.

I've always had blonde lashes and brows and although I wouldn't go out without mascara, I've shied away from getting anything done to my brows. I know the latest trend is for heavy caterpillars on your face, but I baulked at the idea of those, and was innately afraid if I went to a beautician to tint them, I'd end up looking like a child who'd been playing in her mother's make-up bag. Feeling brave I selected a brow pencil in 'light brown' and added it to my basket.

It was then I caught sight of my neck in the mirror. Shops seem to be cleverly lit to make you look as hideous as possible under the harsh fluorescent lighting, and my neck looked like an old crone's. Apart from only ever wearing roll-neck jumpers or scarves for the rest of my life, I had absolutely no option but to invest in the best neck cream around.

'It's never too late to take pride in your appearance,' I told myself sternly. 'Self-love is the best love.' Or so the MAAF app had lectured me this morning. Spotting an age-defying neck and décolletage serum, I popped it into the basket as well.

When I saw the total amount for half a dozen items, I nearly put them all back on the shelf, but then I remembered how glowing Claire had been and how envious I'd felt, so I pulled out my cash, paid and then threw the receipt in the bin.

James would have been furious at how much I'd spent on 'frivolous nonsense', so it was best if I hid it from him.

I secretly called him The Bank Manager as he gave me an allowance each month, and we would sit down at the weekend so I could tell him what I had spent it on. It makes sense really as he's so good with money and I'm so bad. I get £100 per month from my pay that I can spend on anything I want.

On the train a little later, I considered that disturbing question that Claire had asked.

Did I feel happy today? If not, why not?

Would I feel happier if I was going home to an empty house, or would I be watching the tendrils of mist clinging to the craggy face of Cave Hill, wishing that James would be waiting for me? The thought of going home to be greeted by his usual cry of 'What's for dinner?' made me want to sit on the train all the way up to the last stop, then get out and book myself into a B & B for the night. I was sorely tempted. Then reality hit as the train pulled into my station, and I reluctantly disembarked.

Suddenly a lightning sharp thought sliced across my mind.

Why have I never discussed any of this with James? Maybe he was feeling the same and all we needed to do was to discuss it, devise a plan of action to rekindle romance and Bob's your uncle. Cue the violins, marriage sorted, happily ever after.

As I drove home from the station, I deliberated about that some more. We'd always been a couple who dealt with our issues by talking them through. When I was struggling with my teaching job, he encouraged me to resign. When I had the two miscarriages, he gently said we shouldn't try for another baby as I struggled so much after each loss.

Perhaps the only way to survive this was to discuss it and find a way forward together. Feeling more optimistic than I had for some months, I concluded that as it was Valentine's Day at the weekend, I'd cook us a lovely meal, pour a couple of glasses of wine and raise the subject.

When I arrived at the house, he was still typing away in the study so I had some time to myself for once. I had promised Kate I'd drop over a pashmina she had asked to borrow, so I nipped across the street and knocked on her front door. There was no answer, but her car was in the driveway, so I knew she was home. Rather than knocking again, I went around the side of the house and opened the back gate before slipping inside.

I heard a raised voice as I rounded the wall and spotted Kate standing in the middle of their conservatory in front of her youngest daughter, Sophie. Instantly I halted, gaping as my friend shouted at Sophie, who looked like she was trying to sidestep past her to get away.

To my horror, Kate lifted her arm and appeared to be about to slap her when her son Luke appeared from behind and grabbed her arm. I heard Kate give a bellow of anger as she swung round to face him and Sophie raced past, clearly upset.

Luke towered over his mother and it was obvious he was trying to talk to her while restraining her right arm. Kate started to cry and Luke dropped her arm as she then tried to hug him.

A brief look of disgust crossed his face as he walked away and disappeared from view. Kate seemed to stumble as she looked after him and then she too disappeared into the kitchen.

The whole thing had taken less than a minute, but it seemed like my feet were rooted to the spot as I tried to make sense of what I had seen.

One thing was sure, I did not want to be caught lurking in their garden or for anyone indoors to realise that the whole sorry scene had been witnessed. Sneaking back through the gate, I closed it as quietly as possible before crossing the road back to our house. I shut the front door behind me and released the breath that I had been holding.

I peeled off my coat, went to put the kettle on, musing about what I had seen and relieved that James was still in his study. In all my years of being friends with Kate I had never once seen her angry or even close to losing her temper, and I was seriously shocked that it seemed she was about to strike Sophie. Thank goodness Luke had been there to stop her.

I felt caught between a rock and a hard place. If I said anything to Kate, she would think that I had been snooping on her but if I didn't say anything, would Sophie be at risk?

I reasoned with myself that Kate was one of my best friends and there was no chance that she smacked her children. We had been friends for years and there had never been any hint of this type of behaviour towards them so I had to be mistaken.

Slowly I recalled the night of the dinner dance when Kate had been distressed and confided in me that she thought her children despised her. Reminding myself I had only seen the tail-end of what had happened, I thought that maybe Sophie had pushed Kate to her limit in the way that only teenagers can. Tempers can quickly fray when buttons are pushed.

I poured milk into my instant coffee as I tried to figure out what I should do. In the end I decided I would not say anything to Kate unless there was an opening the next time I saw her. Confiding in James was also out of the question, as there was every chance he would either dismiss me completely or even worse, insist on marching over to Kate and having it out with her in his own imitable, bossy manner.

For now, I would bide my time and see what, if anything else, was said or done by my friend that was a red flag.

And with that, I promptly stuck my head firmly back in the sand.

CHAPTER TWELVE

At the beginning of our relationship James used to make a big deal of Valentine's Day. He would brandish a dozen red roses, book a table at a fancy restaurant or even a night away at a country house hotel.

Over the years the nights away to the country house hotels stopped, then apparently red roses became a symbol of commercialism at its worst and eventually the fancy restaurants became too busy and overpriced on Valentine's.

Ultimately it became something that only other people enjoyed and I never intimated that a cheap card bought last minute at the garage would have sufficed. I'm not even slightly high maintenance but it seemed James couldn't meet even my low standards.

This year I decided that it was as good an excuse as any to cook us a nice meal then to broach the subject that was causing me so many sleepless nights. Perhaps by the end of the most romantic weekend of the year we would have wiped the slate clean and the future would be laid before us in glorious harmony. I felt it was worth a try anyway, for what did I have to lose?

Therefore I spent a couple of evenings perusing my recipes,

and opted for one of James's favourites, seafood mornay for the main course followed by tiramisu, in the hope that it would remind him of our trip or our silver wedding anniversary. We had spent three weeks inter-railing together and ended the holiday with three blissful days in Venice. A tiny part of me grieved for the contentedness I had felt then, how could our marriage have become so unhappy since?

The fishmongers at St George's Market in the centre of Belfast are renowned for their fresh catches on a Friday morning, so despite the rush-hour traffic I drove into the city with the cool box in the boot of the car, and was there for the market opening at eight o'clock. I swallowed my queasiness at the ripe pong so early in the morning and bought prawns, mussels, scallops, and cod. Transferring them into the cool box a short time later, I then navigated the congested streets in my nippy little Mini and still got to work on time. I felt a rush of optimism that James and I would be able to steer the rocky path that was our marriage as easily as I had negotiated the traffic.

It was the start of half term and the drive home was a bit of a nightmare as the dual lanes of the Westlink were congested with cars, trucks and buses pumping exhaust fumes into the overcast sky.

Whoever had designed this section of road did not have 21st century volume of traffic in mind. Which was exactly why I avoided the city centre traffic as much as possible, instead commuting by train after driving to a local station and leaving the car there. In due course, I made it onto the country-bound stretch of road, and once I reached the outskirts of the village breathed a huge sigh of relief. City driving is not for the faint-hearted.

This relief was, however, short-lived, as with a sinking heart I spotted Kate getting out of her car at the same time as me, and as she waved, made her way over. She was wrapped up in a long pink jacket to combat the chilly February day, her shoulder-length black hair windswept.

'Hello stranger.' She smiled as I made my way to the back of the car. 'I kept meaning to pop over to get your pashmina, I just never got round to it.'

My wobbly smile must have thrown her a bit, because she looked uncertain, and asked if it was still all right to borrow it.

'Oh yes, of course.' I forced a grin, while reaching into the boot for the cool box. 'I kept meaning to pop over with it but the week has run away with me. I've been concocting a special meal for James and me for Valentine's night, so much planning and prep you'd think I'd never cooked for him before. Originally, I was going to do duck à l'orange but then I decided on seafood mornay and even went into St George's Market this morning to get the best ingredients.' My mouth kept on talking, desperate to say anything other than *What was going on the other day with Sophie?*

At last I stopped whittering and Kate hastily intervened. 'How lovely and thoughtful you are. I do envy your great relationship and the peace and quiet you'll get to enjoy your meal.' Her smile faltered as she followed me into the house, where I deposited the cool box in the utility room.

I handed her the pashmina, which had been lying on the wicker chair in the hall since my thwarted attempt to give it to her on Wednesday.

As she took it, I blurted out 'Is everything okay?' before I could stop myself.

'Oh yes, absolutely great.' Her eyes slid away to the left, which I'm certain I had once read in the *Daily Mail* means someone is lying. 'I'm so looking forward to this dinner with David's work colleagues tonight. Though I've got to be on my best behaviour as he's hoping to impress his boss and maybe get a pay rise. I'm hoping he does, as having three kids costs so much nowadays. Did I tell you we're going for drinks at the City Hotel

Observatory before dinner?' Now it was Kate who was babbling on.

Before I could ask her anything else, she thanked me for the pashmina again and left. The odour of garlic from her breath as she leaned in for a hug was a bit overpowering, and again I debated if a real friend would be honest enough to tell her she needed to quit chewing the stuff as her breath was rank. However, I could never bring myself to tell her, as I could picture her pretty face falling and I didn't want to hurt her.

I had no time to give it any more thought when James appeared from upstairs and was obviously tetchy, as he could barely grunt hello before making himself an espresso.

'Is everything okay?' I asked for the second time in ten minutes.

'Just great,' he growled. 'That stupid editor is harassing me for a story and I can't get it finished. I've told her it will be submitted before the end of the weekend; I don't need some menopausal woman taking her failings out on me. She either needs to up her HRT or get a job that doesn't involve dealing with people. It's beyond me why she even got the promotion when she has the brain cells of an ant.' Absent-mindedly he rubbed at his left arm but before I had the chance to ask him if it was painful again, he turned on his heel, leaving me alone in the middle of the kitchen.

What a complete plank my husband is sometimes.

He hadn't as much as asked me about my day or why Kate had popped over or even offered me a cup of coffee.

My blood boiled as I took off my coat and sat down at the table. I really don't know why I was even bothering to cook a nice meal tomorrow night for someone who was as wrapped up and self-involved as him. If I hadn't spent a small fortune on the fresh fish, we could have made do with frozen pizza. I was absolutely itching to have a row with him, and it took a great deal of restraint not to go upstairs and unleash the full extent of my temper.

It was five o'clock somewhere, I thought as I reached for a bottle of Pinot Gris from the wine fridge. Pouring myself a healthy measure, I took a large slug and tried to calm down. There was no point in starting a row with him now if I was going to attempt to devise a rescue package for our marriage tomorrow evening.

I commanded Alexa to play chill-out music and sat unseeing, sipping my wine. But even that failed to mollify me and I could feel my temper continue to fester.

Just as quickly as it had flared, it dissipated, and tears slowly filled my eyes. I felt an agony of despair as my poor mind leapt from anger at my husband to abject despondency at the thought of a never-ending road together, with us snapping and snarling at each other.

I used to think our differences complimented each other, that I was the yin to his yang, but now it seemed our differences only contradicted each other. Instead of a future filled with promise, I felt that it was a vast wasteland devoid of colour and hope.

No matter how many positive affirmations I made or how much gratitude I expressed, deep down I was desperately unhappy and desperately afraid of acknowledging it. Even in the middle of yet another weeping session, part of me was terrified to unpick the slow, inexorable disintegration of our relationship. Another part was furious with myself, because, after all, this was James, the man I had tied my star to since I was eighteen, the father of my son, the person who I had vowed to love, honour and cherish till death did us part.

Or some such naïve, innocent nonsense.

Shakily, I shouted at Alexa to play something cheerful and got up to prepare dinner.

Sometimes I get so fed up with my heartache, that it simply exhausts me. Although I wasn't in the mood for dancing or laughing or optimism, listening to sad songs was bad for my mental health today, and as the kitchen was flooded with Pharrell Williams singing 'Happy' I tried to bury my emotions.

But from the remnants of my desolation, I recognised two small but pertinent facts.

No one was forcing me to stay.

Equally, no one was forcing me to go.

For once the ball was in my court and no rash decision had to be made, as no timer had been set for a final verdict. And for that I had to be grateful.

If I thought it all through and broached it in the right way tomorrow, perhaps we could start afresh. Possibly, if we were brutally honest with each other, we could find some common ground.

Almost as if he had sensed what was on my mind, James came up behind me and wrapped his arms around me as I stared out at the darkening garden.

'I really miss having you around all day, it makes me feel so isolated, especially when you're late back,' he quietly said into my ear.

I leant against him, resting my head naturally into the curve of his neck and inhaled his clean, fresh smell. A smell as familiar to me as my own hands.

'I'm a bit late because I drove into work today to get some fresh fish from St George's Market. I plan to cook us a special meal for Valentine's tomorrow night,' I replied.

'You are an old romantic,' he murmured. 'I'll look forward to that. Would you like to go for a walk at Whitehead tomorrow after I've been cycling?'

'Sounds lovely,' I answered, my mood perceptibly lifting.

With a bit of TLC maybe there was hope for us yet.

CHAPTER THIRTEEN

The following morning while James was out cycling, I happily pottered around the kitchen making the tiramisu and preparing the seafood mornay. The weather was looking much brighter than the day before and once he had arrived home and showered, we drove to the picturesque village of Whitehead for a walk beside the sea. With its quirky painted houses and pretty promenade leading to the lighthouse towering over the bay, Whitehead is usually busy with visitors even on cool winter days.

We ambled along together, chatting about Robbie and his plans to come home for Easter. I deliberately avoided any discussion about 'us' as I wanted nothing to spoil the day and I was still unsure what exactly I was going to say.

When we returned home, James disappeared into his study to work on his article and I went for a run. I'd learned that going for a run helps me feel less guilty about overindulging. It also makes me feel smug which may be a sin, but it's worth it to see James eat his words.

Following my shower, I dressed in lacy lingerie and a teal wrap dress that James likes. I dried and straightened my hair, then applied some make-up. I never usually bothered straightening my hair or wearing make-up if it's just the two of us in the house, but I really wanted to make an effort tonight.

Pouring us both a glass of wine, I took his up to the study where he barely glanced at me, he was so engrossed in his work.

I refused to let this annoy me, went downstairs to set the table with our best crockery and started to cook dinner. When it was ready, I instructed Alexa to play romantic music, then called for James as I lit a few candles.

The seafood mornay was absolutely scrumptious and I was glad I had gone to so much effort, as even James complimented me without his usual criticism. Setting the tiramisu in front of him, I could no longer avoid the conversation I was dreading.

'Do you remember saying a few weeks ago that I don't seem very happy?' I started, a bit nervously.

'No.' He looked at me quizzically, eyebrows raised.

'Well, you did. It was after the row about you discussing our holiday plans with your dad.'

He nodded. 'Yes and you said you were letting things get you down a bit.'

'That's right.' I sipped my wine, still not really sure what I was going to say. 'How do you feel things are now?' I watched his reaction anxiously.

Carefully he avoided eye contact and instead studied the wine in his glass. 'Frankly you still don't seem particularly happy. It doesn't matter what I say or do, you always seem to be annoyed with me.' He sighed heavily before raising his beautiful blue eyes to look directly at me. 'I never thought you would be one of those women who would struggle so badly with the menopause. It makes living together extremely difficult sometimes, as you make it all about you.'

I almost recoiled at the stringent words. But when I opened my mouth to reply, it appeared he hadn't finished yet.

'You keep telling me you're having a hard time but it's hard for me too. The wife I had seems to be buried under a neurotic, irritable shell and I'm worried she'll never reappear. I never know what mood you're going to be in and I don't think your fixation on Robbie being away is helpful at all.'

My stomach reacted so violently I thought I might be sick. Leaning forward on the table, I had to hold my head in my hands to stave off the nausea, for it was as though he had delivered a sucker punch to my solar plexus.

And still he continued, even in the face of my obvious distress. It was clear he had immense pent-up anger and bitterness and the floodgates had opened.

'I'm sick to death of hearing about your menopause, sick of you using it as an excuse for everything. If you feel as bad as this, you need to see the doctor and get pills or something to sort you out. It can't be that difficult as half the world's population go through it and don't make such a song and dance about it.'

I could listen to no more. Scraping my chair back I stumbled from the room sobbing. Instead of coming after me, I was aware that James simply reached forward for the wine bottle. I couldn't bear to be in the house with him, so I grabbed my coat and unlocked the front door. Praying that none of the neighbours were about, I slipped out into the street and started walking, my tears mingling with the rain that was steadily falling. I had no idea where I was going. My shoes were not made for walking any distance and certainly not in the pouring rain. Reaching the end of the street I turned towards the country and away from the street lights.

I was so horrified about the sudden deterioration of the evening that it took me a few minutes to even begin to process it.

James had spoken with a vitriol I had never heard before; it seemed that he hated me. And there I was thinking that I was the unhappy one. Was I really such an awful person, so difficult to be with? Had I been the problem this whole time, not James?

When I could walk no more, I leaned heavily against a field

gate. Nausea again threatened to overwhelm me as I wrestled with the thought that when I returned home, maybe James would tell me it was over and that he wanted a divorce. Although I had been slowly coming to the realisation that our marriage was indeed in serious trouble, I had never allowed myself to consider that divorce was even an option. My legs would have given way if I hadn't got the support of the gate to keep me upright.

Every time I thought about being on my own, I was terrified. Having married straight from university, James had always been in charge of our finances. I had no idea how to take the car for an MOT or anything about our house insurance. I didn't even know who our electricity or oil suppliers were. I could never survive on my own. But what would happen now if I had no choice? If instead of me taking time to think everything through, what if James made a life-altering decision for me?

Where would I live? What would I live on? Would our friends side with James and I'd end up friendless and penniless? What would my son think if our family split up?

Then without even being conscious of it, I asked myself another question. *Would the initial nightmare of a separation ultimately lead to a happier life?*

Belatedly I acknowledged it had been partly my choice not to bother about things like insurance and utilities, though I knew millions of independent people around the world dealt with it every day, so I could learn. If my friends were so shallow as to abandon me, were they ever real friends? Money would definitely be an issue as my running-away-from-home account was not huge, but I could economise and downsize.

I just needed to have a little self-confidence.

After a few minutes, I felt calmer as the sickness passed. I was still no closer to making a final decision but I had realised something of vital importance tonight.

I would survive no matter what happened.

It was time to learn how to stand on my own two feet, and

start thinking about finances. Ultimately it was time to pull my head out of the sand and face the future properly armed and knowledgeable. Therefore even if we separated, I could be independent.

A cow lowed at me from the field, making me jump and I allowed myself a small smile.

It was time to go back to the house and face James.

It didn't take long to reach the front door, and again I was thankful that none of my neighbours were outside to see me. For I knew that I looked like a drowned rat. My carefully applied make-up would have run and my sodden hair was sticking to my head.

I turned the handle and held my breath, unsure what reception I was going to get.

James appeared at the kitchen door and appraised me coolly. 'What on earth did you run off for? You're soaked through. Honestly Laura, I really don't know what to do with you anymore.' His tone was resigned.

'You upset me,' I replied, stung that he wasn't the slightest bit concerned about me.

'It doesn't take much to upset you these days, does it?' The retort was quick. He appeared to soften a little as he told me to take off my wet coat and handed me a towel.

'It's obvious that things have been better between us than they are now,' he continued. 'But I meant what I said, I don't know what to do to make you happy anymore. It's like the Laura I know and love has gone somewhere I can't reach.'

'What about couples therapy?' I had no idea where that came from but the minute I voiced it I realised it was a genius idea.

'I don't believe in therapy,' he answered abruptly.

'What do you mean you don't believe in it? Like you don't believe in the Tooth Fairy or in Father Christmas? James, this may surprise you but therapy exists and it may even help us.'

'Help us in what way? Help us to talk about our practically

non-existent sex life? Help you to see that your hormones are dictating our marriage? You might need therapy but I don't.'

'Maybe I do need therapy but our marriage needs a lifebelt, James, because I have this awful feeling we are sinking.'

That seemed to get through to him, because his head flew up. 'I won't go to therapy with you, Laura, but I do agree that we aren't in a good place. You need to speak to someone that will help you get into a better headspace. It's up to you whether that's therapy or medication, as I can't see a way forward while you're as unstable as this. And I'm not alone in thinking you're losing it: my parents think so too.'

Unstable? I almost laughed in his face. It was clear that James thought our issues were exclusively my fault. He either couldn't or wouldn't see that it had anything to do with him.

'I'm tired of this conversation tonight, you've given me indigestion,' he said. 'The dishes are done and I'm going up to bed. Please think about what I've said. I can't put up with your mood swings and your unhappiness for much longer.'

Striding past me after this not-so-veiled threat, he climbed the stairs and left me thinking about what he had said.

If two people love each other, hope is not lost.

If two people no longer love each other, there is no hope.

The big question is, do we even like each other anymore?

CHAPTER FOURTEEN

Next morning I felt surprisingly calm. It was almost as if the row the night before had forced us to address our mutual unhappiness. And now we jointly had to decide if our marriage was worth fighting for, or if it was time to lay it to rest.

I thought this would shatter me but I simply felt relieved. I would still like to find a way through, but unless we approached this together, there was no chance. Obviously James had been as unhappy as me, so maybe this could be a starting point?

I wrapped my dressing gown tightly around me before creeping out onto the landing, where I was surprised to see that his bedroom door was open, the curtains pulled back, the bed neatly made. I hadn't heard him go downstairs and it was only eight o'clock. The silent house seemed to mock me as I checked each room and found them empty. Not even a note had been left for me.

For goodness' sake, he really was like a child flipping between tantrums and ignoring me. He seemed to get a perverse pleasure out of tormenting me sometimes. Except I was growing tired of him and his antics.

I texted Mum and asked if she would be in later before

making myself an oregano omelette and treating myself to a cappuccino from the usually forbidden Nespresso machine. I drank it while browsing the internet and enjoying the peace and quiet of our sunny kitchen. As I cleared up afterwards, I surveyed the back garden and thought again how lovely it would be if we had a garden room. Somewhere I could sit on warm, sunny days, making it feel like I was on holiday. But James still dismissed it as a silly notion, claiming it would never be used.

Irritated with him, I ran a bath. Soaking in it until the water cooled, my mind flitted between last night's conversation and thoughts about the future. On the face of it, this was out of character for my husband, but the more I dwelt on it, similar episodes from the past would pop into my mind.

There were the multiple times he diminished my opinion in front of family or friends. Once he had announced in front of his work colleague that it was a surprise I'd ever got a degree because I could barely remember my own name. I had bitten my tongue on that occasion to stop myself reminding him I'd got a first while he got a 2:2.

Once I let myself think about it all, it seemed I couldn't stop. From the patronising nickname Teeny, to the sly digs about my weight. His assumption I would do all the cooking and cleaning, when the only cleaning he did was of his three bicycles. From him making a fuss about my one weekend a year away with my friends, to him going to Majorca for a week in both May and September with his cycling club.

It slowly dawned on me that it was usual for him to spit out a caustic comment followed by a morsel of kindness, for which I used to be pathetically grateful. This behaviour had been repeated over the years until it was ingrained in us both.

The trickle of annoyance grew within me until it became a deluge. I could practically feel my blood pressure rising the more I thought about all the ways he had denigrated me over the years.

In fact, I became so enraged that if he had been in the house, there was a real risk I would have exploded.

Just as well he was elsewhere or he would have felt the full force of my meno-rage.

I dried off, then dressed in grey jeans and a blue striped sweater before driving up to my parents without leaving a note. I would have kept my phone switched off, but part of me was worried I would miss an important call from Robbie.

Me and my catastrophising. The source of much scorn from my husband.

It must have been obvious that I was in need of maternal care, because Dad made himself scarce after a quick hello.

'How are you?' Mum asked, while waiting for the kettle to boil.

'I've been better,' I replied, stroking Paddy who had automatically nestled onto my lap. 'James and I have had a row.'

Her look was guarded as she said nothing.

'I tried to discuss some issues with him last night but he turned on me, told me I was impossible to live with and everything is all my hormones' fault,' I blurted out in a rush.

'Men do like to blame hormones, don't they,' she replied sagely, taking a seat opposite me at the table. 'They never like to admit they can be complete and utter pains to live with.'

I looked at her with surprise for she'd never spoken like that before.

She passed me a cup of coffee and a slice of date-and-walnut loaf, then said, 'Look Laura, living with someone else isn't easy at the best of times but reaching middle age? Well, that adds a whole lot of spice to the mix. I think most of us wake up one day, look at the person opposite and think, *How did that happen? Where did that young person I fell in love with go? Do I even like them anymore?*'

She smiled at me as I asked, 'Did you ever feel like that about Dad?'

'Once upon a time, yes. When your dad had retired from the

bank and you and your siblings had all left home. I was concerned that it was going to be just us at home, all day every day. Just the two of us looking at each other every minute of every day. I wanted to run to the hills and not look back. Then we discovered that we still quite liked being together, gardening and caring for the animals. It worked itself out.'

She stared fondly out of the window at my father who was disappearing down the lane, wellingtons and flat cap in place. Paddy gave a muffled bark and made himself more comfortable on my knees.

'Why did you never say any of that before?'

'You're a born worrier; you didn't need to worry about me and your dad on top of dealing with your own issues.' She paused for a moment before continuing. 'Menopause can change you and not always for the worse. It can make you take stock of your life and reassess if you are really, truly happy. And if the answer is no, it can give you the strength to change things. It's always amazed me, you know, your inner strength and your innate sense of right and wrong. However, you're a people pleaser, my love, maybe it's time you realised it's okay to please yourself as well.' She stopped and then ploughed on. 'Sometimes I've felt that you've lost a little bit of who you are.'

She didn't say *Because of who you're married to* but it hung unspoken in the air between us.

'You've never really liked him, have you?' I asked, wanting an honest answer to a question I'd been afraid of for years.

'I liked him because you chose him. But there's things about him I haven't liked over the years.' She turned her tired, worn eyes to me and reached for my hand. 'No one should make themselves feel better by putting someone else down. How you make someone feel about themselves speaks volumes.'

'I'm scared, Mum.' Easy tears filled my eyes. 'I don't know if we're going to be able to come through this. Or if I even want us to.'

'No matter what you decide, you aren't alone. You have me, Dad and all your family who love you. If you come through it together, all well and good. If you come through it on your own, you will survive, Laura, for you are stronger than you think.'

I was sobbing. My sweet, wise mum had said the words I needed to hear. If James and I didn't make it as a couple, it would still be all right. I would cope with it, whatever 'it' might be, because I had people who loved me and accepted me no matter what.

It was amazing how good it felt to talk about it all rather than hiding behind the pretence that everything was perfect. For years I had hidden the truth of how James spoke to me behind closed doors, never confiding in either my family or closest friends, but now I felt like the proverbial weight had lifted off my shoulders. The world had not come crashing down. I was not told to grin and bear it or that many women had a worse husband than mine. I was being told that no matter what, I wouldn't be on my own.

The relief I felt at that moment was immense.

I stayed on for lunch, a hearty vegetable soup made like only Mum could do. One day I'd have to learn her secret because no one else could make it as good as her. Before long two of my siblings, Sarah and Harry, and their kids appeared and I spent a contented few hours chatting and laughing with them.

No one asked about James or why my eyes were red from crying. No one commented on how relaxed they felt without his prickly, critical presence. Sarah had obviously been tipped off by Mum, because she told a long story about a 'friend of a friend' who had ended an unhappy marriage and was thriving. I had to suppress a giggle at Mum's attempts to keep an innocent look on her face throughout.

Soon the hiatus had to end, and after giving my parents one last hug, I started for home. Of course, I was worried about what would be waiting for me when I arrived. Would James still be stropping? Or would he unleash the full force of his anger the minute I walked through the door? Or would he simply ask what was for dinner as if nothing had happened? The unpredictability of his response left me feeling panicky on the drive back to the village.

It was with some trepidation that I pulled into the driveway and noticed straight away that his Mercedes was not in its usual place. Which meant he had come home from his bike ride and then gone out again.

Opening the front door, I called his name but only my voice reverberated back at me. Stripping off my coat, I went through into the kitchen. No note. Which in one way was a respite, but in another, it simply was delaying the inevitable.

Without thinking, I searched through the top drawer until I found the menu for the local Chinese takeaway. Opting for honey chilli chicken and fried rice, I mentally parked my diet for another day. Comfort food was what the doctor ordered tonight, not something green and leafy and full of goodness. I would have just enough time to have my weekly phone call with Robbie before it was delivered.

My lovely son was full of chat for a change; he had submitted his dissertation and he and his friends had spent the last two nights partying. Even better, he let slip that he was applying for a graduate job in Belfast. Feeling almost giddy with pleasure, I made sure not to be too effusive in my response.

He asked if James was about to talk too, but I waffled on about him being out at the minute and if it was important, he could call him back. Finally, he told me he loved me and hung up. I savoured the knowledge of his job application in Belfast like a warm hug. He wanted to come home!

By the time the tasty stodge was delivered, I was already on my second glass of wine and there was still no sign of or communication from my husband. Enjoying every decadent mouthful as I watched *Countryfile* on my own, I debated what to do with the next couple of days. It was half term and originally

James had talked about booking leave as well, so we could spend it together. Then his boss had created a furore so fortunately he wasn't able to. I now looked on this as providence as I had two days entirely to myself.

Also, as we apparently weren't speaking, I could do anything I wanted. Within reason.

Without giving it much thought, I put a message in the Book Club WhatsApp.

> Me: Anyone free over the next couple of days for coffee? Lunch? Shopping?

> Kate: Prosecco?

> Claire: Lunch and prosecco?

> Annie: I'm free on Tuesday, fancy a drive up the north coast and a walk on Portstewart Strand?

I smiled to myself. I was ready to face what was ahead.

CHAPTER FIFTEEN

I t took James a full two days before he would look at me
properly or do more than grunt if I asked him a question.
Each day I would get up, have a shower and then leave as early as
I could to spend the day walking, lunching and having a pleasant
time with my friends. By Tuesday night, it was clear James was
fuming that I wasn't upset by his bad form, and when I came in
from a lovely day spent at the north coast, he met me in the hall
to demand what was for dinner and what time was it at.

'Takeaway at about half seven,' I replied airily, before going
into the snug and flicking on the telly. Reclining on our denim
blue sofa, I rested my feet on a small leather footstool,
determinedly watching a news report about the biggest octopus
ever to have been caught in a shelter pot.

'Takeaway during the week?' He followed me into the room,
clearly still in a filthy mood.

'I'm on holiday, so if you want something else, then cook it
yourself.'

He glared at me and asked, 'Have you contacted the GP about
medication for your moods yet?'

'I'm not going to, James. I don't need medication for my

moods, I need a husband who gets over himself and accepts some responsibility for our issues.' I tried to ensure my voice remained firm, although the telltale chest tightness and racing heart gave my true feelings away.

With a face like thunder, he stormed out of the room and I heard the door to his study slam.

Opting for an Indian takeaway, partly because I wanted something different and partly because I knew James wasn't keen on it, I rang through the order and asked them to deliver for half past seven. Sure enough, it arrived on time and I shouted up the stairs to let James know. By the time he came down, I was settled in front of the telly again, eating my chicken korma out of the takeaway box on my knee.

Which I knew would really, really exasperate him.

My snob of a husband thinks only lower-class people eat their food on their knees in front of the telly.

Much to my disappointment, he simply threw me a dirty look before setting a place at the kitchen table complete with placemat, proper crockery and a napkin. I felt like a rebellious teenager as I finished my dinner and instead of automatically clearing it away as I normally would, left the congealing food box on the coffee table while I watched *Sex and the City*.

After dinner he avoided me and retreated upstairs.

———

When I arrived home from work the next day, I was surprised to be met by him at the front door. Adopting a wounded expression, he pulled me in for a hug without speaking. I allowed him to hold me and then relenting, hugged him back.

'I hate it when you fight with me,' he said, releasing me from his grip. 'You said some awful things to me the other night. But I forgive you. Can we be friends again?'

'Of course,' I replied warily. This change of heart was so sudden, I waited with some trepidation for his finale.

'I only said what I did because I'm so worried about you. You seem to get such pleasure from hurting me these days, it really breaks my heart.'

And there it was. No apology. No admission of the deliberate upset he had caused me.

Inwardly I sighed. He has always been good at paying lip service to things. Only this time I didn't believe him. He had meant what he said the other night; he probably just felt a bit guilty about how he had said it, as he expected me to defer to him at all times. Nonetheless, I was no longer in the mood for a fight, so I appeared to acquiesce and put it behind me.

'I'm sure we'll muddle our way through like we always have.' I tried a reassuring smile as I hung my coat and scarf up.

'What are we having for dinner tonight?' Back to his usual.

'Sea bass with samphire and parmentier potatoes.'

'Lovely, just make sure you don't burn the fish like the last time.'

And on the face of it, harmony was restored.

The rest of February was uneventful as the days grew longer and brighter. We had no more run-ins but equally no resolution. I did my wifely duty once a week since James had made that barbed comment about our sex life during his monologue. I would have rather watched paint dry, but perfected my acting skills and he never appeared to notice. Instead, I passed the time by wondering if I should lie back and think of England, or because I was in Northern Ireland, I should lie back and think of the Mournes.

By the start of March I had lost six pounds and could run for twenty-eight minutes without stopping. Sadly, my expensive face and neck creams had not worked miracles, but I had regained some of my mojo and a tiny bit of confidence in myself. I was proud of my achievements and was looking forward to Claire's birthday party in a few days.

As a reward for sticking to my diet and exercise regime, I decided to treat myself to some highlights. My hair had darkened to a dull auburn over the winter and I felt the need for a change. To be honest I'd taken a positive quote on the MAAF app a bit too literally.

Brighten your mind and replenish your soul with light

I decided 'Brighten your mind and replenish your soul with highlights' is what they really meant, so I booked myself in with my hairdresser and returned home with a shiny, Titian head of hair. As I got out of the car, I spotted Vicky and nipped over for a chat.

'You look great!' she cried, her face wreathed in smiles. 'Love the new hair-do. Do you have time to come in for coffee?'

'I've got about half an hour,' I replied, following her into her house. I couldn't help but notice that she, as usual, was looking amazing. She wore a green and brown Boden wrap dress with knee-length leather boots the exact shade of her hair.

Not only is Vicky gorgeous, intelligent and funny, she also has impeccable taste in décor. As I sank into her smoky-grey sofa at the end of her open-plan kitchen, I felt the tiniest flame of jealousy as I surveyed her Aga, kitchen island and Emma Bridgewater crockery. Soft hues of white and grey had an immediate calming effect, and even her British shorthair cat Keiko blended in seamlessly. Quashing my resentment, I asked her how Alex and Flora were.

'They're fine, busy with their own lives,' she replied while grinding the beans for my coffee. 'Tom is flying all over the place at the minute, I can't keep up with his schedule at all. One good thing about the lockdowns was pilots were stuck at home. It's taken a bit of readjustment now he's away so often again.'

Tom was first officer for an Irish airline, and much to my

shame I even begrudged Vicky having all that time to herself when he was working.

As we exchanged village gossip, she repeatedly got notifications on her phone. She appeared oblivious but the incessant vibration was distracting to say the least. A little agitated, I asked her if she wanted to respond, but she dismissed it with a wave.

'Probably just the kids wanting something,' she said airily, as she turned the phone face down so I could no longer see the screen. 'They constantly disagree about whose turn it is to have the car. If I ignore them, they'll have to sort it out themselves.'

Vicky and Tom could easily have afforded two cars for the girls, but insisted they had to share, which was a repeated source of friction. Changing the subject, I asked her how work was.

'Lots of pressure after Covid,' she reflected cautiously. 'I hate having to triage patients on the phone; I'm always so afraid of missing something vital. I don't think it helps being part-time either.'

'How's the new practice manager working out?' I asked, munching on a chocolate biscuit.

'He's good,' she replied as she stood up and offered a top-up of coffee. 'Working out well I think.'

'So even though he's young, he's able to keep all you GPs in check?' I laughed.

'Yes, he's got a nice way with him. Easy going but well able to be assertive when needs be. And needs be very often with that nightmare of a receptionist.'

Vicky softened her words with a faint smile, but it did bother me that she always turned work chat back to the receptionist. I wondered briefly if there was more to the story than she was admitting.

Not wanting my friend to start another monologue, I hastily asked what she was wearing to Claire's party.

'I've got those sparkly black jeggings I might wear with a lacy blouse. I don't really want to wear a dress because then I'll need to shave my legs.'

She grinned at me and I giggled back. Never in a million years could I imagine someone as perfect as Vicky walking around with hairy legs. Is that why she was wearing the knee-length boots?

'What about you?'

'No idea,' I answered without thinking. 'Maybe a slinky little black dress. Of course, it wouldn't be either slinky or little on me.'

'For goodness' sake, Laura, you're gorgeous. Why do you always put yourself down?' Vicky was looking at me intently, eyes flashing with annoyance.

I hesitated, unsure what to say.

She stared at me, then just as quickly as she had flared up, she leaned over and touched me lightly on the forearm. 'I don't know where you've got this idea that you're not fantastic because you are, you really are, my friend.'

I wanted to scream *Because all I ever get is criticism at home* but of course, I couldn't. I had to bury that secret in a deep, dark place. My eyes dropped to the table as I could barely look at her, my shame was so great.

'Because I don't feel fantastic. I feel fair, fat and fifty,' I managed quietly.

'Fair, fit and fantastic,' she replied quickly. 'Instead of repeating some nonsense affirmations every day, repeat that until you actually believe it.'

I lifted my eyes and looked directly at her. Her stare was steady, and she looked like she was about to say something else, but remained silent.

'We can't all be as perfect as you,' I said, trying to lighten the mood.

But instead she withdrew her hand as she said, 'No one sees

what's inside someone else's head. What's gleaming on the outside is not always gleaming on the inside.'

'Did you get that on the MAAF app?' I asked, a bit disturbed by the darkness in her eyes.

'I must have.' She suddenly grinned at me. 'Worst thing I ever did was download that flipping app. Even when I'm in bed at night I have those sayings floating round my head.'

'My favourite is "Wearing big knickers leads to small pleasures".'

'Mine is "Life's journey is brief, make it sparkle".'

We spent the next ten minutes mixing up our mid-life metaphors and quotes until we could laugh no more. I hugged her as I left.

It was possible that Vicky was right and behind every glossy exterior is a messy, mixed-up interior.

Maybe all it took was a frothy coffee and a leap of faith to confide in a friend to confirm it.

CHAPTER SIXTEEN

Claire had booked the function room in a local hotel for her fiftieth birthday party. The ten of us had, as usual, booked a minibus taxi and we were first to arrive so Claire and Will could greet their guests. Claire had spent the best part of the afternoon decorating the room with her daughters Eva and Poppy. There were a dozen tables festooned with confetti-filled gold balloons, tissue pompoms and the centrepieces were light-up wine bottles. Happy Birthday banners hung from every wall; there was a photo booth and sweetie cart; and I even spotted party bags for each of the guests. We were offered sparkling gold champagne flutes filled with chilled champagne by a uniformed barman on arrival.

Air traffic controllers are clearly better paid than journalists on the local paper, was my uncharitable thought. However, I exclaimed, 'Wow, this is incredible!'

It made my tiny get-together at home for my fiftieth seem positively mundane by comparison.

'Do you like it? I went a bit overboard with all the gold decorations. Gold for my golden years,' said Claire, laughing, resplendent in a shimmering silver and gold minidress.

'I love it. And there's even a dance floor for later,' I answered affectionately.

The DJ was warming up by playing some eighties hits as we chose a table near the back of the room.

'All the better to people-watch,' Annie said with a wink.

People-watch is code for scrutinise and criticise.

I had decided against wearing a dress and opted for a pair of faux leather leggings that I had purchased on impulse in Primark after work. James had looked horrified when I appeared in them earlier, making a sarcastic comment about dressing appropriately for my age. I had smiled sweetly, ignored him completely and flicked my hair back. From now on, I would wear whatever I wanted, despite James's derision.

The room filled with the guests and I was pleased to see that there were a couple of other women around my age who had opted for faux leather leggings as well. For once in my life, I might actually be a little on the trendy side.

The four of us had a great time drinking the complimentary champagne and gossiping about the other guests, while our husbands stood at the bar downing pints of beer and Claire mingled.

'I hope I look as amazing as Claire's mum when I'm that age,' said Annie, who rarely had a bad word to say about anyone.

'Whoever told that blonde she suited short skirts should have told her to take a good look in the mirror,' commented Kate, as an already worse-for-wear woman tottered past us in high heels.

'If I ever apply my fake tan as badly as that one there, please be honest enough to take a scrubbing brush to me,' whispered Vicky.

Okay, so we could be a bitchy bunch sometimes, but I'm pretty sure that every other woman in the room was making a snide comment to her friend about us. Probably along the lines of 'Look at that mutton dressed as lamb' about me or 'I bet that gorgeous brunette has the personality of a lump of wood' about Vicky.

It's human nature to instinctively compare and contrast yourself with others. Or maybe this is just a female thing, this automatic judgement. By finding other women wanting it somehow helps to make yourself, your looks, your achievements seem better. Conversely, if you find them more attractive or funnier, it can make you feel worse about yourself. Do you think that men go into a room, appraise the other men and think, *Who told that bloke to wear that shirt? It makes him look like an ageing hippie?* Or *Someone should be honest with him and tell him skinny jeans don't look good on anyone with a beer belly.*

Somehow, I doubt it. I think that men are hardwired to take it for granted they are attractive to every woman present. Think how many unfit, sweaty, greasy, boring men assume they are God's gift to women. It is a conundrum indeed.

Soon the room was full, some guests dancing, some drinking, some bitching. The room was humming with chatter and laughter. To quote my son's generation, it was vibing.

Claire was speaking to our husbands, who appeared to be superglued to the bar, so we joined the other women on the dance floor.

I happily danced with my friends, self-consciously moving to the music. One by one they gave up and went to have a seat, until it was only Annie and me still dancing. Then she too indicated she needed a drink, but I wasn't quite ready to sit down so I joined Claire's daughter Eva and her friends who whooped and clapped me into the centre of their circle. Laughing, I got into the spirit of things until I was gasping for breath and needed to rest my aching feet.

As I walked past James and the other men still standing at the bar, he motioned me over with a furious look on his face. Tightly grasping my upper arm out of sight of the others, he leaned forward before hissing into my ear, 'Sit down and stop humiliating yourself and me. Haven't you learned by now you can't dance?'

Pointedly I looked down at the hand squeezing my arm, and said clearly in front of Will and Tom who were within earshot, 'Let go of my arm, you're hurting me.'

His hand dropped as though I had burned him and he forced a laugh. He was normally so much cleverer at hiding his true colours in front of other people. 'Sorry, I didn't mean to.' Automatically he glanced around to see if anyone had witnessed this charming domestic scene unfolding in front of them.

'Does anyone fancy a dance?' I turned to the men standing beside James, as that classic 'The Only Way Is Up' by Yazz played. One of Will's friends Jonny, who was all of five foot four in his heels said yes, held his hand out and led me to the dance floor.

Incensed with my husband, I moved my ungainly body to the music, Jonny encouraging me all the way. For a few minutes I was able to forget James, forget the others and abandoned myself to the music, the beat ricocheting around my brain. At the end Jonny clapped me, reached up to give me a kiss on the cheek and breathlessly I went to sit down with my friends, avoiding the bar and my miserable excuse of a husband.

'Well, you can dance when you want to.' Vicky grinned.

'Don't you make a lovely couple,' said Kate with a giggle.

Sod James, I thought, although I suspected I would pay for it when we got home. I knew his response to my disobedience would be irrational. Our fragile truce was in tatters but I was learning that it didn't hurt anywhere near as badly as I had thought it would.

After a while the finger buffet was served and the men came to join us. James blatantly avoided me by taking a seat at the opposite side of the table, so I ended up sitting beside Matt, Annie's husband. Friendship groups are a funny thing. Although the ten of us regularly socialised together, I very rarely spent any one-to-one time with my friend's husbands and found it a little bit awkward. Matt and Annie were unlike the rest of us in that they had no children, so we didn't even have that in common. Matt was a primary school principal so inevitably we resorted to talking about work, as that was our only connection. He was, however, very witty and had a huge repertoire of one-liners, which kept me entertained while we ate the beef empanadas, roasted artichokes, buffalo chicken wraps and parmesan bread bites.

'Where are you and Annie going on holiday this year?' I asked, chewing on a delicious fried mac and cheese ball.

'We haven't decided, but maybe the Algarve to Annie's family apartment. Annie wants to go with Iona and her current boyfriend, even though he's a bit of a pain.' Iona was Annie's younger sister and they were especially close. 'Although between you and me, I don't think either of them can afford it as they are "between jobs" again.' Annie had mentioned to me in passing that she worried constantly about Iona who was drifting her way through a series of poorly paid jobs, and was back living with their parents, even though she was in her thirties.

Obviously not wanting to discuss them further, Matt dropped his voice and asked, 'Laura, is everything okay with Vicky?'

I was surprised to say the least, so stalled for time. 'In what way?'

'I'm not sure. I was grabbing a coffee from Costa after school the other day, and happened to see her at the back of the coffee shop on her own and she looked like she was crying.' He seemed a bit embarrassed but continued quietly. 'I know you and her are especially close and that Tom is away with work a lot again. I hope everything is all right.'

'She hasn't said anything to me,' I replied, unsure why he was discussing this with me and not Annie. Maybe she had enough on her plate worrying about Iona. 'I know she's had issues at work with the receptionist, so perhaps she'd had another run-in with her or something.'

'You're probably right.' He smiled at me, and then turned to speak to Kate who was sitting on his other side.

I felt a stab of worry as I looked around my group of friends. I thought I knew them so well but did I really know what was going on in each of their lives? Kate with her worrying outbursts and Vicky crying in public. I suddenly realised I was seeing a lot less of Claire than usual, which I hadn't even twigged until now as I'd been so wrapped up in my own personal turmoil. Annie had always been a bit of an enigma to me, so bright and cheerful, but who played her cards close to her chest.

Like me, did they have deep, dark secrets in their centres? Maybe I only knew the gleaming front of each of my friends. All of a sudden I felt like the worst friend in the world, so self-absorbed that I wouldn't have noticed if one of them was in the middle of a crisis.

I had no time to mull this over any further, as Claire stood up to cut the cake. It was two-layered like a wedding cake, decorated with sparklers and mini bunting. So much thought, effort and money had gone into making this night a success. As we sang 'Happy Birthday', I again covertly studied my friends. Had I been a rubbish friend recently? So consumed by the misery of my marriage that I was somehow failing them? Resolving to try harder and to be a better friend, I smiled at them all.

But I still wouldn't tell them about James.

The night ended on a high note as we were handed our adult party bags. I didn't even know such a thing existed until tonight. Excitedly we delved in to find mini bottles of bubbly, chocolates, tinned candles and sweet thank you notes. The men got miniature bottles of Scotch, bottle openers and hangover kits.

Before we left, Claire hugged everyone, thanked them for coming and also for the enormous stash of gifts that were piled up on one of the tables. She was laughing with Tom who offered to help her carry some of the gifts out to Poppy's car before we filed out to the waiting taxi. James had no choice but to sit beside me on the way home, but although he conversed pleasantly with our friends, he studiously ignored me.

I felt something almost imperceptible shift within me.

He was making my decision easier.

CHAPTER SEVENTEEN

Oh, how I love the springtime, when March comes in like a lion and out like a lamb. My mood was lighter and so was I. I had lost a total of half a stone and had finished the C25K. I could now run my way around five kilometres without collapsing in a heap, and although I still looked like a beetroot after it, I was chuffed with myself.

James and I were co-existing in relative peace, though it seemed we were more like polite strangers doing a house share, apart from our once-a-week quickie on a Friday night. The unsettling thing was that he had never confronted me about dancing with Jonny at the party. I knew deep down that it wasn't the end of it, so the anticipation of my punishment hung between us. He had taken to visiting his parents each weekend, ostensibly to help Donald with the garden that was too big for him. He never asked me to accompany him and I never offered. I contemplated asking him if all that gardening was making his arm pain worse, but his frequent scowl prevented me and I figured if it was that bad, he'd see someone about it.

It seemed the lighter days had generated more energy within me, as I was tempted to try the local park run but James didn't want me being committed every Saturday morning. I nearly pointed out that he was usually out cycling 'getting the miles in before Majorca' or with his father, but it wasn't worth the argument. I would stick to plodding my way around the village on my own.

I did, however, sign up for yogalates on Tuesdays with Claire and Vicky. James was not at all pleased when I said I was going to join the class, but I reassured him I would make dinner for him before I went, and that I'd be home by eight o'clock at the latest. It started at six o'clock in a local leisure centre and as it was only three quarters of an hour long, it wasn't as if I would be out all evening.

I had never heard of yogalates before Claire suggested it, but was intrigued when she attempted to explain it. 'It uses a mind-body connection which improves your emotional, physical and spiritual being. A fusion of Pilates and yoga,' she enthused one Saturday afternoon when I had popped over for a chat.

'Can we go for coffee after?' I'd queried hopefully. Surely James couldn't complain about a quick coffee with friends.

'Yes, if you want.' She grinned. 'I knew there was no point in asking you to come if you didn't get your coffee fix after. Should I ask the others?'

'Good idea,' I agreed. I'd been making an effort to see more of them all since the party.

In the end only Vicky was interested in joining us, so every Tuesday we would go and lie on a mat in the draughty hall of the local leisure centre and stretch, breathe and plank. I always felt so virtuous after that I sneaked the odd pear, blue cheese and walnut scone with my coffee, as I didn't have time to eat much before it started.

It was a catharsis after the unrest I had been feeling for the past few months. As I felt myself relax into the exercise and regular debrief with my friends after the class, I found a contentedness that a few weeks ago had evaded me. I didn't know if it was the exercise, the self-care or the gradual realisation that I could find happiness in things other than my marriage. When I practised gratitude each morning now, I wasn't simply paying lip service to it. There was no simple explanation for my more positive outlook; it just seemed I was able to face the future with a certainty that everything would work itself out.

One Tuesday evening towards the end of the month, Vicky couldn't make the class as she was busy so it was just Claire and me. As we sat together sipping our coffees, she mentioned that she had booked a spa break again with her mum.

'Going to the Averie again?'

'No, we're going a bit further this time, to that new place in Donegal that gets great reviews. Can't remember what it's called as Mum has taken care of the booking. It's a belated birthday treat.'

'Sounds lovely. When do you go?'

'The weekend after we get back from London.'

Raising my eyebrows, I thought to myself there would be no way James would allow me to go away without him two weekends in a row.

She obviously knew what I meant, because she shrugged and said, 'Yes I'm married to a saint, I know.' There was a distinct trace of bitterness in her tone that was out of character. 'He works such an odd shift pattern that he doesn't view weekends the same as the rest of us. With both the girls living their own lives at college the weekends can be quiet on my own.'

She smiled as she changed the subject. 'I'm so glad you decided to come to the class with me. I hope you don't mind me saying this but you hadn't really seemed like yourself for a while there. You seem happier now and you're looking great. Not that you didn't look great before; you just seemed, well... sad.' She looked directly at me.

I steadily held her gaze, taking my time before replying. After a moment, I confided, 'I have been struggling a bit over the past few months. Not really sure why, but everything got on top of me. Since I started running and eating better, I feel I've got a bit of the old me back.'

'Why didn't you talk to me about it?' Her green eyes were warm and concerned.

'Because I bore even myself with the whole mad meno lady bit.' I grinned to lighten the mood. 'Seriously, how often can you talk about hormones, moods, weight gain and hot flushes before all your friends desert you?'

'Has James been supportive?' Now her look was probing, as she rested back in her chair.

Just in time I stopped myself from rolling my eyes and said, 'James is a man who likes his life to be ordered and orderly. Mood swings and rogue hairs aren't really his forte.'

'Like most men. I doubt Will would be much better.' She smiled in solidarity with me. It was nice of her to put Will down so James didn't seem like such a prat on his own.

Deliberately we moved the conversation away from our husbands, and discussed our upcoming Book Club trip away. We had booked tickets to *Mama Mia! The Party,* planned cocktails on a rooftop terrace and had made dinner reservations at a riverside restaurant in Greenwich. The others were keen to take the cable car between Greenwich and the Royal Docks, but the thought of swinging ninety metres above the Thames was enough to give me palpitations.

'Are we going dressy or casual?' I asked.

'Have you seen our friends on a night out? Dressy I'd say.'

'Then I'm going to have to raid my wardrobe for something stylish! And I'll need to pack a big hat in case it gets above twenty degrees.' Like a true friend she giggled at that old joke.

We nattered on about our trip and I felt better than I'd done in a long time.

The following Saturday, as James was at Donald's again, was spent browsing the shops in Belfast city centre. They were brimming with spring colours, fabrics and accessories. Whereas a few weeks ago it had seemed incongruous against the bleak winter sky and frigid air, today it hinted at sunshine, barbeques, cloudless skies and flip-flops. I was so looking forward to our break in London, when the weather should be sunny and warm, anticipating long lazy lunches and cocktails before five o'clock. Friendship and gossip.

After a browse in House of Fraser of all the clothes I couldn't afford, I decided to cheer myself up with a quick coffee before going home. Distracted by my thoughts, I walked out of the shopping centre and straight into a man walking along the street.

'I'm so sorry!' I exclaimed, hitting him on the arm with my handbag.

'No problem at all,' he replied. Then quizzically, 'Laura?'

I looked at the silver fox standing in front of me, unsure who it was. It wasn't until he smiled that I recognised the dimples. It was Sam, my first boyfriend – the one before James – who had gone to study medicine in Edinburgh.

'You haven't changed at all! I'd know you anywhere.' His smile was wide.

'You haven't changed at all either.' I returned his grin, my stomach doing a little flip.

'That's nice of you but I look every day of my age. You don't.' Idiotically I kept grinning. Thirty years ago, before the internet and mobile phones, when someone went away 'across the water' to university, it was either handwritten letters or a phone call from a pay phone in the street. We had decided to split up, not because we wanted to, but because we knew I wasn't going to follow him to Scotland.

Then I met James and forgot about Sam.

'I'd love to hear what you've been up to; I don't suppose you'd have time for a coffee?'

'I was about to get one,' I answered without thinking. 'Are you back for a holiday or living in Northern Ireland?'

Without needing to discuss it, we headed into a coffee shop nearby and he insisted on buying. As he stood with his back to me at the counter, I studied him from under my eyelashes. He was tall, that goes without saying. I'm tall so I've never been into short men. He had blue eyes, but unlike James his were a darker shade of sapphire with thick black lashes. His hair was cut in the short back and sides that I've always found irresistible. And he was fit. So fit. How could I have forgotten that?

We chatted in the way that old friends can, even if they haven't seen each other in years. He'd married his university girlfriend but they had divorced and had no children, so he moved back home a couple of years ago and was a doctor in one of the local hospices.

Attractive, self-depreciating and altruistic.

And those biceps! I couldn't take my eyes off his arms. What was wrong with me? I basked under his interested gaze in a way I hadn't done for years. Actually, make that decades. He genuinely wanted to find out all about me, my family and my life. And he made me laugh. I realised that I had missed him, his easy company and his decency.

We reminisced about the year we had dated, me watching him play rugby on cold Saturday mornings, so proud to be the girlfriend of the first XV captain. It reminded me of carefree, joyful times when the future lay ahead teeming with possibilities.

The time flew past until I needed to leave, as the Book Club was getting together to finalise details of our trip. But I didn't want it to end and I found myself in a bit of a quandary. I knew I should say goodbye and leave. That to keep in touch would be a bad idea.

But aren't bad ideas good for you sometimes?

'Are you on Facebook?' he asked, as we gathered up our belongings.

'Yes, under my married name of Remmington.'

'I've finally given in and joined. Would you mind if I sent you a friend request?'

The perfect excuse to keep in touch, as I was friends on Facebook with lots of people I'd gone to school with. So innocent and harmless. No one would ever think anything of it. He sent through the request and I accepted it before we parted.

'It's been so lovely to bump into you. I'm really glad we had a chance to catch up.' He smiled that cute, boyish smile again.

'Lovely to see you too.' I knew I was smiling too much, but couldn't seem to stop.

He leant forward for a hug and as those biceps wound around me, it didn't even feel a teeny, tiny bit wrong to hug him back.

I managed to prise myself away and with a final wave, I turned in the direction of the car park with the smile still on my face.

And it was still on my face in the car on the way home as I replayed our meeting over and over again. I felt attracted to him in a way I had forgotten you could be attracted to someone, in that way that makes your insides contract each time you accidentally brush his foot or his hand.

In a dangerous, exciting way that a woman aged fifty-two and married shouldn't feel.

But I didn't care.

CHAPTER EIGHTEEN

Easter was at the beginning of April and school always takes a fortnight's break to give us a chance to recharge our batteries before the summer term. Robbie was only going to be home for a few days as he needed to study for his finals, but I was delighted to be able to spend any time with him. He had a list of things he wanted to cram into his visit home, so I knew it would pass in a flash.

I was a bit concerned that he would feel the distinct coolness between James and me. Arguing with myself how best to respond if he commented, one minute I felt we should be (almost) completely honest, the next I wanted to protect him as long as possible. Robbie was not a child and he has a few friends whose parents have separated, but I was still worried about breaking up our family.

If we didn't talk about it, we could pretend all was good.

By the time he was due home, James and I had agreed long enough to plan the next few days together. We would spend Saturday afternoon at his parents, hopefully without the Dimmocks this time, and then my parents had planned a barbeque for all the family on Easter Sunday.

Robbie arrived home on the Friday afternoon, which was a sunny, still day with a light breeze. Such a contrast to when he had arrived home for Christmas. Watching the ferry dock, I thought back to that freezing day and how low my spirits had been. It was as if a completely different person had been waiting for him then.

Just then my phone screen lit up with a Facebook Messenger notification. Instinctively I knew it would be Sam. He'd sent his first message a short time after we'd parted, a simple:

> Great to have bumped into you and to catch up, maybe we could do it again some time?

I'd messaged back without a second's hesitation to say that would be nice. *Nice.* Such a bland little word that meant so much more to me that day. Nice that someone made me feel young, attractive and interesting. Nice that there had been no disparaging remarks.

Nice that when I closed my eyes, I could feel the warmth of his smile on me.

It barely crossed my mind that a mild flirtation with an old flame could be considered cheating on my husband. Not in the proper sense of the word. Cheating is not sending teasing messages or having coffee or going for an innocent walk. Is it?

I messaged Sam back to say I was waiting for Robbie to disembark, and that we had a busy few days planned. He told me he had volunteered to work over the Easter weekend and perhaps once Robbie was back in Stirling we could meet up for coffee. We arranged when and where and I felt exhilarated as I got out of the car and waited for my son. Harbouring my secret within me, I suppressed a smile. All I seemed to do these days was smile. I felt a stone lighter and twenty years younger. Surely that couldn't be a bad thing?

Easter Saturday was the first time I had seen Donald since Christmas. I would meet up with Heather occasionally for lunch, but I had no time for my father-in-law and preferred to see as little of him as possible. After we arrived, Donald led us through to the back garden, where straight away I was confronted with the reason James had been spending so much time at his parents.

Pride of place in the back garden was a brand new garden room. Exactly like the one I had been trying to persuade James to buy for the past couple of years, but which he had stubbornly been refusing. I was suffused with rage.

'What do you think of our little surprise?' he asked, appraising my reaction with frosty eyes, while barely concealing his smirk.

It was then that I understood this had been deliberate. His punishment for embarrassing him in front of Tom and Will at the party. That particular axe had finally dropped.

With difficulty, I controlled my temper, instead making some appropriately pleasant comment as I went to take a better look. It had a pale-grey exterior, with sliding glass doors along the entire front and whitewashed wooden decking that matched the interior floor and walls. A sea-green linen sofa stretched the full length of the space, and tasteful knick-knacks from Heather and Donald's many travels were displayed on floating white shelves. It, of course, was the epitome of good taste and James was bursting with self-congratulations.

I detested it. Detested everything it stood for and at that moment detested my husband and his underhand plotting.

I hid my distaste, lavishing compliments on him and Donald for doing such a great job and on Heather for the impeccable décor. Donald reached for a chilled bottle of bubbly from the wine fridge nestled in the corner, and we toasted it as if it were a royal ship.

Robbie immediately made himself comfortable on the sofa and asked, 'Isn't this a bit like the one you've been wanting, Mum?'

'A bit,' I managed to reply evenly, 'but I don't think we'd have the room in our garden.'

'We don't,' answered James imperiously. 'This is nothing like what you wanted, Laura. You were after some twee little playhouse.'

Ignoring that barb, I turned to my mother-in-law and we discussed the garden. There was an abundance of multicoloured spring flowers in pots edging their patio, early hanging baskets and I admired the well-tended flowerbeds.

I presented a calm and agreeable front throughout the whole torturous afternoon. Heather served a delicious array of canapés followed by roast lamb studded with rosemary and garlic then a summer fruits trifle. We chatted about the Dimmocks and Donald boasted about how well the children were doing at fencing, dressage and surfing. They were spending the Easter holidays at their holiday cottage on the north coast. I didn't even have the heart to play Snob Bingo today, as I just wanted to get the day over and done with. To go home, get into my slippers and watch television. Thankfully Robbie was going out to a concert with his friends, so we could make our excuses and leave early.

At home as soon as Robbie had left, James again raised the subject of the garden room, prodding at what he assumed would be a sore point.

'Isn't Mum and Dad's garden room amazing?'

'Very nice,' I replied firmly. 'Luckily it didn't aggravate your arm pain.' *That you've been moaning incessantly about,* I thought to myself. I wasn't going to rise to his bait, so sat with my tongue touching the roof of my mouth, a new trick I employed when I was nervous my mouth would open without engaging my brain.

'A bit like the one you've been nagging me for years to get.' He observed me, like a spider with a fly caught in its web.

'Like I said earlier, yes, a bit like it. But I'd rather get an arbour for the gable end of the house. Don't you think it would be perfect there on long summer evenings? I could grow wisteria and honeysuckle up it and we could light the fire pit under it when we have friends over.'

He sneered a little at that. I had no intention of getting an arbour, but was quite enjoying sparring with him, and would not give him the satisfaction of letting him see I was upset by his deception.

'I shouldn't think so and you've never been successful at growing wisteria before. The best you could manage would be something artificial.' Getting up from the sofa, he said he was going to watch the World Tour cycling in the living room and left me in peace.

The following day Robbie offered to drive up to my parents for the barbeque. By the time we arrived the garden was filled with the sound of my many relatives gossiping and laughing together. Thankfully the weather was dry and warm, and we could sit outside under the carport while the kids bounced on the trampoline and kicked a ball about. My nieces were huddled together stalking handsome boys on Instagram.

James considers himself an expert at barbequing, so without discussion, appointed himself head cook while ordering my brothers around.

My sister Sarah sat beside me watching him flip the burgers and sausages. 'How are you, Laura?' she asked quietly. She had been visiting that Sunday when I'd confided in Mum.

It's like the bush telegraph in our family and nothing remains secret for long.

'I'm okay. I take it Mum had a chat with you?'

'She's the soul of discretion and didn't say much when I asked her about your red eyes the other week.'

My youngest sister is so different from me in many ways. While I am tall and pale, she is small and dark with caring brown eyes and a gentle nature.

'We're going through a bit of a rough patch,' I disclosed. 'It isn't the first time and it probably won't be the last.'

'All marriages have good times and bad. But remember when the bad outweighs the good and it doesn't change, you don't have to stay.'

Normally such a comment would have me scrabbling about making excuses for James, concealing what was really going on in our relationship, but I no longer wanted to do that. Sarah is a counsellor and has an abundance of empathy. I knew the fact she had initiated this conversation meant she had been thinking about it since I last saw her.

'I'm beginning to realise that.' I smiled at her to hide the depth of my feelings. 'I won't make any rash decisions when there's Robbie to think about too.'

'I know this is hard to accept but Robbie isn't a child anymore; he's a fully-fledged adult who I'm sure would prefer two happy parents who are apart than two unhappy ones who are staying together for the wrong reasons.'

'Tell me what you really think, Sarah,' I snapped. 'I know he's an adult, you don't really have a clue what's going on so maybe butt out.'

Instead of apologising she laughed.

'I knew that quick-tempered redhead was still in there under the genteel exterior. You've been living with the hobs, snobs and sophisticates too long.'

I couldn't help myself, as I too started to laugh. Why is it that families can drive you to distraction, but at the same time are the only ones who tell you the brutal truth, no matter how unpalatable?

As James served up the meat and we tucked into plates of salad, sausages and burgers, I thought about the Remmingtons. I'd been impressed by their extravagant lifestyle and moneyed existence when I first met them. Now I recognised it was all a brittle front that hid deep and bitter cracks.

It was becoming clear to me that I didn't want to be part of it anymore.

CHAPTER NINETEEN

I thought that I was doing a great job of hiding the growing rift between James and myself until the day before Robbie was due to return to Scotland. We had been blessed with a lovely sunny week and Robbie and I decided to go for a walk in Glenveagh Forest followed by lunch at the castle tearoom. James had been on good form all week after the dismal day spent at his parents. That was him all over, perfectly lovely when he wanted to be, leaving me unsure from one day to the next what mood he would be in.

We wandered through the forest enjoying each other's company and chit-chatting, then stopped to catch our breath after climbing up to the waterfall. I rested on the stone wall while listening to the water crash on the rocks below.

'Mum, are you okay?' Robbie was facing the waterfall with his back to me.

'Yes of course, what do you mean?'

He came over and sat down on the wall beside me. 'You and Dad, I mean. I don't know what it is, but you don't seem very happy with each other at the minute.'

'Oh, all couples go through rough patches,' I responded as reassuringly as I could. 'This is just a patch.'

'Mum,' he said again and then stopped, clearly trying to say something but finding it difficult. 'Dad… Well, sometimes I don't like the way he speaks to you. He puts you down a lot.' My poor son, his face flaming, his words tumbling out.

I reached for his hand, squeezing it lightly. Robbie was no longer a child and even though he was away for months at a time, he could see all was not right at home. Still my instinct was to protect him.

'Everything's all right, Robbie. Your dad and I have been married a long time. People speak to each other in a different tone when you've been together as long as we have.' Even as I said it, I realised I was lying. James spoke to me like I was beneath him, that I should be grateful he had married me and I should spend my life thanking my lucky stars I was the chosen one. I didn't want my son, when he met a girl he liked, to speak to her that way. He couldn't think it was normal or acceptable.

'Look, maybe he does say unkind things sometimes and that's not right. But we'll sort it out, pet, I'm sure we will.'

'If I get this graduate job back here, I'd like to live in Belfast with my mates and not in the village. Is that all right with you?'

'Of course it's all right with me!' I exclaimed. 'I don't think it would be right for you to move home, as you're used to city living now. How could you even think it would be a problem?'

'I'm a bit worried about you.'

'Pet, you've nothing to worry about I promise. I'm fine. Really.'

I did not want my lovely son to waste time worrying about me when he had finals around the corner. It was enough that he had spoken to me. I hoped I had reassured him everything would be all right, so he could go back to university and focus on completing his degree. We walked on, talking about irrelevant things and then treated ourselves to bacon baps and coffees. He didn't bring the subject up again before he went back to Stirling, and I deliberately behaved pleasantly towards James that night.

When Robbie had returned to university, James's mood darkened as my weekend away with the girls grew closer. First, he demanded that I make evening meals for each night I would be away and leave them labelled in the chest freezer. Then he wanted to know exactly where the hotel we were staying in was. None of this bothered me greatly, as I was well used to his behaviour when I was going to be away from him. I just had to put up with it, and make sure it didn't sound like we'd had too much fun when I came home.

One thing I was doing out of the normal was meeting Sam for a coffee again. Our messages had been light-hearted and cheeky, a welcome respite from the tense atmosphere at home. And completely, utterly innocent, just two old friends reconnecting.

But of course, I didn't tell a soul.

This was my little secret, a balm for my bruised heart. Sam probably didn't even think of me as any more than a platonic friend anyway.

Fortunately, I was going to be leaving work early on the Thursday before London, as there was some training I didn't have to stay for. It wasn't that I was lying to James, I just wasn't being completely honest with him. If he found out I had arranged a coffee rather than bumping into Sam, well I couldn't think about his reaction. I had plotted it out carefully. Sam suggested the coffee shop attached to his hospice, so I deduced if I drove all the way into work instead of to the train station that day, James would be none the wiser. As long as I arrived home at the usual time.

Deep down I knew it was reckless and that if James found out he would be incandescent, probably in much the same way that once upon a time I would have been enraged if he was meeting an old girlfriend without telling me. But I had felt so cheerful after meeting Sam and so buoyant for once, that I was prepared to risk it to meet up again.

Unconsciously I spent more effort on my appearance that day. I dressed in my most flattering pleated skirt with a royal-blue blouse that I knew complimented my eyes, straightened my hair and tucked a small make-up bag into my handbag so I could touch it up later.

The day was spent in a state of nervous excitement. Part of me tried to play it all down, while the other part felt like a teenager on a first date. I hadn't arranged to meet another man for coffee in thirty-four years, which was a rather sobering thought. I'm pretty sure if it had happened a year ago, I would never have agreed to it. For I knew that as much as I was struggling with menopause, it had changed my perspective for the better. The 'couldn't give a toss' attitude I was developing towards life in general these days, had given me a new sense of freedom. One result was my dissatisfaction in my marriage. The other was in me not feeling especially guilty about this meeting.

Maybe I could start a new bucket list.

1. Reconnect with an old boyfriend who makes you feel seventeen again.

2. Tell your husband to go feck himself once in a while.

Definitely not a list I would be sharing on Facebook.

I sneaked into the staff toilets to refresh my make-up before leaving school, adding a bit more blush and a slick of lip gloss. Then I set off towards the hospice and parked the car before messaging Sam to let him know I'd arrived. With one final glance in the mirror to ensure I'd nothing stuck in my teeth, I got out of the car and walked into the coffee shop. I took a seat with my back to the wall facing the door, that way I could make sure that no one would see me before I could see them. Just in case.

A few minutes later Sam came through the front door and his face broke into a smile as he spotted me. He looked even better than I remembered. I've always been a sucker for a man in a shirt and chinos. Today he was wearing little round glasses, which gave him an aura of authority. My hands felt a bit clammy, so I wiped them discreetly on my skirt.

'Hello, can I get you a coffee?' he asked.

'It's my turn,' I replied, standing up. Straight away I felt completely at ease, no longer nervous or excited. It was as though it was the most natural thing in the world to be meeting an ex-boyfriend behind my husband's back.

Once I'd bought the coffee we sat talking together, oblivious to the other patrons or staff. I asked about his marriage and he simply said, 'There was no big drama. We grew apart and realised we wanted different things from life. Then my mum became unwell with heart issues and Dad needed help to look after her. My sister Marianne emigrated to Australia about ten years ago, so I couldn't leave Dad to manage on his own.'

'I'm so sorry,' I blurted out. 'Your mum was always so lovely to me.'

He looked wistfully at his cup. 'She doesn't complain, but she's in pain and short of breath all the time. I don't regret moving back to help Dad.'

Changing what was obviously a difficult subject, he asked me about my family. I talked about my parents, my siblings and their relatives, regaling him with funny stories that are part and parcel of a big family. Then he asked me about James.

'Oh, he's fine.' My mind went blank, that menopause-related emptiness in your brain that leaves you unable to think of one sensible thing to say.

'Fine?' He raised his eyebrows quizzically.

'Umm yes, fine.' Total blank. I should be extolling his virtues not describing him as *fine*.

'He sounds absolutely fascinating.' Sam beamed at me and I burst out laughing.

'Fascinating in his own opinion anyway.' That slipped out without thinking. 'He's lovely. Thoughtful. Caring.' Liar. I should have said *Not often lovely, thoughtful or caring.* But I didn't of course.

Not wanting to think about James any longer, I spoke about the one person I could genuinely enthuse about. Robbie.

'I think it's great he went to Scotland to study as it will give him a bit of life experience,' said Sam. 'And probably great for you he wants to come back here to work.'

Astute as well.

I glanced at the clock on the wall and was horrified to see it was later than I expected. If I was to make it back without James being suspicious, I needed to leave immediately. 'I'm so sorry,' I blustered, already gathering up my things, 'I need to go now.'

Sam looked at me askance. 'Did I say something wrong?'

'No, no, I need to get home before James asks me where I've been. Obviously, I didn't tell him I was meeting you or he would have tried to stop me. I'm so sorry I need to go. It's been lovely. We'll have to do it again sometime. Or not. Whatever you want. Or don't want.' I was already out at the car and my mouth still kept going. No thought, just a blind panic that I had to get home before James noticed I was late. I should have had an excuse ready but I couldn't even think straight. If he asked me where I'd been, I had no alibi. Close to tears, I tried to open the car door but kept hitting the lock button.

Gently Sam took the keys from me and hit the unlock button. 'Laura, I don't know what's going on here but it's all right. You haven't done anything wrong. Are you afraid of James finding out we had coffee?'

Silently I nodded. I was afraid. Not of him physically but afraid of incurring his wrath should he find out.

'We're two old friends catching up. Nothing else. We don't have to meet up again if it's going to be an issue for you.'

I knew I should tell him straight away it was going to be an issue. An enormous issue.

But he looked so forlorn I instead said, 'I do want to, Sam. I just don't want it to be behind my husband's back. I'll maybe message after I get back from London. I'm so sorry.'

He nodded and handed me the car keys. 'Do whatever feels right, I'll understand either way.'

Without another word I got into the car and sped out of the car park as though being chased by the hounds of hell. For that is what it felt like at that moment. My glittering fantasy world had smashed with the reality of my situation.

Deep down, I was afraid of James.

CHAPTER TWENTY

When I arrived home, I expected to see James's Mercedes parked under the carport as usual but instead there was a black Range Rover. I barely had time to register it and get out of the car when he appeared at the front door.

'You're late, Laura,' he commented dryly.

'Sorry, I had a meeting that ran over and I missed the early train.' Once the panic had subsided, I had thought of the perfect excuse on the drive home. I'd recited it over and over to ensure the lie would slip out easily.

'You should have messaged me. You know how I worry when you're not home when I expect you to be.' He said nothing else, just stood quietly waiting, arms folded across his chest. 'Well, what do you think then?'

'Think of what?' Pathetically grateful that he hadn't made a fuss about the time, I was genuinely confused about what he meant.

'The car, Teeny. Surely even you know the difference between a Mercedes estate and a Range Rover.' He sighed theatrically.

'Well yes, of course. Whose is it?'

'Mine.' He smiled at me in a self-satisfied way that dared me to question it.

'Yours? When did you get it? You never mentioned it to me.'

'I know you expect me to ask for your permission every time I buy something, but this time, I decided all on my own. I got a pay rise in December and thought it was time I upgraded the car. The Mercedes was five years old after all.'

I was so bemused, that I genuinely couldn't think of anything to say except 'It's lovely, very nice.'

And went over to ooh and ah at it.

But then my temper rose. He had got a pay rise in December and never said a word? He never asks my opinion anymore, rather he tells me what my opinion should be. And most galling of all was that my Mini is ten years old and has 120,000 miles on it. I couldn't afford to upgrade to a new one in a million years. I was so angry at that moment that I wanted to punch something hard.

Especially his smug face.

It all made complete sense. This had been calculated. He had got the car delivered today because he was counting on me to be furious. Then he could start a row to ruin my weekend away. He was becoming so predictable. I inherently knew that it was essential to pretend I was neither concerned nor annoyed, otherwise I was simply walking into the trap he had laid so deliberately for me.

I held my tongue and smiled at him, as though it was the loveliest surprise ever. I could almost taste his disappointment. A short time ago I wouldn't have thought there was anything wrong with this scenario at all, but I could see clearly now.

My husband could be a complete tosser sometimes.

He insisted on taking me for a drive to show it off, although I was pushed for time and still needed to pack. Trying to act as though everything was normal between us, I made dinner and helped him with the dishes. He was clearly still expecting a fight, anything to put a dampener on my time away, so I felt on edge all evening.

It was after eight by the time I got a chance to pack, but as we were only going from Friday night until Sunday, it didn't take me long. The forecast was good and I was taking lightweight clothes. I even tucked my big sunhat into the case. You can never be too careful.

I ran myself a bath before bed and studied my phone while waiting for it to fill. Torn about what to do but still livid with my husband, I quickly sent Sam a message apologising for running off and thanking him for coffee. I wouldn't have been surprised if he didn't bother replying as I'd acted like such an idiot. But as I was lying under the water a few minutes later, my phone vibrated, and I got a reply from him.

> Please don't worry about it at all. It was lovely to catch up and if you want to meet up again let me know. My treat next time 🙂

My grin was so wide, my cheeks hurt and I told myself that I really need to wise up and calm down. For I needed to perfect my lying skills or it would be transparent something strange was going on with me.

Later that evening as I read in bed, James appeared wearing only his dressing gown. 'I can't let you go to London without a proper goodbye,' he murmured, slipping naked under the covers beside me.

I managed to suppress a groan of frustration, setting my book on the bedside table and turned to face him. As I lay beneath him playing the best role of my life, I felt him gnawing on my neck. On and on it went until I wanted to push him off and scream to go away, but at last it was over and he rolled off me. Swiftly getting up, he went to his dressing gown which was hanging on the back of the door and reached into the pocket. I could see him withdraw some cash, which he set on the bedside table on top of my book. Then he leant over me and gave me a kiss on the forehead.

'I know you are angry about the car and that really hurts me, I was so excited to show you it. But I forgive you, so I'm giving you some money to spend in London.'

He left the room before I could reply, and I lay there stupefied. Reaching for the cash I counted £80. He had done his business and left me money.

Like a whore.

My cheeks burned with shame. It wouldn't be spent on my trip, I would put it into my secret savings account.

I hurried into the bathroom, where I despondently studied my reflection in the mirror. It was then I admitted to myself that he sometimes disgusted me, and I wondered what on earth I was going to do.

Finally I let myself concede the truth I had been hiding from.

It had been insidious, a gradual realisation that I no longer liked my husband.

There was no big fanfare. I just faced the indisputable fact I no longer liked the man I shared my life with. Would I ever be brave enough to do anything about it? I vowed that when I came back from London, I would make a list of things I needed to learn in order to become self-sufficient. I could put it off no longer.

I tossed and turned all night, acutely aware that I must not rise to his bait, as this was not finished yet. If I went downstairs and lost my cool, he would play the injured party and wouldn't be satisfied until he had upset me all over again. It took all my willpower to smile, give him a kiss on the cheek and converse normally as I made breakfast.

'I got a bit carried away last night didn't I?' He stood right in front of me.

I forced a smile, murmured something unintelligible and went to move but he blocked my way.

Laura, please don't sulk. I thought you would love the car as it's just like Olivia's. You are really ruining the enjoyment for me.'

'I love the car, James, it was just a surprise as you hadn't said anything about it.' Then I kept on talking. 'I wish you had told me you got a pay rise in December.' I could have kicked myself for saying anything. I must repeat, *Engage brain, then open mouth* before speaking in future.

'I did tell you, Laura.' He looked sad. 'You really have the brain of a gnat these days, don't you?'

Had he? I was consumed with self-doubt. He could well have done, because I had a tendency to not listen to him. Now I wasn't sure.

'In fact, I told you several times and you said you were so pleased for me.'

He had overplayed his hand. Once I could just about believe, several times was simply not possible. I had seconds to decide what to do and, in the end, I went with playing dumb.

'I'm sorry, I really am so forgetful these days.'

'That's why you should see the doctor about pills, Laura. I'm so concerned about you, darling.'

'Maybe I should.' I pretended to think it over. 'Thanks for being so understanding, I'm lucky to have you.'

It seemed I had said the right thing because he broke into a genuine smile, and with a final kiss disappeared towards his study. I watched his retreating back with complete distaste. I couldn't wait to get away from him tonight.

The day passed quickly, and in no time at all I was home, had changed out of my work clothes and was ready to leave. James made a song and dance about helping me out to the taxi with my small case, offering to lift all my friends' suitcases into the boot as well. He was the epitome of good manners, encouraging us all to have a great weekend and reminding me to message him every day so he knew I was safe.

'He's so thoughtful,' said Annie. 'I don't think Matt even remembered I was going away until this morning.' She made a face. 'You have no idea how much I've been looking forward to this!'

We grinned at each other. With each mile the taxi took us from the village, the happier I felt. Two days of no James. Two days of fun with my friends with no brooding presence, ready to berate me for the slightest thing. Watching the countryside speed past, the tension drained from me. When we arrived at the airport, we got through security quickly and made our way to the bar. I don't normally drink in the afternoon but it's a Book Club tradition we start every trip with a glass of prosecco.

'To the best weekend ever,' toasted Annie.

'To fun, frolics and frippery,' I said, clinking my glass with my friends. *And to being James-less,* I thought to myself.

All too soon London was just a memory. We had a fantastic time enjoying each other's company, free from the mundane daily stresses.

The only fly in the ointment was that James messaged me several times a day and expected a daily phone call as well. If I didn't reply quickly enough, he would keep sending me texts asking if I was all right, was I safe, what was I doing, he needed confirmation NOW. It seemed like he was determined to keep tabs on me even from 500 miles away.

On the plus side, it was only a few days until he would be off to Majorca and I would have the house to myself with nobody to answer to for a whole week. Bliss. I was going to do what I wanted, even if that was to spend the entire day in my PJs. I could meet up with my friend Sam with no worries that I would forget the time and panic that I was going to get caught out. All I had to do was behave myself for a few more days to keep the peace and give James what he wanted.

No questions asked.

CHAPTER TWENTY-ONE

It seemed all was going well as James had been in a surprisingly good mood since I got back on Sunday night and I felt myself relax a bit. As usual, Claire, Vicky and I headed off to yogalates on Tuesday. After our class we went for coffee in the leisure centre café. It's situated right beside the sea, next to the promenade and we made the most of the beautiful sunny evening as we sat at a table by the windows. Looking out at the flat calm Irish Sea I was aware that Scotland was only a few miles away, so close it seemed I could reach out and touch it.

'Are you looking forward to your spa break, Claire?' asked Vicky, spooning the chocolate sprinkle from the top of her cappuccino into her mouth.

'Yes, it should be nice.' Claire didn't seem too enthused which surprised me. She had been pretty excited about it when we were in London. Changing the topic, she turned to me. 'Any plans for the next week on your own, Laura?'

I thought, *Meeting my ex-boyfriend for a walk, not putting the plastics into the recycling, eating crap at any old hour.* And then I said, 'Nothing really, though it will be lovely to have the bank holiday Monday off.'

'If you're at a loose end over the weekend, give me a shout,' said Vicky. 'Tom's off on some long-haul trip and before you ask, I have no idea where to. As long as he's on the end of the mobile if I need him, I've usually got no idea where he's going.'

Then I saw a surprised look cross Vicky's face and she glanced at me. Claire too threw a look in my direction, and although she smiled tightly, I knew her well enough to know she wasn't particularly happy.

'Hello, lovely ladies. I thought I'd come and see what all the fuss is about.'

James.

I swung around to look at him, casually standing there in front of me wearing jeans and a polo shirt the exact same cold blue of his eyes. Then he pulled over a seat beside me, flung his arm nonchalantly around my shoulders, giving me a none-too-gentle squeeze.

'What are you doing here?' I tried to keep the resentment out of my tone.

'I thought it was about time I checked out the gym here and saw your class in the hall. I see there's men in it too so I might join you one evening.'

My stomach sank. Seriously? I couldn't even go to an exercise class with my friends without him spoiling it?

Claire, however, was having none of it. 'Great idea, James, I might ask Will as well. How about you Vicky, do you think Tom would be interested? We could do with a row of nice butts in front of us when we're doing down-dogs. Make sure you wear something tight and short, James, to give us all a thrill.'

Her smile did not reach her eyes. She was clearly throwing down the gauntlet.

His jaw almost imperceptibly tensed as he flashed the briefest smile. It was the tiniest change of expression, probably not even noticeable to other people, but which I dreaded and would have done anything to avoid.

'Only if you wear something tight and short as well, Claire.' His rejoinder fell flat and there was an awkward silence. Flipping to charm mode, he asked about London. Then, 'What did you both think of *Mama Mia*? I can't imagine Laura dancing on a podium like a teenager.'

'We were all dancing on the podium, James, though I don't know where we got the energy from,' replied Claire. 'Reliving our youth, no doubt.'

'Were there men there too? Laura was cagey about that.' He laughed awkwardly.

'What goes on tour stays on tour,' replied Claire.

'I must remember that.' He looked at me deliberately.

By trying to defuse the situation Claire had inadvertently fanned the flames. Now he would think we were hiding something. That I was hiding something. Instantly I felt drained. I couldn't face another row, another quizzing session, more bad feeling. After we finished our coffees, we headed for the car park. Vicky had given me a lift over, but I obviously now had to go home with James.

Outside, I said goodbye to my friends. 'Have a great weekend away with your mum, Claire.' I wanted to make a point that Claire was going away again without Will. 'Give me a shout at the weekend if you want to go for a walk or whatever.' I waved at Vicky before getting into the Range Rover.

James was completely silent on the way home. Not a word. No fight. No row. Somehow it was worse, the apprehension of what he was going to say or do.

Without a word he got out of the car at home and went into the house. Submissively I followed him inside, before shutting the front door.

He was waiting for me in the hall.

'Your friends think I'm a laughing stock, don't they.' It was a statement not a question. 'Clearly something happened when you were away that you didn't tell me about. Something they know and I don't.'

I knew there was no point even bothering to correct him. It was best to let him whinge on, to get it out of his system. His whole injured party act was wearing so thin I could spit through it. Idly I visualised a row of fit men wearing shorts while doing down-dogs in front of me, and I had to chew the inside of my cheek not to laugh.

'Do you know how lonely I am sometimes? Do you want me to be on my own all the time while you are out having fun?' He'd obviously been stewing in his own juice for the weekend, and was now using this as an excuse to let rip. He continued. 'I think the best thing would be for me to come to the class with you, Laura. Claire is becoming a bad influence.'

For goodness' sake, I was sick to death of this pathetic self-serving drivel. There is little less attractive than a grown man acting like a child.

'You can come to the class if you want, James. Really, it's up to you and I don't mind either way.' What I really wanted to say was, *Make a fool of yourself again if you want. I'm pretty sure my friends can see through you.*

'Then I will. We can go together, so you won't need to go with Claire and Vicky.' He watched me, awaiting the first wrong move.

'If you want,' I said as unconcerned as possible. 'Though I should probably let you know the men in the class are all part of a mental health support group. You know, men with addiction issues, PTSD, that sort of thing. I'm sure they'd welcome you into their fold; just don't stare when Paul's hands shake.'

As I had hoped, he looked horrified and said he'd think about it. I was becoming a convincing liar for there was no Paul and no men's mental health support group. If there had been, I would never have saddled them with James. He had no understanding, no compassion for anyone struggling with mental health issues, as I had found to my own cost when I went a bit mad pre-HRT. I knew there was no chance he would come along to the class again.

He was leaving early on Saturday morning for his flight to Majorca and spent the rest of the week packing, making an almighty fuss about dismantling his bike to get it into its special travel case. I noticed that he again had been on a spending spree, having bought several new polo shirts and shorts for his holiday.

My plan during my week's holiday from him was to make out a checklist of things I needed to learn in order to become more independent. Researching how to access our bank accounts was top of the list. I couldn't even log online onto the account my pay went into, to see how it was being spent. It had also registered with me that I had no way of accessing our joint savings at all, leaving me totally reliant on James if I wanted to spend anything from it. Which I never did as he had warned me that it was savings for holidays and the like, and if I spent it on impractical things we would have nothing to fall back on.

When I took a long, hard look at myself, I was mortified for having become so totally, utterly dependent on James. It hadn't seemed so important when we were happy together, but now I was miserable with him, it was imperative I learned these things.

The night before he left, I casually asked him for the log-in details for both my current account and our joint account.

'What do you want to know that for?' He was clearly on the defensive.

'Just in case I need to access either of them for something when you're away.' I had thought this through and planned to keep it simple.

'You don't need to worry about that, I'll leave you some cash. Though you've had your allowance for the month plus the extra I gave you for London.' His body was rigid, his eyes flinty.

I tried again. 'What if something happened to you in Majorca? You've told me about a couple of cycling accidents out there and I would hate something like that to happen to you. I couldn't even transfer you money if you needed it.' The sentence petered out, as my bluster ran out of steam.

'All right,' he snapped. 'You can have complete control of our money from now on. Welcome to the world of balancing our finances, budgeting, saving, paying the bills on time. You who can't even remember where you've put your purse half the time can be in charge of it all now. You're welcome to it. I've only ever tried to protect you from money worries and you are implying I'm some sort of ogre. As usual you are determined to ruin my week away, Laura.'

Easy tears filled my eyes. How could he manipulate such a simple thing to make it my fault? I knew what I was asking for wasn't some terrible thing, and that I only wanted to have some sort of knowledge about my own money. How could that be wrong?

'Great! Try and cry now to make me feel bad before I go away. I don't know what has happened to you. You seem to get pleasure out of inflicting pain on me these days. Please go to the doctor like I keep asking and get some happy pills before I come home next week.'

Back to my need for pills again. If someone throws enough mud at you, some of it will stick. I didn't think I needed pills but maybe I did. He made me feel so confused at times, I was forever questioning my sanity.

'I'm sorry, James, I didn't mean to make you feel bad. I was concerned about what I would do if something happened to you. I didn't mean to imply you are some sort of ogre.' A heat that started within my chest rose steadily, until my face felt that I had stood too long in front of an open fire.

He ignored that, turned his back to me and went upstairs without another word. As he slammed his bedroom door shut, I sat alone in the kitchen with my thoughts. How did he have the ability to play with my mind? Had he always been like this and I had ignored it? Or was this a new thing? I was no longer sure.

But it seemed the more I distanced myself emotionally from him, the tighter he held on. It was suffocating me and driving me away.

I just wanted peace and my own space.

The week ahead was going to be an important one.

CHAPTER TWENTY-TWO

After a poor night's sleep, I woke the next morning to find a silent house. Glancing at the bedside clock, I could hardly believe it was half past nine. James had been due to leave at seven o'clock. Which meant he had gone without waking me.

Prat.

I sat up quickly and pure joy coursed through my veins as I realised he was gone. Hooray!

Filled with energy, I jumped out of bed and flung back the curtains. Sunlight did not flood the room as it was a grey overcast day with a fine mizzle, but for once I didn't care. It could be snowing for all it mattered. I felt a little nervous as I opened my bedroom door. What if it was all a con and he hadn't left, but instead was waiting for me downstairs, metaphorical straitjacket at the ready, prepared to take me to the doctor for happy pills. As quietly as possible, I stepped into his bedroom. Empty. No suitcase. I looked in all the rooms upstairs then padded silently downstairs, inspecting every space including the garage. Empty.

He really was gone.

'Alexa, play the happiest songs you can think of,' I shouted ecstatically. Alexa replied immediately, 'Playing happy mix' and cheerful music flooded the kitchen. 'Up!' I commanded and the volume got louder. Dancing along, I happily toasted my pancake then slathered it in Nutella, before I placed chopped strawberries in the shape of a smiley face on top. I was going to stay in my pyjamas all day, binge-watch Netflix, then open a bottle of wine and order in a takeaway this evening.

Day one completely to myself doing exactly what I wanted to do and answerable to no one.

Tomorrow, I had planned to go with Sam for a walk with his dog to a place I figured no one would know me. Not that I was paranoid, it was completely innocent after all, but there was no point in going somewhere I would be looking over my shoulder.

It didn't take long for me to change my mind for I didn't want to stay in my pyjamas and watch TV all day; I was going to take the bus into Belfast and go for a wander around the shops. I hadn't been charity-shop shopping for ages and with summer around the corner I could peruse their lightweight clothes. Taking the bus was a novelty as well, as James was such a snob about public transport.

It was nearly lunchtime before I got into town and spent a fabulous couple of hours wandering around the charity shops. I found a lovely patterned skirt from Mistral and a brand-new T-shirt from Seasalt which would be perfect for Dubrovnik.

It was time for coffee, so I headed towards the Marks and Spencer café on Royal Avenue, which was busy with shoppers having a breather, and I had to take a high seat facing out of the windows. The café is on the second floor so it gave me the perfect view over the city's main shopping street. I sipped my coffee and ate my caramel shortbread, while watching the oblivious shoppers bustling about below me. I could have sworn I saw Claire's mum coming out of the Boots store opposite, but that was impossible: she was away with Claire on the spa weekend to Donegal. The woman who looked like her even had the same handbag I had noticed her carrying the last time I saw her, a distinctive black, daisy stem Orla Kiely one. A bit odd, but I dismissed it as one of those strange coincidences you get from time to time.

I forgot about it when I felt my phone buzz, and my heart sank as I read a message from James.

> Arrived safely although I'm not sure you even care.

Prat.

Without replying I put my phone back into my bag. *'He will not ruin my week; he will not ruin my week,'* I recited to myself.

Extracting it again, I opened the MAAF app which I hadn't checked all week. Today's quote hit me in the face:

Only be anchored by love, for if it is not love, set yourself free.

Suddenly the corny sayings didn't seem so funny anymore. What happened to quotes like:

Wrinkles, wrinkles everywhere, not a drop of Botox to spare.

Annoyed with the app – which was supposed to be helping me live my best life – I thought, *Whose side is it on?* Then I smiled to myself. Who cared? I had a whole week ahead of me and I wasn't going to let anything upset me.

Returning to James's message, I deliberated how to reply. Unexpectedly I remembered something Robbie had cheekily said when he was about six and I was trying to make him do something he didn't want to do. 'You're not the boss of me,' he had furiously shouted. Should I send that to James? Tempted but deciding discretion is the better part of valour, I simply replied:

> Glad you got there safely, enjoy x.

Then I deleted the 'x' and hit send.

As I sat on the bus home a little later, I messaged Vicky.

> If you fancy a wee glass of something chilled
> later let me know.

She was on her own this weekend too as Tom was away with work. By the time the bus deposited me in the village, she had replied, *Yes please!* and we agreed she would pop over around eight. I sent similar messages to Annie and Kate, and before I had reached home, they had both arranged to come over as well.

I felt almost deliriously happy. We would order takeaways, drink wine and put the world to rights. No tetchy husband to demand sex or dinner at half past six. Freedom Week as I privately called it, lay before me like an early Christmas present, to be unwrapped slowly while savouring every moment.

Once home, I tried on my new purchases, surveying myself in the full-length mirror and thought I looked quite nice. It could have been the exercise or the brighter days. Or perhaps I was finding myself again, the self that I had buried for years in an effort to make James happy. The self that was beginning to blossom again under a little attention and genuine compliments. I had been like a flower ravished by drought, wilted and drooping that suddenly gets a shower of water and blooms again.

How fanciful! I laughed at myself.

When my friends arrived over, we gathered in the living room, which gets the late evening sun. The room was bubbling with happiness as we chatted and joked, reminiscing about our trip to London and debating where we should go next year for our girls' weekend.

'Lisbon.'

'Valencia.'

'A wellness retreat in Thailand!' Vicky suggested.

'Ohhh,' we all replied simultaneously. A little voice in the back of my head thought, *I'll never be able to afford that,* but I went along with the others. It would probably not come to anything, as we had a habit of considering exotic places and then ending up closer to home.

The conversation moved on to my plans for James's week away.

'Have you anything exciting planned?' asked Annie. I could have sworn she glanced at Kate before catching my eye. What was that about?

'Nothing really, just going to visit my parents and then the usual; yogalates, running, cocktails on the beach.' I smiled back.

I tell my friends everything but I couldn't tell them I was meeting Sam.

'Why don't you do the park run with me next Saturday morning?' asked Annie. Again, she seemed to glance at my friends as she was speaking.

Quickly, I understood what was going on. She'd regularly been asking me to the park run with her, but I'd been fobbing her off, making excuses as to why I couldn't. I'd never actually said, 'I can't because James won't let me' but maybe she had realised? Perhaps Claire and Vicky had told her about James turning up unexpectedly at the yogalates class, and they had been discussing it behind my back.

How mortifying if they'd worked out James was becoming so overbearing that I couldn't even go for a run without his permission.

'Sorry, but I promised Mum I'd go with her to visit my aunt.' The lie slipped out like a professional, as I sipped my wine.

It seemed I was becoming a pathological liar. Could you develop it in mid-life like heartburn or varicose veins? Why did my brain go off on little jaunts when I should be concentrating on all the subtexts in my friends' conversation? Dragging it back from its meanderings, I turned to Kate.

I admit I was a bit harsh, but I wasn't thinking straight.

'How's parenting these days, Kate? Do your kids still hate you?'

'What the actual…?' She spluttered into her glass of prosecco.

'Only joking!' I hastily tried to make it into a not-at-all funny joke. I had forgotten that she'd told me all that stuff in confidence. And it was so long ago I had no idea why I said it.

Kate just replied grimly. 'Yes, most of the time they still do. And some of the time I can't stand the sight of them too.' She drained her glass and reached for the bottle in the wine cooler. 'I'm a terrible, terrible person, aren't I?' She grinned and we all laughed. Thank goodness for my friend's good nature.

Soon it was time to call it a day, and they left shortly after midnight. Kate stayed on for 'one for the road' and I apologised for my stupid, thoughtless comment earlier.

'Don't worry at all,' she slurred slightly. 'I've got used to the fact my kids think I'm awful. In fact, my lovely son told me recently I was the worst mother of all time and if there was a prize for the biggest waste of space, I would win it.'

Horrified, I rushed to defend her but she waved me away.

'Well, he's probably right as I'm pretty awful. I mean it's obviously awful if your mother finds your hidden stash of vodka, and finishes off the bottle before you can sneak it to your mate's party. Or who forgets she promised to drive you to the train so you could go to Dublin to the 1976s. Or is it the 1975s?'

I had no idea. What the hell was the 1976s? Was it a disco? Why would you go all that way just to have a dance? Maybe it was a new pub in the Temple Bar area. That would make more sense since she'd been talking about vodka. I let her ramble on. Then, although she was obviously a bit drunk, she said something so clear and honest I was dumbfounded.

'I'm sorry to say this, Laura, but James is a bit of a dick sometimes.' She nodded to herself before continuing. 'Claire told me about him turning up to check on you at yoga-thingy. It's all a bit *possessive*, isn't it? Did he think you were going to run off with one of the men in your class?'

I opened my mouth but couldn't actually think of anything to say.

'I'm sure he's really lovely,' she had put on a posh voice, 'but he's a bit *bossy*, isn't he?' Leaning forward she reached for the prosecco bottle again but it was empty. 'Well, I really should be going.' She stood up and stumbled a little. 'And forget what I said about James.' She put a finger to her lips. 'Don't tell him I said he was a dick, will you?'

Dumbly I shook my head and asked if she wanted me to walk her over the road. She declined, gave me a final hug and slowly crossed the street. It took her ages to finally get her key into the lock and I waited until the front door had closed and she was safely inside before I went back indoors myself.

I knew I shouldn't, but I giggled when I thought about her calling James a dick. I had always assumed my friends thought he was great and that his smooth talk had them fooled.

It gave me a shiver of pleasure to realise that he hadn't after all.

CHAPTER TWENTY-THREE

When Sam and I had dated back in the late eighties, we used to love walking on the beach together with his family dog. We had usually gone to the north coast, but I had a fear the Dimmocks would be at their holiday home on the north coast, so instead I suggested we go in the opposite direction towards Newcastle. I had spent a weekend as a teenager at Dundrum and remembered the fantastic Murlough Beach, with its sand dunes and seals basking by the water's edge.

I also knew it was not somewhere my Remmington in-laws would go so it was ideal. Though it was all perfectly innocent: two old friends catching up.

I spent the best part of an hour deciding on what to wear. I wanted something casual but flattering. Something it appeared I hadn't spent time carefully choosing, but that I had just flung on at the last minute. For some bizarre reason I was no longer self-conscious about my weight gain. Although I would still love to lose that last stone, I wasn't going to fret about it any longer. Nonetheless, I found I was anxious in case it was all a disaster, that we wouldn't have anything else to talk about and there would be painful silences. Or that he would regret ever arranging to meet me again.

Observing myself in the mirror before I left the house, I thought I looked all right. Bootcut jeans and a navy cashmere cardigan from M & S that I'd found in a charity shop for ten pounds. Winding a cream and coral scarf around my neck, I was ready to go.

We had agreed I would drive to Sam's house, leave my car there and he would drive us to the beach with his black lab Nigel in the boot. Minis don't have big enough boots for dogs the size of Nigel, I had joked. It never crossed my mind to suggest we drive there separately. Sam gave me directions to his home located in the Cave Hill part of the city, near Belfast Castle. As I drove up the hill towards his house, I was impressed by the wide leafy street and affluent homes. It was a lovely part of the city with incredible views over the lough. The weather was kinder today than it had been yesterday, with a weak sun breaking through the clouds, hinting at a lovely afternoon.

Sam's home was a red-brick period house with bay windows and small garden that was in need of attention. The black front door had an arched, stained-glass panel and traditional doorbell, which I pressed anxiously. It was answered quickly and it seemed as though he had been waiting behind it. He too was wearing jeans and a navy top, as though we had deliberately coordinated beforehand. No glasses today, meaning I could look straight into his warm blue eyes.

A big smile greeted me and then Nigel came bounding down the hallway.

'Sit,' instructed Sam and the well-trained dog obediently sat at his heels. Chocolate-brown eyes considered me mournfully, as I reached forward to say hello and his tail wagged happily.

'He's like the Nigel you had at home!' I exclaimed.

'Meet Nigel the fourth. It's hard to beat a black lab, so I've always had one.'

'All called Nigel?' I laughed.

'Perfect name for them,' Sam replied.

We were just standing there grinning inanely at each other, so I admired his home and he took me on a quick tour of the downstairs. Leading me through to the back of the house I saw that it had been renovated, so there was an open-plan living room and kitchen. Although the front garden had been small, the back garden was long and wide with high hedges to prevent nosy neighbours looking in. A few pieces of wooden garden furniture huddled together on a brick patio.

'I'm not much of a gardener,' he confessed, 'but the garden is great for Nigel to run about in. He goes to doggy daycare when I'm working, and my neighbour's teenage daughter walks him if I'm stuck late in work.'

We chatted easily as we went out to the car. He drove a Ford Focus, no expensive Range Rover here. We needed to drive through Belfast to get on the Newcastle Road and stupidly we had forgotten it was the Belfast Marathon, meaning roads were closed and diversions in place all around the city. Sam took it in good grace with no complaints and no whingeing.

Soon we left the city roads behind and headed towards Murlough. The closer we got, the sunnier it became and when we finally arrived the sky was clear with the sun shining brightly. I was glad I had put a T-shirt on under the cardigan, so I could strip off layers if it got too warm. Nothing is less attractive than a sweaty red face when you're trying to impress someone.

I shouldn't have worried earlier, for there wasn't a single lull in the conversation. We reminisced about school, and how straightforward life was when all you had to fret about was exams and being allowed out late on a Saturday night. He told me about his life in Scotland and how he missed it sometimes but didn't regret moving back.

We had arrived at the car park for the beach, and strolled up the wooden boardwalk which looped between the sand dunes.

The sun was high in the sky now, tiny wisps of white cloud scuttering across it from time to time. Tasting the salty air, I anticipated my first glance of the sea.

'Do you have any regrets?' Sam asked me out of the blue, concealing his eyes with a pair of sunglasses to reduce the glare of the sun, as we rounded the last corner on to the sand.

'Not really, though I do wish I'd had another child. I'm afraid I'm an overprotective mum.' I glanced at him ruefully.

'Was it through choice you didn't have another one?' he inquired gently.

'I had two miscarriages after Robbie and James thought it would be best not to try again.'

Sam nodded and I was grateful he didn't delve further, as I did not want to discuss my husband.

Nigel was bounding about in ecstasy, running backwards and forwards to the water's edge but never quite venturing in nor going too far ahead. The golden beach stretched in front of us for what seemed like miles, with only a few people on it. I felt myself relax as it was highly unlikely I would know anyone here. We walked side by side in companionable silence for a time until we came to some black rocks jutting out of the sand. Nigel appeared with a stick he had uncovered, so we sat on the rocks and took turns throwing it for him.

I sneaked a look at Sam sitting beside me and was struck with how comfortable it was to be here with him. It was almost as if we were teenagers again on the cusp of adulthood with the future bright ahead of us.

'Laura, can I ask you something? Don't answer if you don't want to.' Taking off his sunglasses he turned around to face me. 'Does James make you happy?'

I wanted to look down, to look away, but forced myself to maintain eye contact. 'Not really, not anymore.' I couldn't believe I had said it, voiced what I was feeling inside. I was terrified but elated at the same time.

'I didn't think so.' His voice was barely more than a whisper.

Now I couldn't meet his eye, so instead stared at the horizon. 'He's just... moody. Quick to anger. Or to sulk.' I was murmuring it, admitting it aloud for the first time. 'He doesn't like me seeing people or doing things without him; it makes him jealous.' I was close to tears and this wasn't even all of it, but I couldn't say any more.

'I don't want to put you in a difficult situation by meeting me. I'd love for us to be able to meet up, as friends of course, but I'd never force you to do something that would jeopardise your relationship with your husband.' I sensed Sam was looking at me, but I couldn't make eye contact with him.

'I want to see you too, Sam, but I can't tell James. He wouldn't understand we're just friends. So I need to be careful. Is that okay?'

Sam looked relieved which cheered me up enormously. He smiled at me, dimples reappearing like the sun coming out from behind a cloud. 'I'd like that, Laura. To be friends.'

We didn't need to discuss it further as we walked back towards the car park. Nigel was tiring and was trotting along beside us now, ignoring the waves. When we reached the car, Sam poured some water into his bowl and he lapped thirstily. Once he had drained the bowl dry, he jumped up into the boot and curled up on his blankets.

'Fancy a coffee before we head back?' I asked.

'Sounds good. We passed a café just before we turned down the beach road, shall we try there?'

I nodded as I slipped into the passenger seat and Sam turned the car towards the village. Instantly I had déjà vu, the sudden feeling we had been here before. It was just a memory, long buried, of us sitting together like this in a car. I remembered how I used to tuck my right hand under his thigh as he drove along. I would keep it there for miles. My cheeks flushed a little at the thought, it was so long ago I'd forgotten what it was like to even touch another man.

Fortunately, it was a dog-friendly café and we were lucky that it was almost empty. We took a table at the window overlooking the overgrown garden and I went up to the counter to order the coffees. The pastries looked delicious so I got a chocolate one and an almond one. I hadn't thought to ask Sam what he wanted and I didn't know what he liked anymore.

'I didn't know what to get, so I chose two different ones,' I said, setting them on the table between us.

'Good idea, we can cut them in two and have a half each.' He made a great show of splitting them evenly so it would be fair.

As we sat together with Nigel asleep on the floor between us, I briefly wondered what anyone who saw us would think. Would they think we were together, a proper couple? Or on a Tinder first date? I nearly giggled aloud with nervous tension as I re-crossed my legs under the table and brushed Sam's leg. Accidentally of course.

Excusing himself, he got up to use the bathroom. As he passed me, his hand rested briefly on my shoulder. Instant desire flamed within me and it became clear.

My sex drive was low with James because the connection between us had fractured. I no longer liked him and for me, emotion and libido are entwined.

In a flash, I understood that I was feeling again whereas for so long, I had simply existed. Of course, I had no idea if Sam felt the same or if he viewed me as an old mate.

When he returned to the table we made our way to the car and retraced our route, hardly speaking this time. I found it hard to think of things to talk about, as my shoulder still blazed from his touch. He too was quiet and by the time we drove into his driveway, I was certain he was going to tell me thanks, so long, see you around.

'Thanks for a lovely day,' I babbled, getting out of the car, ready to make my escape. He came around to my side before letting Nigel out of the boot.

He stopped right in front of me, looking directly at me without speaking. My breathing grew shallow, my body tense as I waited, unsure of myself.

He spoke quietly, almost as if to himself. 'I'm really glad we can be friends again, Laura.' My heart stilled for a moment. Reaching forward, he touched my hair and tucked a strand of it behind my ear. My too-flat ear that I usually tried to hide. 'I meant it when I said you haven't changed at all. You're still that same girl who turned my head in school. You're the one that got away.'

Impulsively I reached up and held the palm of my hand to his cheek. There was no denying the attraction between us. It was not just a figment of my imagination. I felt a yearning within me for the first time in years. But I had to pull back, as I couldn't make my awful situation with James worse by adding an affair to the mix.

'Thanks for a lovely day,' I repeated stupidly. 'I'm so glad you're as amazing and understanding as you are.'

I had to leave before I said or did something I would regret later. Promptly I turned on my heel and got into my Mini without looking back. But inside I was delighted.

I think he likes me.

CHAPTER TWENTY-FOUR

After our walk along the beach, I really wanted to see Sam again. But I knew that I had to be careful or I could be in trouble. Instead, I went to work, then ran a few miles in the evenings to try and forget his touch, the tenderness in his eyes as he told me he was glad we were friends again. Lying in bed each night, I closed my eyes and saw dimples. Biceps. Kindness reflected in sapphire-blue eyes.

My mother-in-law had rung me to ask if I'd wanted to get together while James was in Majorca, so we met for an early dinner in a city centre restaurant on Wednesday after work. Heather asked me how I was finding being home alone, and I found it difficult to look her in the eye and lie that I was missing James. Swallowing down my discomfort, I pretended that I was looking forward to seeing him, but the words stuck slightly in my throat. I regretted having to lie to her, but I had no option.

For I was dreading James's return on Saturday night, and couldn't say no when Sam messaged to ask if I wanted to go to the Ulster Museum on Saturday morning. He added, teasing:

> Knowing your love of history, I'm hoping you can educate me a bit.

I replied:

> I'll bore you stupid about all the fascinating exhibits.

I was like a silly schoolgirl with her first crush.

I changed my clothes several times before I took the bus into Belfast. One last day to myself before my husband was due home. I'd chosen teal cargo trousers, a white T-shirt and a sea-green cardigan, with my ancient denim jacket on top.

On the walk up from the Europa bus station to the museum, I enjoyed the bright day, weak sunshine and warmth in the air that heralded early summer. Passing through Shaftsbury Square, I was reminded of my student days at Queen's University. How quickly my time there had passed as I spent every spare moment with James. How in thrall I was to this exotic city boy, at odds with the country boys of my youth.

I wished now that I could talk to my younger self, knowing I would say 'All that glitters is not gold. Take a breath before committing your life to him.' But as I made my way through the lush Botanic Gardens, I reminded myself that if I hadn't met and fallen for James, I would never have my son. No matter what was happening with us as a couple, we would always have Robbie in common.

Quickly I glanced around to ensure there was no one nearby that I recognised and stood in the foyer of the museum waiting impatiently for Sam to arrive. It was only a few minutes, but they seemed to drag past until I caught sight of silver hair and little round glasses. My heart beat a little faster as I watched him unnoticed.

He smiled kindly at a frazzled-looking woman dragging two reluctant children in her wake before he spotted me lurking in the corner and his smile grew warmer. Making his way over to me, he stopped to pick up an information leaflet from the stand.

'Hello. Ready for an exciting morning of dinosaurs, meteorites, mummies and sailors?' he asked, dimples enticing me.

'Nothing quite like new perspectives on ancient Ireland,' I replied, reading from the leaflet, feeling a warmth spread across my cheeks. We were standing stupidly beaming at each other so I suggested we pay and start our tour.

I have no idea what we looked at for I was acutely aware of the nearness of him, his deep laugh, his witty comments. Forgetting to keep a wary eye out for anyone I knew, we browsed our way around the exhibits in record time. I could have been looking at anything, I simply didn't care. If he had suggested going to an exhibition of crochet blankets I would have agreed. Occasionally we stood together so we were almost touching, but not quite.

The illicit pleasure of being so close yet so far was intoxicating.

Before long we stopped pretending that we were engrossed in the exhibits and bought takeaway coffees from the café. The sun had broken through the clouds as we went outside and made our way into the Botanic Gardens. Conversation flowed as we passed the palm house, that great cast-iron glasshouse; the rose beds which were already a riot of colour; and groups of friends huddled together. We settled under a large, leafy tree.

'Did you come here as a student at Queen's?' he asked, lying back on the grass.

'All the time if the weather was warm. I love to wander through now as well,' I answered, settling beside him. 'City life bustles past, but in here you could be anywhere. I love the calmness against the chaos of life.'

'I've only been here a couple of times before.' He lay beside me, close but not touching. If I crept my fingers a fraction of an inch to the left, we would be. I felt parts of me tingle that hadn't tingled in forever.

'I'm only getting to find out what Belfast offers since moving back. For so long it wasn't exactly at the top of anyone's tourist list, but it's like a different world now.'

'You need to do the tourist Hop-on Hop-off bus tour then,' I murmured while shading my eyes against the brightness of the sun. I could feel the heat of his body tantalisingly close.

'Maybe we could do it together one day?' he remarked casually.

Tilting my head, I looked at him. He was so close now I could smell his aftershave. I found I could barely speak. Instead, my eyes were drawn to his mouth, until with an effort I raised them to his.

'I don't know, maybe.' I got my voice back as I turned my head away. Lowering my hand to the grass, my fingers grazed his and without thinking I left them there. I felt the softest touch as his finger slowly moved up mine to the sensitive skin on my inner wrist. Such a tiny thing but also the most erotic thing I had experienced in years. Decades. We lay beside each other in silence with our eyes closed and I felt the sweet flicker of longing. I involuntarily tensed to his touch as I held my breath, waiting to see what he would say or do next.

'Sam, is that you?' A booming voice broke the spell.

My eyes flew open to see a tall, slim man staring down at us.

Sam leapt to his feet and bade the interloper hello, shaking his hand and introducing us. 'This is my colleague Mike. My friend Laura.' He motioned to me.

I said hello as I sat up and felt unexpectedly guilty, as if we had been doing something reprehensible. It dawned on me that it could have been anyone strolling past us. How would I have explained myself if it had been someone I knew? As Sam chatted easily to his colleague, my phone vibrated in my bag. Using it as an opportunity not to have to stand up and talk to Mike, I reached for it and read the message.

> Flight is on time. Will be home at around half past five. Will need dinner.

My heart sank. Back to the same soul-destroying routine of making dinner every night, asking permission to go out, long evenings at home with James watching my every move. A deep, black depression rolled over me, suffocating my very core. This past week had been a taste of independence, of lightness and laughter, of doing what I wanted when I wanted. Of answering to no one. It was as though the sun had broken through for a short time, but had been consumed by a blanket of thick, impermeable cloud stretching as far as the eye could see.

> See you then

I texted back before despondently shoving my phone back into my bag. Mike was saying goodbye and I managed a polite wave before Sam sat back down beside me.

'Are you okay?' he asked, concerned.

'Yes, I'm fine,' I lied. 'But I need to think about getting home.'

'Already?' He looked crestfallen but then said, 'No problem, if you need to.'

I wanted to scream, *I don't want to, I want to stay here all day with you and never have to go home again!* But of course, I didn't. He'd think I'd lost the plot if I did that. Instead, I made myself smile, as he stood up and reached out a hand to help me to my feet. I thanked him as I brushed off the back of my trousers, and we strolled over to a bin to throw the coffee cups into.

'Did you drive?' I asked. Parking spaces around the Queen's area are notoriously scarce.

'No, I got the train for a change.'

Damn, I should have got the train in and then we could have spent a bit longer together.

'I need to walk down to the bus station so I'll have to go this way.' I pointed down the street towards the Europa Hotel, which had the dubious honour of being the most bombed hotel in the world.

'And I need to go this way.' Sam pointed behind me. We stood at the junction with the red brick of the main university building to our right, sunlight dappling through the trees and looked at each other.

'Thanks for the tour of the museum. I think we may have raced through it in record time.'

'You're welcome.'

'Laura, if this is too difficult when James comes home then I will understand.' Sam was looking intently at me.

'We're just friends,' I said firmly, quashing my fears and my hopes along with them. 'Although I don't think I'll be inviting you around for a drink with James any time soon. Not sure he'd appreciate that!' I grimaced a little at that.

'Good. I'll be in touch?'

We parted without touching and I mooched along the street thinking about how happy I felt when I was in Sam's company, and how unhappy I felt at the thought of James coming home. By the time I had reached the bus station, I had decided nothing. It was as though I was incapable of making even the slightest decision about my future or my marriage.

I watched the city zip past from the bus window a short time later, and did accept that I couldn't stay forever in this state of misery. Robbie was going to be graduating at the end of June and hopefully would be successful in getting a job, so we wouldn't need to support him anymore. He wanted to live with his friends in Belfast, so he wouldn't be at home to act as a buffer to mask our problems.

There were only five more weeks of school then I would have

the long break throughout July and August to help make my decision. By the time summer was easing into early autumn, I was determined to have made some sort of choice. Should I stay or should I go? Giving myself the next few months to see if it was possible to rescue my marriage or not, I would be better prepared to face the future.

One thing I knew for certain. I couldn't factor Sam into this. He might be a catalyst for a life change, but I couldn't make this out to be more than it was at the minute. If I was going to leave James, it had to be for the right reasons and not because a tall, blue-eyed blast from my past had reappeared in my life.

Even if he did make me feel better about myself than I had for years.

CHAPTER TWENTY-FIVE

I t was just after five o'clock and I was sitting in the living room waiting on James's return. I felt anxious and uncertain about what mood he would be in, and if he would continue to sulk about our finances. He hadn't phoned me at all in the past week and only sent a few short texts, which was unlike him.

On the rare occasions he was away from home he normally rang each evening to ensure I was all right. Did he think I'd been fretting all week about him and his bad mood? Little did he know that I'd had a complete ball, putting food waste in the black bin and living on cheese on toast in the evening. I'm a girl who knows how to party hard.

Soon the taxi drew up in front of the house, and my handsome, tanned husband appeared from the back seat. Dispassionately I watched as the taxi driver unloaded his suitcase and bike case from the boot. Laughing and shaking his hand, I could see charming James in full flow. The façade of bonhomie as ever.

He made his way to the front door, while I waited restlessly in the hall.

'Laura, my darling,' he announced as he came through the

door. 'I've missed you so much.' Opening his arms wide, he pulled me into a tight hug, as though there had been no issue at all before he left. After a minute he released me and bent down to give me a kiss on the cheek. 'Did you miss me or were you too busy going out with your friends?' he asked lightly.

'Of course I missed you.' The fib slipped out effortlessly. 'Are you hungry?'

'No, I ate on the plane,' he replied, waiting to see if I would make a fuss. He had deliberately sent that text earlier, ensuring I would have his dinner ready for him coming home.

Always playing games.

'No problem,' I retorted sweetly. 'I'll do the chicken stir fry for myself then.'

Smirking coolly in response, he left his suitcase in the hallway before taking his bike case through into the garage to unpack it. While he fondled and stroked his bike, I cooked myself the stir fry in the wok before opening a bottle of Pinot.

'Would you like a glass?' I offered, as he reappeared in the kitchen. 'Then you can tell me all about your week.'

'Yes please.' He took the glass from my hand as he settled himself at the table.

For the next hour I listened with half an ear as he regaled me with stories about the steep hairpin climbs, vertiginous sea views and lush scenery. He was animated and relaxed, although he complained about the food, as he'd been suffering from indigestion all week. I saw traces of the man I had fallen in love with and it seemed the trip had broken down some of the barriers that we had jointly erected. I felt great relief that I was enjoying his company again.

It didn't even bother me a short time later, when he took me by the hand and led me upstairs and into his bedroom. I was able to participate without thinking about dimples. Or biceps.

The following evening, we had our weekly phone call with Robbie, who only had one last exam left to do.

'I've got news for you,' he said excitedly. 'I've been offered a job in Belfast with GJG, the engineering firm. I just heard for definite this week. Provided I pass my degree of course.' He was overjoyed and I could have wept I was so pleased for him. He would be coming home!

Even James was thrilled for him, though he did make a snide little comment about Robbie having to pay his own way once he was back with us. I didn't confide in him that Robbie wanted to live with his friends. I'd keep that to myself for another while. We discussed our trip to Stirling for his graduation at the end of June, when we would be moving him out of his flat and I felt an unfamiliar peace wash over me.

'You'll be pleased he's coming home,' said James after we hung up. I agreed cheerfully and then he continued blithely on. 'Maybe your moods will settle down a bit now and you can give me some attention instead of always obsessing about Robbie.'

It hadn't taken him long to start whining about my moods again. I ignored that comment, nodded and switched on the television. I wasn't going to let him ruin my happiness tonight.

Somehow, we got on well enough over the next couple of weeks. It was coming to the end of the school year with summer tantalisingly close. School was filled with trips, sports day, little work and mostly play.

I had received a message from Sam to let me know his dad was going through a difficult time with his mum, and they were hoping to get her a respite place in a nursing home. I was concerned about them all and arranged to meet him for a supportive coffee after work. Selecting a day I knew I could get away a little earlier, I again drove into work rather than taking the train. If I was careful to keep an eye on the clock, I should be able to get home at the usual time and not arouse James's suspicions.

We were meeting at the hospice coffee shop as before, and I was a few minutes early, so took the same seat in the corner as I had done the last time. I must have been getting better at the subterfuge, as I wasn't nearly as worried as the last time, or as concerned about being spotted by someone I knew.

Sam was running late and when he arrived looked a bit frazzled. I supposed that he had been speaking with a patient or their relative, breaking bad news in a sympathetic manner and meeting me was taking up his precious time.

When I said as much, he replied, 'You're a bit of brightness in an otherwise dark day.' He didn't say any more, but I squeezed his hand and went up to the counter to order the coffees without asking what he wanted.

I no longer needed to.

We spoke about his parents and it was obvious that he was heartbroken about his mum. She had always been a vibrant, caring person who had juggled a busy home life with her job as a legal secretary.

'Dad's struggling to look after her at the minute, even with carers helping out,' he said sadly. 'He needs a break and Mum needs specialist nursing care, but I think just for a short time. There's a couple of really good nursing homes close to them, so hopefully she will get a place in one of them soon.'

The time flew by and before I knew it, I had to leave. We stood facing each other in the car park and Sam thanked me for meeting him, saying it was good to talk with someone who knew his mum before her illness. I was itching to give him a hug but made do with a rather feeble wave and a promise to meet up again soon.

When I arrived home, I went straight upstairs to change into a pair of shorts and a T-shirt as the sun was shining, and I fancied sitting out in the garden before dinner. When I got back downstairs, my way was blocked by my husband.

'What have you been hiding from me, Laura?' He was standing by the kitchen table, brandishing my mobile phone, which I had left in my handbag in the hall.

'What do you mean?' I managed to reply in a steady tone, though already my heart rate was quickening.

'Who is Sam?' He stood close to me, towering over me, seemingly twice as broad as usual.

My mind went blank. My mouth dried instantly. I couldn't think of anything at all to say.

He read the message on the front of my phone.

> I think we got away with it but it was a close thing

His voice was even, his jaw clenched, eyes of steel. 'Well? Do I need to repeat myself?' Now his voice held a warning. 'Who. Is. Sam?'

Thankfully it dawned on me in a dazzling ray of relief.

'Sam. Samantha. One of the other classroom assistants who's organising a baby shower for Simone the chemistry teacher. We're trying to keep it a surprise, but she walked in on us chatting about it today.'

'Okay.' He nodded. 'I wouldn't like my wife to be messaging some man. I wouldn't like it at all.'

My legs were trembling as I forced a smile.

Then. 'Have you changed your passcode on your phone? I can't get in.'

'Yes,' I answered as firmly as I could. Thinking on my feet, I told a half-truth, 'We did a cyber security training thing in work and they recommend changing passwords regularly. To protect accounts, that sort of thing.'

'I doubt they meant protect them from your husband. What's your new code?'

My stomach filled with acid. Was he going to go through my messages? Was he going to see the ones from Sam? I gave him the six digits of my passcode.

As he punched in the numbers, our landline phone rang. The only people who use our landline are his parents so he set my mobile down on the table before going to answer it. Knowing I only had a couple of minutes, I snatched it up, deleted the Facebook Messenger app, changed my phone notifications and set it back on the table where he had left it. James did not use Facebook and I had to hope without the Messenger app he wouldn't think to search for anything there.

By the time he returned, I had taken a seat at the other end of the table, more to hide my shaking legs than anything else.

Without a word, he lifted my phone and made a point of silently looking through my texts, my WhatsApp messages and my emails.

Please don't find anything, please don't find anything, I prayed over and over to myself.

Seemingly satisfied that all my messages were innocent, he handed me my phone back saying, 'Don't change your passcode again without telling me,' and strode from the room.

I sat where I was, trying to make sense of what had just happened. My immediate feeling was one of relief that he hadn't discovered my messages from Sam. Then I digested what had happened. He had demanded I hand over my phone so he could snoop through all my private messages. Leaving the whole Sam situation to one side, he had calmly stood there reading my personal messages to my family, my friends and my colleagues. Worse, I had sat there meekly letting him.

Raging both with him and myself, I grabbed the sun-cream and went out to sit on the patio. Plonking a baseball cap on my head, I flipped open the MAAF app. What would today's words of wisdom be?

Only you can plot the story of your life.

Great. The Mad As Absolute Feck app was now listening to my conversations.

As quickly as my temper had risen, it subsided. I wasn't going to stop messaging Sam, therefore I had to stay one step ahead of my increasingly autocratic husband.

Idly I wondered about using Snapchat or Instagram instead, but wasn't really sure about either of those.

Thus I planned to have a chat with a younger colleague who could tell me the best way to message an old boyfriend without my husband finding out.

CHAPTER TWENTY-SIX

I counted down the days of June to both my trip to Stirling for Robbie's graduation, and my next opportunity to see Sam.

It was increasingly difficult not to fight with James over the smallest things, but I was afraid to upset him in case he became even more unreasonable. Claire, Vicky and I were still going to our yogalates class on a Tuesday and thankfully he didn't reappear there, probably because he sensed my friends were less than impressed with him. And even though I desperately wanted to, I never mentioned doing the park run with Annie again. I had downloaded Snapchat and that was how Sam and I now communicated, the messages disappearing after reading.

I felt I should now introduce myself as 'Remmington, Laura Remmington' I was becoming so adept at deviousness.

Sam's mum had been offered a respite placement in a nursing home and she was due to move into it at the weekend. It was only a short drive from my parents so I hatched a plan to visit them briefly, then to meet Sam after he had settled his mum into her new room.

Just so he had a friend to talk to after such an ordeal.

The night before, I arrived home from work to find James

sitting on the patio, eyes shaded by his Ray-Bans and nursing a beer. That was so unlike him that I went straight outside to ask if everything was all right.

'Who is he?' he asked dolefully, taking a long drink from the bottle of Bud.

'What do you mean?' I was genuinely puzzled.

'I'm giving you a chance to explain, Laura, so don't play the innocent with me.'

'I really don't know what you mean.' My chest tightened. This was it. He had found out about Sam. I braced myself.

'I decided to take my wife out for lunch today as a surprise. Then when I was walking past that café beside the school, I saw you having lunch with a man. You were laughing like a foolish girl, all over him like a rash.' His tone was vicious.

'I was having coffee with Timothy, my boss. We were discussing my new student for next year.' Was James being serious?

'You expect me to believe that?' His voice rose. 'That was no work meeting.'

'For goodness' sake, James, Timothy is ten years younger than me and has a fantastic boyfriend called John-Paul. I've told you about him before!'

'Why were you laughing like a hyena then? You looked very cosy in the corner together; how could a husband not think there was more to it than work colleagues?'

'I was laughing because he's one of the most lovely, funny people I know and we've worked together for the last six years so yes, we probably were very cosy-looking.' Why did I have to explain a coffee and a chat with a friend? James's paranoia was becoming more and more out of control.

'You have no idea what it's like having no one to talk to all day every day,' he started. 'It's all right for you going out to work when I'm here on my own. I look forward to seeing you in the evening but you insist on going to that class with your friends or to visit your parents at the weekend. Do you know how lonely I am sometimes?'

I scrutinised him sitting there in his expensive clothes and his Ray-Bans, self-righteousness oozing from every pore and I understood something profound. I not only disliked my husband; he was making my skin crawl. But more importantly, I was afraid of him and afraid to stand up to him. So instead, appalled with myself as much as him, I went over and sat on the Adirondack chair beside him, before taking his hand.

'Do you think it might help if you went back into the office a couple of days a week?'

'No, what would help is if you gave up your job and were at home every day.'

I laughed immediately, thinking he was making a joke. But one look at his face told me he was deadly serious. Dread filled the pit of my stomach.

'I've been giving it some thought. Now Robbie is finishing university and has got a graduate job, there is no need for you to work. I've done the sums and if we halve your monthly allowance and sell the Mini you could be a lady of leisure at home every day with me.'

'But James…' I didn't know what I was going to say. He had blindsided me. 'But James,' I repeated. 'I need a car. We live in a village with sporadic public transport. How would I even do the food shop? And I need to work, I love my job.'

'Love it more than you love me?' Turning to face me, he removed his sunglasses. His hangdog expression repulsed me.

How could I have spent so many years thinking that this man had my best interests at heart, when it was becoming clear the only person he was concerned with was himself. If I didn't make a stand now, I could wave goodbye to a job I loved and instead would fill my days cooking, cleaning and serving him. The thought of it terrified me so much that I quickly stood up, before saying quietly, yet as emphatically as I could, 'I'm not giving up my job to become an unpaid skivvy here. You may not value my job but the children I help do.'

I defiantly held his stare and at last he had the decency to drop his eyes. 'Okay, it was just an idea,' he muttered sulkily. 'If you prefer to work rather than be here to support me then fine.'

I gritted my teeth with frustration at such an asinine comment. 'Just because I'm working doesn't mean I can't support you. The two are not mutually exclusive.' I turned towards the house, calling over my shoulder, 'I'm going for a run. Dinner will be a bit later tonight.'

Upstairs I swiftly discarded my work clothes and dressed in my running kit. Pulling my hair back into a ponytail I removed my make-up – no need to have mascara running down my face as I sweated my way round the village. Tightening the laces of my trainers, I kept replaying our conversation over and over. Something was jarring but I simply couldn't figure out what it was. As I jogged round the village past the sheep, past the wood, over the bridge, it suddenly hit me.

Timothy and I had used a back gate to sneak out of school an hour before my usual lunch break. So how could James have spotted us in the café if he had just been walking past? Instantly I stopped running and gazed unseeingly past the sheep. Timothy and I had been sitting in the back corner of the café so as not to be spotted by any errant pupils or staff.

If James had been passing the café, there was no way on earth he could have seen us. So how exactly had he known where I was and who I was with?

A cold chill ran down my spine. Was he following me? Had he been lurking outside the school grounds all morning on the off-chance I would appear? No, I reasoned, there was no way he even knew that I used that back gate as it is supposed to be for vehicles only. And I'd never mentioned the café as it's a bit grotty but did the best bacon baps in the city.

So how did he know I'd been there with Timothy?

I walked the rest of the way so I could consider it all in peace. I couldn't figure out how James knew where I had been, until I reached the end of our street. It was obvious that there was only one explanation.

He was using my phone to track me.

Nausea swept over me. My phone was a hand-me-down from James as usual. He always got the new one and gave me his old one. Tearing it from my arm holder, I shakily unlocked it and scrolled through the icons on my home page. There was nothing out of the ordinary. I searched through them all to see if he had somehow uploaded a tracker. Then I spotted the green icon on the last screen.

Find my iPhone.

Hands sweating, I pressed it and there in all its hideous simplicity I read it.

James can see your location.

The little blue dot sat steadily on the map of my street.

I had no idea if he'd downloaded the app himself, or if it had always been there, but I knew with absolute certainty that I had never added him, or agreed to share my location with him. He had done that all by himself.

I plodded on towards the woods and my mind was in turmoil as I processed what I had uncovered. Making my way to the bench beside the pond, thoughts swirled relentlessly around my head.

He knows exactly where I am at all times.

He can watch me any time he chooses to.

Which meant that today he hadn't accidentally seen me with Timothy like he claimed; he must have been spying on me via the app. He must have seen me leave school early and then come to investigate.

His deception was complete and I felt incapacitated by it. How long had he been tracking me for? Was this a new thing after I had changed my passcode? I couldn't think straight.

Eventually though, the shock wore off and I was able to logically process it.

It had to be a recent thing, otherwise he would have questioned why I had been at Murlough Beach or the hospice coffee shop in a strange part of the city. Therefore, he must have only done it in the past couple of weeks.

I knew I now had an advantage in this strange game of love versus hate that we seemed to be playing, as he was unaware that I had rumbled him. One thing was certain though, from now on I had to be very careful and to assume he was spying on me at all times.

Still, I couldn't think about marching up to him and screaming in his face that I knew what he was doing before packing my bags and leaving. I was still too unsure of myself, too afraid of confronting him and of facing a life on my own.

I sat there alone beside the pond and felt deeply ashamed of myself. How could I stay married to someone who was slowly and inexorably snuffing out every bit of affection that I felt for him? Deep down I blamed myself for the demise of our marriage. If I had been able to continue exactly as I had done for years, maybe he would never have felt the need to know what I was doing all of the time. If I could have been a better wife, there was a chance he could have reverted into the man I fell in love with.

Having committed to giving myself the next couple of months to figure out what I was going to do, I couldn't let this new discovery affect that timescale. I didn't have enough money to up and leave today and I had nowhere to go – after all, I could hardly run back to my parents and ask to move back into my childhood bedroom.

As much as I detested having to go back home and pretend I had never discovered this, I would have to.

But it would only be a matter of time until I made that final decision.

CHAPTER TWENTY-SEVEN

On my return home, I knew it would be extremely difficult to be civil to James and to act as though nothing was different, but I truly felt I had no option. For if I confronted him now, he would simply deny adding the app and I was too afraid of provoking him. As hard as it would be, I would have to act as if I was completely oblivious to it, while being aware he could be watching my movements any time he chose.

I prepared myself for a continuation of the argument about me giving up work, as I reluctantly walked back towards the house. The very thought of giving up my job or my car made me feel sick and I couldn't imagine being alone in the house with him day after day, with nothing to do but look after him. I would have to ask for his permission to go out for the day or explain why I wanted to go and see other people. It was essential I remained strong about this or I would be buried under the depression that again threatened to immerse me.

Surprisingly it was as though a light switch had been flipped when I got in. Instead of being in a morose mood, he asked me about my run as though the previous conversation had never happened. Like so often before, he left me unsure if I was coming or going. After my shower, he even offered to barbeque the chicken breast I had left out for dinner and as he did so, prattled pleasantly about our forthcoming trip to Stirling for Robbie's graduation.

Because he seemed to be in a good mood, I risked mentioning that I was planning on visiting Mum and Dad the following day. 'Would you like to come with me?' I asked, fervently hoping that he would say no.

'I would, but the cycling club have planned a long ride around Strangford tomorrow. I'll be away all day, but I'd like you to be home before I get back, so don't be late,' he commanded.

Relieved that I wouldn't have to cancel Sam, I nodded.

Next morning he rose early and disappeared with his club on his bike. I had plotted my day carefully. First, I would visit Mum and Dad and then I would make an excuse to go into their local town 'to suss out the charity shops' when in fact I would meet Sam for a coffee.

During the entire drive up to their house, I debated with myself about confiding in Mum about my rekindled friendship with Sam.

Mum, I wanted to let you know I'm seeing that old boyfriend I was crazy about in school until he left me for Scotland.

Possibly not. How about: *I'm popping into town for coffee with my ex who gives me butterflies in my stomach. Behind my insufferable husband's back of course.*

Did Sam give me butterflies in my stomach? With a bit of a start, I realised that is exactly what he gave me. And yes, my husband was increasingly insufferable.

By the time I was driving up the hill to their house, I still wasn't certain what I should say. In the end as we drank our coffee together, I merely asked Mum if she remembered Sam Brown.

'That lovely, kind boy who went to Scotland to become a doctor? Wasn't he captain of the rugby team?'

'That's the one.'

'The one who broke your heart when he left?'

'Did he?' I was surprised she remembered, for I thought I'd buried that hurt deep.

'You cried every day for a month at least. Told me you'd never find anyone who made you feel as good about yourself again.'

My broken heart had been pretty transparent then.

She carried on, 'I heard his poor mum has health problems.'

Without thinking I replied, 'I bumped into him in Belfast. He came back to help his dad look after his mum. You're right, she has heart issues and as Marianne is in Australia, it's just him and his dad to care for her now.'

Mum looked at me, saying nothing. So of course, I kept talking to fill the silence. 'He's a doctor at Belfast Hospice, divorced, no kids but has a dog called Nigel. Do you remember he had a badly behaved black lab called Nigel who ate my leather sandal?'

'You know a lot about someone you "just bumped into".' She took a bite of her fruit scone as she studied me knowingly.

My cheeks grew warm as I admitted, 'I met him for coffee after I bumped into him. Was that awful of me?'

'I take it you didn't tell James?' She knew me too well.

I shook my head, waiting for her to denounce me as a harlot and a deceiver.

'No need to tell him. If you're just friends it would only cause a fight.'

I was so shocked I couldn't answer.

'Assuming you are just friends of course.'

Hurriedly I answered yes of course we were just friends, nothing more.

'Anything else you need to tell me?'

'I'm meeting him for coffee today after he moves his mum into Clover Field Nursing Home.' I said it in a rush, wanting to be honest with her.

'And you don't want James to know?'

'No,' I replied in a quiet voice.

'Well, I won't be telling him if that's what you're worried about, but I won't lie for you either. Go for your coffee and if anyone asks, you were here and went for a dander around the town after. That's as much as I know.' Then she leaned forward before saying firmly, 'Ask yourself this, Laura. Are you playing with fire? You said things are difficult with James at the minute, so is adding this friendship with Sam to the mix making it more confusing?'

I denied it vigorously and after a time left, feeling slightly guilty.

Sam and I met in a bustling coffee shop in the centre of my hometown. Ballyburn had changed greatly over the years with a host of new developments, thriving shops and café culture. Hanging baskets brimming with summer blooms decorated every lamp-post, there were throngs of teenagers chatting over their takeaway skinny oat milk caramel lattes and we were lucky to find a free table in the busiest café in town.

Sam looked drawn, his demeanour quiet. It had obviously been a stressful morning and as we sipped our bog-standard coffees, he filled me in on how his mum had cried as they settled her into her new room.

'I left Dad with her for a bit, but I need to go back and collect him in a couple of hours. He's feeling very guilty about it all, but he needs the break.'

Covering his hand with mine – nothing sensual, just a friend supporting another friend through a difficult time – I let him talk. When we finished our coffee, he suggested we take a short drive to a neighbouring village so we could walk along the edge of Lough Neagh. Squashing the worry that James could be monitoring me via my phone I agreed, reassuring myself he could hardly spy on me while riding his bike. I drove us in the Mini to the village that I hadn't visited for about twenty years. It had changed greatly in the intervening time and the marina now boasted a children's play area, a viewing platform over the lough and even glamping pods. There was a nature trail signposted through the woodlands and we wandered along it reminiscing about the many times we had explored these woods when we were dating.

'Do you remember the day you insisted on us coming here for a walk and the midges were so bad we were both covered in bites for a week?' I smiled at the memory even though it had been no smiling matter at the time.

'Or the time we came here in the evening and stumbled across that couple in full view of everyone?'

'I remember being mortified anyone would have sex outside!' We laughed together at the memory.

'Such innocent times,' Sam said softly. 'Really we were just kids with no idea of what was ahead.'

It remained unspoken between us that we had never had sex in the year we dated. Lots of smooching and petting, but refraining from total intimacy. That's how things were in the eighties. Times were changed indeed. As we reached the water's edge, the first spots of rain fell. Of course, I had left my coat in the car thinking that it would stay dry but no such luck. I should have known the only thing reliable about the weather in Northern Ireland is its unreliability. We ran towards the nearest public shelter which was enclosed on three sides and exposed at the front. Hardly ideal cover from a sudden downpour, but we were so far from the car we had no other option.

By the time we reached the shelter I was soaked through. Breathless and wet, I retreated as far back into the shelter as I could, trying to escape the rain. Sam stood in front of me to protect me from the worst of it and as I recovered my breath, I felt his proximity to me. It took immense willpower not to reach out and wrap my arms around him.

Giddy with longing, my breath was now ragged not from the

exertion, but the desire rising within me. I became aware that Sam's breathing too had changed, as if he was holding his breath, waiting to see what I would do. As I felt an overwhelming urge to touch him, a small snappy dog appeared at his heels and we heard a voice call 'Fred.' The spell was broken as Fred's owner appeared and apologised for him.

'No problem at all,' said Sam politely, stepping away from me.

Fred and his owner disappeared back into the woods as the rain tailed off, and we stood side by side watching it fall onto the still surface of the lough.

'I should be getting back for Dad,' Sam finally said and held a hand out to me as he started to make his way towards the trail. Reaching out, I grasped his hand, which was large and warm. My own felt small and cold, and he laughed as he rubbed them both within his.

'You always got cold so quickly, Laura, I'd forgotten that.'

I liked that my little quirks caused Sam amusement, whereas they provoked derision from James.

In fact, there was nothing I disliked about Sam. Each time we met up I felt myself draw closer, unable to stop comparing him to my husband and finding James sadly wanting. Kindness emanated from Sam whereas ridicule emanated from my husband.

We drove together back into Ballyburn and I dropped him off in front of the nursing home.

'I hope your mum settles in and your dad benefits from the break.'

'I hope so too. Thanks for today.' He reached out and held my hand, fingers interlocking. 'Just checking you've warmed up,' he said gently. 'Have a lovely time in Stirling.'

Reluctantly I let his hand go and said goodbye. Watching him in the rear-view mirror as I drove off, I realised something.

Mum was right.

I was playing with fire.

CHAPTER TWENTY-EIGHT

Before I knew it, it was finally time for our trip to Stirling for Robbie's graduation. Filled with excitement, I packed with great care. I'd found a flattering blue and white floral maxi dress in a hospice charity shop that I was going to wear with wedge sandals if it was dry, or, more likely, white trainers if it was wet. Scotland is not renowned for its sunny climate.

The crossing was calm, and as I watched the horizon from the comfort of the leather sofa, I fizzed with the anticipation of a lovely few days ahead. As we neared the rugged Scottish coast, I savoured the thought of the return journey with Robbie. It was hard to believe that his four years in Scotland were finally ending, as in one way it had flown past and in another every day had dragged.

Once we reached the hotel in Stirling city centre, I started to unpack my small case, even though we were only going to be there for a couple of nights. As I was hanging my lovely dress up in the wardrobe, I heard James clearing his throat. Turning round, I saw him standing beside his suitcase and with a flourish he pulled something out of it.

Initially, I couldn't make out what it was, something small

and black. Then with my heart sinking, I recognised lingerie that he had bought me a lifetime ago from Victoria's Secret. Truthfully I never wore it nowadays as thongs were clearly designed by a man who had no idea getting flossed between your butt cheeks is about as sexy as skinny jeans on middle-aged men.

'I brought you this to wear as a special treat.' He had a salacious smile on his face.

'Oh right,' I replied unenthusiastically, eyeing the scrap of material.

'Put it on now,' he ordered, holding it out to me.

'Well, it's just that I'm wearing a white top tonight and black underwear isn't exactly a great look under it.'

'You're not going to be wearing it tonight. I want you to put it on now and then I can slowly strip it off you before we go out.'

So that's what he wanted.

Sex.

Great.

Maybe if we get it over and done with now, that will be it for the duration, I thought as I obediently stripped off my jeans and striped top, then slipped into the bathroom to put the scraps of material on. The bra was a wispy lace thing that barely covered my breasts, the strap cutting into my back. It had literally been years and a stone ago that I'd last worn it. Putting on the G-string, I looked at myself in the mirror. The harsh bathroom lighting did nothing for my middle-aged body, every sagging lumpy bit of me exposed in the miniscule silk lingerie.

I had never felt less attractive or less in the mood for sex in my entire life.

Taking a deep breath, I returned to the bedroom where James lay naked on the bed.

'It doesn't look as good on you as I remember, Laura. Go to the window,' he instructed.

'No chance,' I retorted immediately. 'It's broad daylight!'

'I said go to the window,' he replied so firmly that I did it without speaking. Then, 'Do you remember Paris?'

I did remember Paris, which, like the lingerie, was a lifetime ago. We were not long married and had sex all the time. Anywhere, anytime, whenever we took the notion. In Paris we had sex up against our hotel window with the curtains open, oblivious to the fact we could have been seen by anyone who happened to glance up.

'I do remember Paris but no way. That was in the days before CCTV and anyone could record you on a mobile phone!' I exclaimed aghast.

He got off the bed and pushed me hard against the window before I could resist or say anything else. He started kissing my neck, my chest, slipping the bra straps down.

'Please James, I don't want to do this, can we just move to the bed?'

'No, don't be so boring.' He pushed the bra down so my breasts were exposed.

'Please no, I don't want to.'

Ignoring my pleas completely, he briskly turned me around so I was facing the window, breasts displayed for anyone who might happen to be looking in our direction. I was mortified and terrified at the thought of someone photographing or videoing us. Again, I begged him to stop, but was ignored as he roughly took me from behind. Perversely, the more I begged, the more excited he became and luckily it didn't last long.

When he had finished, he moved away from me. 'You love it really, Teeny, how much you turn me on. You can't pretend you didn't enjoy that. I'm going for a shower and I'll look forward to a repeat later,' he said, closing the bathroom door behind him.

Weeping softly, I felt humiliated beyond belief. He knew I hadn't wanted it, that I had asked him to stop. But he had forced himself on me despite my pleas. I didn't want to stay in the room with him now, as he had destroyed all enjoyment of what should have been a special time. How was I going to put on a brave face and act as if everything was all right in front of my son?

Somehow, I had stemmed my tears by the time James came out of the bathroom, and squeezing past him silently, I went in to have a shower. Turning the water up so hot I could hardly bear it, I tried to scrub all traces of him off me.

By the time I had finished something inside me had changed. Irreparable. Implacable.

Stepping out of the shower, my skin red and inflamed from the scalding water, I stared at myself in the mirror. I barely recognised the man my husband had become, for now he was a man who seemed to get pleasure out of demeaning and belittling me.

I do not know when I stopped loving James. It may have been after the tenth casual cruelty or the thousandth. But I knew without doubt as I stood in that small bathroom in Stirling, debased and in pain, when I finally allowed myself to admit it.

I no longer love my husband.

There could be no future with a man who had forced me against my will, who degraded me to such an extent that he left me weeping and sore. All I could do now was to get these next few days over, paste a smile to my face in front of my son, and then my scheming would begin in earnest on our return home.

I forced myself to go back into the bedroom, dried my hair, reapplied my make-up and hid my loathing of my husband, who acted as though nothing was amiss. Inwardly, I reminded myself that these few days were about my son, not about two parents whose relationship was in tatters.

We arranged to meet Robbie for a drink in a city centre bar before dinner, and we made our way there in silence. If James knew I was upset with him, he ignored it. On our arrival at the wine bar, he imperiously ordered me a drink without asking what I wanted, and I made an excuse that I needed the loo.

From the ladies' toilet I messaged Sam. It may have been

wrong, but I felt such antipathy towards my husband, I needed contact with someone friendly. He responded quickly to tell me he hoped I was enjoying my trip and that he was looking forward to hearing all about it when I got home.

Certain he wouldn't want to hear the truth about my trip so far, I replied that I was looking forward to seeing him when I got back. Mindlessly, I added an 'x' for the first time. My finger hovered over the send button for a fraction of a second before I pressed it.

In the same way that I had earlier admitted my true feelings to myself about my husband, I now acknowledged that I didn't simply think of Sam as a platonic friend.

The heart is after all just a muscle, and how I felt about him was only muscle memory. For I felt exactly the same as I had when I was seventeen and we were driving in his dad's car, windows down, radio playing, with my hand tucked under his thigh.

The boy I had fallen for had become a man that I was falling for all over again.

Possibly it was foolish, probably it was because I was so unhappy in my marriage, but I couldn't lie to myself any longer.

I waited in the toilets just long enough for him to reply that he was looking forward to seeing me too and my heart lifted when I saw that he had signed it with an 'x'. I had crossed some invisible line, but instead of feeling guilty I felt happier than I had in a long time.

When I made it back to our table, my gorgeous son was sitting with my husband drinking a pint of beer. Standing up when I reached the table, he gave me an enormous hug.

'I'm so proud of you, pet,' I whispered into his ear, holding him tightly.

He brushed it off modestly with a gruff 'Thanks Mum.'

'Stop clinging to him, Laura.' James's tone was hard, patently annoyed with my unseemly display.

I ignored my husband and sat down beside Robbie, asking him what the plans for his graduation ceremony were the following day. As he filled me in, I was delighted at the knowledge he would be coming home with us, and it would no longer just be the two of us at home. At least for the next few weeks until he found somewhere in Belfast to rent. It would give me a breathing space to plan for my future, which increasingly looked James-free.

The next couple of days were crammed with happy celebrations and packing up Robbie's stuff. James refused to allow me to play my white noise machine at night, but I had discovered an amazing little gadget called a pillow speaker that played it directly into my ear through my pillow. This meant it didn't disrupt James, who snored so loudly anyway, it would have drowned out any white noise. When he tried to have sex again, I avoided it by pretending I developed thrush. He had always been squeamish about things like thrush and periods, so this was the perfect cover.

Most of Robbie's belongings were fit only to be dumped after three years in a damp flat, so everything fitted neatly into the Range Rover. He had whistled under his breath when he first saw it.

'Very nice, Dad. Is Mum getting a new car too?'

'Your mother can get herself a new car any time she wants,' was the dismissive reply.

Robbie rolled his eyes behind James's back and I grinned at him. It would be lovely to have him home.

CHAPTER TWENTY-NINE

S chool was out for summer and I woke on the first Monday of the holidays, threw back the curtains and was met with a sunny morning and the promise of a beautiful day.

The three of us were going to Dubrovnik in a couple of weeks, and as I practised gratitude that morning, I gave thanks that in a rare moment of generosity my husband had agreed Robbie should come on holiday with us. If it had just been the two of us, I would have dreaded every minute.

I scrolled through my Facebook feed and then opened the MAAF app to read today's little gem.

Even without wings you can fly, to deny it is a lie.

Complete tosh as usual. The quotes were getting as bad as a Hallmark card.

My plan for the time before our holiday was to go through my wardrobe and sort out my clothes. Keen to save as much money as possible, I had come up with the bright idea to sell my clothes online, on Vinted, a second-hand clothes website. Having decided that until I had £5,000 in savings, I wouldn't be in the financial position to leave, I really needed another source of income. I was still making a little each month from the jewellery

I sold on Etsy, but it wasn't a great deal. It was important I make more money as quickly as possible and in a way that didn't arouse James's suspicions.

All the clothes I bought in charity shops were in great condition and good high street brands, so I would hopefully make a small profit from selling them. I would use decluttering as the excuse if I was asked any awkward questions.

When I had sorted through the first wardrobe, I was beginning to think I had a hoarding problem. My friends regularly joked I had a never-ending supply of new clothes, and I would laugh it off, but now I realised they had a point. Visions of being featured on one of those television programmes where an expert came in to physically prise the tat from my sweaty hands swam in my head. I bought most of my stuff from charity shops, but did I really need seven navy-and-white-striped tops? Or ten pairs of bootcut jeans?

Hoarding is a form of mental illness, I decided as the pile of clothes to sell grew. As if I wasn't mad enough, I could add that to the mix. Finally, I had a stack of freshly washed and pressed clothes ready to photograph, so I opened an account on Vinted and sussed out how to sell on it when we came back from holiday. If I sold anything, my money could be held in the account before withdrawing it to a bank account eventually and James would have no say over it.

Things were definitely easier at home with Robbie there. With another person in the house James had to temper his behaviour, unable to speak to me in his usual harsh manner, and he couldn't insist on knowing who I was seeing or where I was going. Nevertheless I never forgot that he could be following that little blue dot when I went out, ready to pounce if he noticed anything unusual. It was seared into my mind that he could be tracking me every minute of every day.

I continued to meet my friends for coffee and walks when he was working and it was necessary that the house remain clean and tidy and his food prepared at the expected time in order to avoid any unpleasantness from him. The days passed quickly, and I was even able to see Sam once before we left for Croatia, again in Ballyburn before he visited his mum.

I hadn't seen him since the awful episode in the hotel in Stirling, which had left me feeling violated and as I looked into his gentle blue eyes, I felt like soiled goods. We had gone for another walk along the lough shore, this time with Nigel who ran on ahead of us sniffing every blade of grass. Thankfully Sam's mum had settled well into the nursing home, and they had been offered another fortnight's respite. Although he didn't say it, I suspected that he was beginning to think that she might never make it back home. In due course the conversation turned to his work.

'There's a formal dinner dance being held next month to raise funds for the hospice,' he casually said as we watched a kayaker paddle past.

'Are you going to have to go?' Jealousy swept over me in a surprising wave. He was bound to have to take a date for the evening, and I was already envious of whoever it would be.

'No thanks.' He shook his head. 'Though I'm getting a bit of pressure from management, as they really want all the consultants there to represent the staff.'

Relief followed this comment. I couldn't bear the thought of him getting dressed up and escorting someone else. We strolled back to the car park we had driven to separately, where we had parked beside each other in a quiet, leafy corner. As I stood with my back resting on the Mini door, he came closer to me.

'Enjoy your holiday,' he murmured and leant in to kiss me on the cheek. All it would have taken was for me to turn my head slightly and our lips would have met. He stepped back after the chaste peck, paused then gave an apologetic smile. The atmosphere between us was charged, and I was sorely tempted to pull him back to me. It seemed that we were on the verge of taking a step towards a different kind of relationship, but I knew he would never make the first move. I would have to.

'Laura.' My heart missed a beat as I heard my name being called. I swung round and came face to face with my sister Sarah, who had her cockapoo Winnie on the lead. She inclined her head at us, seemingly oblivious to the tension between Sam and I.

'Hi Sarah,' I stammered. 'Do you remember Sam Brown from school?'

Sarah automatically said hello while looking a bit puzzled. She scanned from me to Sam and back again. 'I vaguely remember you. Were you in Laura's year at school?'

'Yes, that's right,' he replied easily. 'I think I'm quite a few years older than you.'

'Oh yes.' Sarah nodded. Then the penny finally dropped. 'I remember now. Didn't you two date for a while?'

'That's right, a lifetime ago,' I answered firmly. 'Sam's mum is in Clover Field. We bumped into each other. He's a doctor at Belfast Hospice. This is his dog, Nigel.'

STOP TALKING, my brain screamed at me. Why do I lose the ability to act in a rational manner when I'm talking about Sam? Could I appear more guilty if I tried?

'Well, good to meet you again, Sarah, I really need to get going if I'm to see Mum. Have a nice holiday, Laura.' Nigel obediently jumped up into the boot of the Focus, then Sam got behind the wheel and with a final wave drove off.

Sarah wasted no time. 'Well now, what's going on here?' she questioned.

'Absolutely nothing,' I said flatly. I'd read once that in order to be a successful liar you should keep as close to the truth as possible. 'I bumped into him one day in Belfast, we got talking and then he sent me a friend request on Facebook. His mum's health is poor and it's all terribly stressful as you can imagine.' All true so far. 'As I was up visiting Mum and Dad, I suggested a walk in case he needed to talk about it. Sarah, please don't make it out to be something it's not. We're just old friends. I'm a happily married woman.' *Liar.*

She smirked. 'Laura, of course you're just old friends, don't get so defensive. Does James know?'

'No.' I paused then ploughed on. 'Does that make me a bad person?' It was a struggle to look her in the eye.

'If I was married to James, I'd want to reconnect with an old boyfriend too; he treats you like the hired help. He's such a flipping snob and it's been clear for years he can barely tolerate your family.' Flushing, she grimaced. 'Sorry, I've said too much. He's your husband. Who knows what goes on behind closed doors.'

An image of me crying in Scotland came unbidden into my mind.

'Please don't say anything to anyone else and especially not to Jill,' I begged. Our sister was a gossip who got her kicks out of knowing something juicy, and then pretending she was about to spill the beans.

'Especially not Jill!' Sarah exclaimed derisively. 'My lips are sealed.' It seemed like she wanted to say more but instead changed the subject to Robbie being home and we soon parted company.

All the way home I agonised that she would say something, and that I would be the subject of family gossip. I also worried that it could have been anyone who had seen Sam and me together and that I was allowing myself to be sucked into the vortex of something that I couldn't handle. I had worked myself into such a state of anxiety by the time I got home, that I was convinced that James would meet me at the front door with a scarlet letter in his hand to pin to my top.

The relief I felt as I let myself into the hallway and wasn't met by my husband was enormous. Instead, Robbie came casually out of the kitchen eating a bowl of cereal and asked, 'What's for dinner and what time's it at?'

I breathed a bit easier. Nothing was any different than when I had left earlier.

'Takeaway tonight, family tradition the night before our holidays.'

I wasn't completely at ease that evening as we sat together at the kitchen table eating pizza, still concerned that my playing with fire was going to result in me getting badly burned.

It turned out that even James was in good form and he surprised me by saying, 'Laura, Mum and Dad have bought a table at the Belfast Hospice dinner dance at the Dunwoody Hotel in August. They want us to go with them, Olivia and Jasper.'

I choked on the bit of pizza I had in my mouth and started to cough.

Before I could say anything, he cut in. 'This is non-negotiable so please don't argue.'

'That sounds lovely,' I answered sanguinely, once my coughing fit had passed. 'Who else will be at our table?'

He named two couples, friends of his parents that I had met before.

'It will be something to look forward to after Dubrovnik.' I smiled innocently at him.

I'd have to mention to Sam that James and his family were going to be at the dinner dance. Maybe he would decide to go after all.

Playing with fire or a death wish?

CHAPTER THIRTY

A fter we got back from Dubrovnik, I met with the Book Club for a debrief.

'It's been ages since we've all been together,' commented Annie, as we settled into her garden room. There was a freakishly hot spell of weather that had lasted for over a week, practically unheard of in Northern Ireland. Annie and Matt's wooden garden room overlooked the stream which meandered between their garden and the fields behind. It was decorated in a nautical style, with rope accessories and rush matting on the floor. I felt a tiny twinge of envy as it was exactly what I would love for our garden. It was so tasteful and elegant, just like Annie. No chance of getting one though as James had explicitly spelled out.

'How was Dubrovnik?' asked Kate, brushing her hair out of her eyes. She took a portable fan out of her handbag and blew it directly into her face.

'Hot and humid,' I replied. So much for it being cooler than Italy, my clothes had stuck to me from the minute I woke, to the minute I fell into a restless sleep. 'I don't think going in the middle of July was the best idea,' I continued, 'as it was mobbed every day. Although Lokrum was a godsend. When James and

Robbie went kayaking, I took the ferry over and it was bliss compared to the crowds in the city.'

Then I realised how ungrateful I sounded, so instead extolled its virtues. 'I did love the Kravice Waterfalls in Bosnia though and Robbie insisted on going for a swim but said it was baltic! And we did a three-island tour on a wooden boat that included as much wine as you could drink. Sounds great,' I giggled, 'but it tasted like paint stripper, so even I couldn't manage more than one glass! Or should I say plastic mug.'

The girls all laughed as I had hoped they would.

'Kate, you really need HRT,' said Vicky with a wink as poor Kate sat perspiring despite the fan.

'I'm starting to think you're right,' Kate answered, much to my surprise. She had always been adamant that the natural way was the only way. 'I'm getting barely any sleep at the minute, I'm so hot at night!'

We chattered on, but I got increasingly frustrated with Vicky and Claire who were both glued to their phones. We hadn't caught up for ages; why did they have to sit staring at their mobiles? Annie filled us in on her holiday to the Algarve with Iona and her boyfriend, who apparently was called Darth.

'Darth?' asked Kate, 'As in Vader?'

'Apparently it's of German origin but as his favourite T-shirts all had *Star Wars* on them, I doubt that.' Annie had us in stitches as she regaled us with tales from their travels, making even my trip sound like paradise in comparison.

Suddenly Claire interjected, 'Sorry girls, I'm not feeling great so I've messaged Will to come and pick me up.'

That explained her preoccupation with her phone. We said how sorry we were and that we hoped she felt better soon.

'I'm sure I will, thanks,' she replied. 'I think I'll head out into the street so I can meet him on the road. Enjoy the rest of your night and we'll catch up soon.'

The evening wore on, but again I was a bit distracted by

Vicky's obsession with her phone. With a start I recognised the Snapchat icon. Was she messaging someone? She caught me looking and laughed a bit shamefacedly.

'Sorry, I'm stalking the kids on Snap Maps as they're both out in Belfast tonight. Flora is only just legal, so I'm a bit afraid she'll get up to no good with all this new-found freedom.'

Ah ha, a simple explanation. I was so used to my own deceit that I automatically thought the worst of everyone.

The rest of the night was spent gossiping together, and being with my friends was a welcome respite from the angst within my mind. For I had told Sam I was going to the hospice dinner dance with my husband's family, and he had replied with a grin that he would love to attend to see my in-laws in person, they sounded so horrendous.

Now I was in a state of tension at the thought of my two worlds colliding. Would I say or do something that gave the game away? Would James sense my feelings towards Sam? While part of me was overwrought, another part of me was coolly anticipating the evening. To say I wanted to compare the two men in my life was being disingenuous, but subconsciously that could be exactly what I wanted to do.

The following day, I checked out my Vinted shop and was delighted that I had sold another couple of dresses. That was £90 already that I could squirrel away. Selling was addictive and it took a great deal of willpower not to spend my earnings on new clothes for myself. I may have joined the game late but I was throwing myself into it with gusto. Selling second-hand clothes online was becoming a new passion.

Robbie had been looking at flats to rent in Belfast city centre and he was keen to move before starting his new job at the beginning of September. He spent ages browsing through the RentaHome website, and I used it as an excuse to suss out available properties to rent myself. So I would be better informed.

Initially I was horrified at the prices as I had assumed having savings of £5,000 would be a decent safely net, but with rents starting at £700 a month for a pretty basic place in a not-so-nice area, that wouldn't last long.

Completely deflated, I searched again. I would prefer a two-bedroomed place in case Robbie wanted to stay sometimes but knew that although I loved having a garden, I didn't need one. That narrowed it down a bit. Also, as much as I would hate leaving, I knew I couldn't remain in the village. There was no way I could be that close to James, meaning I would either have to move into Belfast itself or a neighbouring town. My anxiety increased at the thought of dealing with all of this on my own. Tempted to forget all about it, an internal battle raged as I tried to convince myself that I could do it. All it needed was planning and savings.

But my stomach churned with worry every time I tried to plan ahead. In fact, it got to be that I was in such a perpetual state of anxiety that I gave in and made an appointment with the GP. Behind my husband's back of course. If he tracked me via my phone to the GP practice, I would tell him I was getting something for vaginal dryness. That would soon shut him up.

During the appointment with the doctor I nervously confessed to my anxiety, poor sleep and for the first time ever, the dark thoughts that threatened to inundate me at times. Empathetically she asked me if I was dealing with any new stress at the minute. I nodded but didn't elaborate. Instead of dismissing me as a menopausal nightmare, she was kind and knowledgeable and explained that although mood swings were common at my age, it sounded like I needed something else in addition to my HRT.

'Happy pills?' I asked bluntly. 'Am I going mad?'

She looked a bit horrified when I said that before replying, 'You're not going mad, Laura, although you might feel you're losing your mind at times.' Faced with her understanding and compassion, I started to cry. Great big gulps that I couldn't seem to stop. Ugly crying at its finest.

After a time, I got myself under control and she passed me a tissue. 'We have a few options. I'd advise counselling as a first step and then there's an online cognitive behavioural therapy course that I can refer you onto. It's very useful to help overcome stress, anxiety or depression. Medication is also an option but that is entirely up to you and I'd never recommend just that on its own. Even then we have some choices, either something you only take when you feel anxious or something you can take daily to help stabilise your mood. You don't have to decide on that today, you can try the counselling and CBT first if you like.'

Relief swept over me as fresh and invigorating as a sea breeze. I was not crazy. I was just dealing with a stressful situation that sometimes left me feeling powerless. Sharing my true sentiments was another step in freeing myself from my tortuous relationship.

'I'll take some drugs too, please.' I managed a weak smile to let her know I was going to be okay.

I replayed my conversation with her as I drove home. I had assumed that my despair had been as a result of empty-nest syndrome and Robbie moving back home would be the solution, but I had been wrong. Robbie moving home was lovely and a tear in my heart had been healed, but I had to face the fact there were other reasons for my black moods. I was hopeful that the counselling would help or the CBT. But the tiny packet of anti-anxiety meds tucked into my handbag would play their part as well.

It was crucial my husband never found them, as the thought of his gloating was enough to make me want to scream. I would take them only when I felt my heart race or my thoughts escalate, I didn't want to become reliant on them. If James ever came across them accidentally, I would say they were cellulite busters or for thinning hair. He could be so stupid at times he'd probably believe that.

Therefore I hid them in my bedside drawer under a pile of old pens, hankies, nail files and general junk that is my private space.

As long as he never discovered that he had driven me to the edge of insanity and I had finally succumbed to pills.

CHAPTER THIRTY-ONE

A couple of weeks later it was the night of the hospice dinner dance. I was so edgy I had resorted to taking two of my little blue pills as I titivated myself.

This was complete and utter madness; why on earth did I think it would be a good idea to have both James and Sam in a room together? I must be certifiable to think I could get away with it.

My hands trembled as I applied my make-up and straightened my hair. The black dress I had worn to the dinner dance in the autumn was hanging on the wardrobe door. My quest to save money meant that it would be getting another outing. Or as the tabloids like to say, I was recycling it.

By the time I was ready, my frayed nerves had settled somewhat. Strangely, I felt calm as I descended the stairs.

Robbie was standing munching a slice of toast slathered in peanut butter as I reached the bottom step. 'Looking good, Mum,' he complimented me good-naturedly.

'Finally ready?' asked James ill-temperedly.

Robbie had offered to drive us to the Dunwoody Hotel, probably delighted to have the house to himself for once.

'Have a nice night and I'll pick you up around midnight,' he said, as we went up the long winding driveway lined with silver birches. We pulled up in front of the imposing white building and a doorman stepped forward to greet us. After welcoming us, he directed us along the hallway to the drinks reception.

James tightly took hold of my elbow before leaning down and snarled in my ear, 'I don't want you making a fool of yourself by dancing tonight. I won't be at all pleased if you show me up in front of my family.'

Straightening his shoulders, he pulled himself up to his full height as I nodded compliantly.

Prat.

I perused the reception room looking for silver hair and glasses, but instead was greeted by my perspiring brother-in-law who looked like overdone meat. His flaming face clashed with the crushed ruby velvet jacket he was squeezed into. Olivia trotted along behind him wearing a tight red dress with a plunging neckline and a split up the side. Money doesn't buy you taste; and they both needed to wear a size bigger.

Dutifully, I allowed Jasper to kiss me on the cheek and tried not to recoil from his sticky hands clutching my bare arms.

'Looking fabulous, Laura,' he declared, making no effort to hide the fact he was ogling me, much like a farmer eyes a prize sow.

'Lovely,' trilled Olivia who also kissed my cheek. Her breath smelled of booze and I wondered how many glasses she'd already had.

Then Donald strode over to us with Heather trailing behind. His strident hello made several guests swivel their heads to see where the noise was coming from as he too kissed my cheek. Heather looked as elegant as ever in a shimmery, long, silver-grey dress, her perfectly highlighted bob held back with a pearl headband.

'You look sensational,' I told her as she kissed my cheek.

So much kissing I wouldn't be surprised if I had a make-up-free spot on my cheek.

A waiter walked past carrying a tray of drinks, and James helped himself to two glasses of champagne before ostentatiously handing one to me. Nibbling on the strawberry from the glass, I cast a surreptitious look around for Sam. There was no sign of him, so I excused myself and made my way to the ladies' loo. Two gorgeous young tanned things with poker-straight hair and skin-tight dresses came into the bathroom giggling together, and I eavesdropped as I washed my hands.

'He might be old but he is hot with a capitol H!' one said with a titter, as she reapplied a deep-pink lip gloss. Her lips were already so shiny she really didn't need any more, but clearly less was not more for her.

'He gives me fanny flutters as well,' said her friend with a snigger, pulling her crimson dress a bit lower on her cleavage. Charming.

Smiling tightly at them, I turned to dry my hands as the pouty one continued, 'Dr Brown, AKA Dr Hot, can take my temperature any time.' She pulled a hip flask from her handbag, took a swig and offered it to her friend. Then she turned and proffered it to me.

'No thanks,' I replied politely, desperately trying to hide my distaste for them.

Simpering together, they left the room.

Dr Hot indeed.

I wasn't jealous at all. Not one bit.

After ensuring that the back of my dress wasn't caught up in my knickers, I took a deep breath and went to see if I could spot Dr Hot.

By the time I had rejoined my family, the room was packed with people dressed in their finery and sipping their aperitifs. The evening sun slanted through the floor-length windows as I surveyed the mature gardens in full summer bloom.

I turned back to the conversation and saw Sam appear through the crowd, talking and smiling at various people as he made his roundabout way over to our group. A short, bald man was making introductions to various people as they crossed the room, but soon he was standing in front of me. I felt slightly light-headed, my senses heightened as I absorbed him, drinking in how distinguished he looked in his dinner suit.

'May I introduce Dr Samuel Brown, our senior consultant,' said the bald man.

Donald stuck out his hand before anyone else had a chance to speak or move. 'Mr Remmington, retired orthopod. I'm considering sitting on the hospice board of trustees, thought this shindig would be a good way to find out more about it.'

'Nice to meet you,' replied Sam cordially.

I wondered if he found Donald as obnoxious as I did. Sam blandly observed my husband as they shook hands. They were the same height, but that was where the similarity ended. For Sam embodied goodness, whereas James embodied self-satisfaction.

'Pleasure to meet you,' pronounced my husband. I noticed he didn't bother to introduce me, so gathering my nerves I said firmly as I stuck my hand out,

'Laura Remmington.'

Sam's touch was electric and I was surprised no one else could feel the sparks that flew between us. Grasping my hand for a second longer than he should have, he smiled wryly at me, eyes boring into mine while I struggled to maintain my composure.

James and Donald vied for his attention, pontificating loudly, and I stood wordlessly beside them, aware that not even my unkind description had done them justice. The icing on the cake was when Jasper interjected with some nonsense about his holiday cottage, and it took immense effort to stop myself from laughing out loud. What a pack of preening peacocks I had married into.

Sam and his escort excused themselves and moved on to the next group of people.

'Nice young fellow that,' Donald stated patronisingly, while scanning the room for a waiter.

'Dr Samuel Brown,' mused James. 'I can't work out why that name is familiar.'

Frozen, I looked blankly at him. Could he have worked out my ex-boyfriend would now be Dr Brown?

'That's because our GP was Samuel Brown when you were a child, James.' Heather unwittingly saved the day.

'That must be it,' he answered, as the master of ceremonies called for everyone to move through into the function room.

As we took our seats at the round table festooned with balloons in hospice purple, I subtly glanced around to see where Sam would be sitting. His table was far from ours, but I was actually glad of that. If he had been closer, I was at risk of giving my feelings away. For there was no doubting that I was longing for his touch. It may have been the allure of forbidden fruit, but I could hardly think beyond the imprint of his hand on mine.

I'm sure the food was delicious, but I could have been eating cardboard for all I tasted it. Small talk with Jasper on my left was difficult in the extreme, but I soon noticed that I didn't need to talk, just listen. My senses were on high alert for any sight or mention of Sam, so ostensibly listening to The Dimwit and nodding along occasionally was all that was required of me.

Eventually the dinner was over and the speeches began. The bald man who had been escorting Sam around turned out to be the hospice CEO, and he gave an impassioned speech about the complexities of palliative care.

When he mentioned the silent auction and raffle, all the pompous attendees reached into their embossed wallets and dug deep. James would no doubt bid in the silent auction and it was obvious to me that he wouldn't be satisfied if he did not get the winning bid on something. Browsing the list, I pondered if it would be the spa break at the Dunwoody? I dismissed that because he would feel obligated to give it to me. More likely it would be tinted windows for the Range Rover. Or a four-ball with Danny Clarkson, the famous Northern Irish golfer. Although James was crap at golf so wouldn't want to be shown up.

I decided that he would bid highly for a personalised whiskey tour and tasting session at a famous local distillery and swallowed down my contempt, as I could practically smell the rancid stench of whiskey on his breath already.

Once the speeches were finished, the band played and my husband glanced warningly at me, as though I was going to get up on the dance floor and start breakdancing. Fortunately he went with the other men to the bar where they all ordered pints, and us ladies were left to make more small talk together. After about half an hour the band stopped so the winners of the silent auction could be announced.

Jasper surprised Olivia with a successful bid on the spa break and she was brimming with delight. I noticed him fondly pat her bottom as she hugged him, and I was surprised at the affection. It seemed he wasn't so bad after all.

James did win the whiskey tour and pumped the air with undisguised pleasure.

Prat.

The band started playing again and a short time later I'd had enough small talk for one evening. I used the excuse that I was having a hot flush, and informed Heather that I was going to get some air, ensuring I left my bag containing my phone on the table. Darkness had fallen as I walked into the gardens via a side door, and although there was a cool air, I hardly noticed it. I passed some flowerbeds, then headed towards the river running through the grounds and leaned against a secluded end wall. Breathing in the delicate fragrance of late summer roses, I closed my eyes and listened to the soothing burbling of the flowing water.

Then I heard the tread of soft footsteps making their way over to me, and the scent was no longer of flowers but of the aftershave I now knew so well.

'So, this is where you are hiding,' Sam murmured, leaning against the wall beside me.

Opening my eyes, I smiled in the dim light. 'Not hiding, Dr Hot, just getting some air.'

'Dr Hot?' I could hear the laughter in his voice. 'Where on earth did you get that from?'

I merrily recounted what I'd overheard in the toilets.

'How mortifying is that?' I could sense his blush, although it was too dark to see it.

As I moved towards him I whispered, 'But you are hot, Dr Brown.'

He stepped around to face me but was not yet touching as he softly said, 'You look lovely tonight. It took a great deal of effort earlier not to let that slip out.'

Tentatively I reached out for him, placing my hands under his jacket and around his back. I felt his muscles tense then relax, as he leaned in towards me. The kiss was the lightest of touches as we finally stepped over the fine line of friendship into the unknown. I ran my hands up the length of his spine and this time the kiss was longer and deeper. I was now oblivious to everything but Sam; his touch, his smell, his lips. Heedless to the danger of being caught by someone and of the line we had crossed.

Before I did something I really regretted, the quiet was broken by a bombastic voice announcing the proximity of my father-in-law. I pulled Sam in close so we blended as one into the shadows and shook with silent laughter. He too was laughing as we heard Donald walk past, boring some unsuspecting guest to death with his monologue. The spell was broken and I knew I had to return to the function room before my absence was noted.

'I'll go back first,' Sam muttered quietly. Then, 'Any regrets?'

'None,' I replied firmly. 'I'll follow you in a bit.'

Alone now, I watched his retreating back and thought about what had happened. It had been inevitable really. I had been fooling myself for the past few months that we were just friends.

Because I wanted him more than I had wanted anything in a very long time.

CHAPTER THIRTY-TWO

The following morning after another night dreaming of strong arms and dimples, I had a rude awakening as James slipped into my room early and demanded his conjugal rights. No foreplay, just wham bam, thank you, ma'am. About as far from my tentative kisses with Sam the night before as could be.

'Thank goodness Robbie will be moving out soon and we won't have to sneak around afraid of getting caught,' he said crossly, lying back with an arm flung above his head. 'We could have a rerun of Stirling, take a few risks. I know how much you enjoyed that.'

He rotated his head to face me and I willed myself to keep my face still. How he could pretend I had enjoyed that was beyond me. What kind of animal was my husband morphing into?

My hope was that by the time Robbie moved out I would have saved enough to seriously start looking for a place of my own. First though, James needed to go away on his next cycling trip so I could examine the contents of the filing cabinet in his study. I had formulated a mental list of things I needed to educate myself on and those precious few days he would be in Majorca meant I could look through the paperwork related to the things I wanted to learn about. The trouble was that I had no idea if he even kept paper copies of things now, or if it was all online.

School would be starting again in less than a fortnight and I was looking forward to getting back into some kind of routine. As much as the long days stretch tantalisingly ahead at the start of the summer break, by the end of eight weeks off, I'm always ready for the new term. Also, with the fractious presence of my husband constantly in the house, this had been no real break.

Sam and I had managed to meet at the cinema the Saturday afternoon James had spent at the distillery. Donald had accompanied him, leaving a few hours free when he wouldn't think to snoop on me. Nevertheless, we arranged to meet at a cinema complex that was situated beside a retail park. Then I 'accidentally' left my phone in the car. On the off-chance my husband decided to check up on me, all he would see was me at the shops.

We arrived separately and Sam had pre-paid for the tickets, so we met in the foyer of the cinema. I felt we were the protagonists in *Brief Encounter*: she too was Laura and he too a doctor. What romantic nonsense.

Both of us knew we had to pretend we had accidentally bumped into each other, should we be seen by anyone we knew. When I arrived, he was studying the movie posters and without speaking, we ambled down the corridor towards the screens. It felt like the atmosphere crackled between us and I couldn't believe the other cinemagoers couldn't feel it too. He subtly passed me my ticket, and I was imbued with delight that he had booked us seats in the back row.

There were only half a dozen other people in the theatre, as the film was a worthy independent movie that had garnered little to no interest. The lights dimmed and I took his hand, pretending to concentrate on the screen as the trailers played. Every nerve ending was on high alert as we sat in the semi-darkness, the nearest person several rows ahead. When I could restrain myself no longer, I leaned over and touched his face. Within seconds our lips met and I felt like a teenager again on a date with the boy she fancied not a married woman on the verge of an affair. At last I ran my hands over those biceps that I had been dreaming about for weeks, it took all my self-control not to take things further. When we parted, and looked at each other through new eyes, he whispered, 'I suppose we should remember we could have an audience.'

Casually putting an arm around my shoulders as he had done so many years before, he pulled me close and we tried to concentrate on the movie, occasionally giving into the urge to snog. Like kids.

When the film ended, we waited till everyone else had left the theatre. Slowly making our way towards the exit, we remained a few steps apart, mindful of any prying eyes. Outside, we stood in front of the cineplex, and said our goodbyes while grinning sappily at each other.

'Hopefully I'll see you soon,' I finally said before getting into the Mini.

On the drive home, I felt elated. No guilt, no worry, just happiness and contentment from within.

Later that week I arrived home from doing the food shop, and James appeared out of his study once I had unpacked the groceries in the kitchen. There was no sign of Robbie, so I assumed he had gone for a workout at the gym.

'Come in here, Laura.' His face was hard.

For goodness' sake, what now? I thought, before meekly obeying him.

He had taken a seat on his brown leather office chair and pointedly looked at his oak desk as I stood in the doorway. There, lying on top of his writing pad was a packet of pills. Little blue pills. Instantly agitated, my eyes flew to his as he raised his eyebrows in an unspoken question.

I found I couldn't speak. My mind jumped about like a flea on a hot stove, unable to process what was unfolding.

Breaking the silence, he asked quietly, 'What are these?' stabbing at the packet with a finger.

Brazenly I replied, 'Where did you get those?' fully aware that he must have rifled through my drawer, as they were well hidden.

'That's unimportant. What is important is that my wife is taking medication without my knowledge. I'd say that was rather underhand, wouldn't you?'

'I'd say looking through someone's personal stuff without consent is the underhand thing here,' I fired back, completely sick of his overbearing ways.

Straight away he stood up, looming over me and although he didn't touch me, he stuck his face close to mine. 'I'm only going to ask you once more, what are these tablets for?' His tone was measured, yet threatening.

Instantly I didn't feel brave or bold, I felt fearful and frightened, so I stuttered, 'Medication for anxiety.'

'Speak up, I can't hear you.'

Clearing my throat, I softly said, 'I've started tablets for anxiety.'

He didn't move back from me, just snarled, 'I have been telling you for ages you needed something. Now you go behind my back?'

'I'm sorry.' I tried to sound sincere.

'Say "You were right, James, I'm sorry for keeping things from you".'

Inside I was screaming, but I deferentially repeated it.

'And while we are at it, why didn't you tell me you were selling your clothes online and keeping the money all to yourself? I'm concerned just how many secrets you seem to be keeping from me.' He must have been searching through my phone behind my back and found the app. What else had he been looking at? The fact he didn't mention messages on Snapchat was good fortune, nothing more.

'I didn't mean to keep it from you. Someone mentioned it and I thought it was a good idea to declutter my stuff.' My words tripped over themselves as I frantically tried to stave off the increasing tension in the room.

Reaching for my chin, he squeezed it hard. 'If I find out you are doing anything else without telling me I will not be happy at all. Have I made myself clear? I can't trust you anymore. It seems you are wilfully trying to upset me, hiding things from me, forcing me to check up on you by...' he caught himself just in time before he said, 'tracking your phone.'

Mutely and close to tears, I nodded, hoping it was over. It wasn't.

'Take off your jeans,' he demanded savagely, recovering quickly.

'No I won't, what if Robbie comes back?' I whispered, horrified.

'So what if he does? I can have sex with you any time I want to, you're my wife.'

'You don't want him to walk in on us, do you? Please don't,' I begged.

'I really don't care. It's about time he left home anyway.'

To my alarm, he grabbed for my jeans, opening the button and pulling the zip down. Roughly he hauled me over to the desk where he dragged my jeans and pants off and forcibly pushed me back on the desk top.

Even when I cried no, he didn't listen. *No* seemed to mean *yes* when he's your husband. He insisted on leaving the door open, as if he wanted Robbie to arrive home and find us. Shutting my eyes, I didn't make another sound. Although he could dominate me sexually, he could never master my thoughts, my memories or my fantasies.

Once he finished, he said in an off-hand tone, 'I don't know why you can't take proper care of yourself like Vicky or Claire. You never see them slobbing about in second-hand clothes or with their hair needing a wash. You may come from a farm, Laura, but you don't need to look like you're about to feed the pigs. Hopefully now you're taking the pills you'll take more pride in your appearance.'

Without speaking, I gathered up my clothes and retreated to the security of my bedroom, where I shakily placed the pills back in the top drawer. No need to hide them now. I was inundated with despair as I sat on the edge of the bed. It seemed that there was no aspect of my life, my looks or my personality that my husband didn't criticise or censure nowadays. It appeared that he detested me almost as much as I detested him. It's funny how quickly I had gone from acknowledging my dislike, to registering my abhorrence for him. Not funny at all actually. It was as though I was living with a stranger who enjoyed making me as unhappy as possible.

Despondently I checked the online balance in my secret savings account, and saw that I now had £3,700. Which meant I needed another £1,300 before I could even think about leaving him. Still shaking, I deleted my browsing history and went downstairs to set about listing more of my clothes online. I could always resort to selling my bits and pieces of gold jewellery that had lain unworn for years in my jewellery box. But first I'd sell as many items of clothing as possible.

I just had to keep on the right side of my husband and not make him angry while I did it.

CHAPTER THIRTY-THREE

The Sunday before I started back to work, James insisted on inviting his parents over for an end of summer barbeque. I voiced no objections, instead savouring the knowledge that I had to play the part of the docile wife for just a short time longer. While the three men stood outside cooking the meat, Heather and I sat companionably together in the snug, as I'd prepared all the side dishes earlier.

She asked about Robbie renting in Belfast, before confiding in me that she had felt quite low after James and Olivia moved out, leaving just her and Donald at home. As she disclosed this, something curdled within me. I'd never considered that she would in all likelihood side with her son when I left him and this could be our last time together. I felt immensely sorrowful that my relationship with her would suffer as a result of our split. So rather than feeling frustrated at my enforced afternoon with them, I tried to make the most of it. As I kissed her on the cheek before they left, I blinked back easy tears. Enforced politeness towards Donald helped to stem them.

The following day I was back at work and the first week of the new term is always a busy one, filled with planning for the year ahead. It was a relief to get away from the intolerable atmosphere at home, especially as Robbie had now moved into his new flat. Mercifully although I knew I would miss him, I felt completely different than I had when he left for Scotland, content that I could see him any time I wanted. Unfortunately it meant my husband was insisting on having sex in every room to celebrate, even when I said no.

I caught up with my colleagues' news and then the work started. Our head teacher Mrs Gribbons had decided the first day of term would be children free and all staff would get some mandatory training out of the way. The morning session would advise us how to recognise harmful sexual behaviour displayed in children, and the afternoon session would be about toxic relationships. I was glad not to be a teenager these days as it was such a minefield.

The first session was interesting, if disturbing. The second session started after lunch and was preceded by a talk by Mrs Gribbons.

'I know this is quite demoralising but unfortunately, it's critical that we are able to recognise and empathise with students who may be dealing with either of these issues. If we teach them about healthy relationships early on, this can reduce the likelihood of them staying in abusive or unhealthy relationships.'

We settled down to watch the presentation but my mind was only half on what was being discussed. I was too busy thinking of when I would be able to meet Sam again.

First slide – How to recognise coercive control.

Coercive control is a strategic form of ongoing oppression used to instil fear.

Those poor girls, I thought absent-mindedly. *They need to tell him to get lost and leave him before it gets to that stage.*

Next slide – Major signs of coercive control.

One by one, the signs were listed.

Persistently putting their partner down
or belittling them.

Trying to isolate them from family or
friends.

Limiting their freedom, such as stopping
them going to work or school.

Making unreasonable demands for their
attention.

I started to feel a little uncomfortable.

Accusing them of flirting with other
people.

Controlling how much money they have and
how they spend it.

Telling them what to wear or who to see.

Blaming them for arguments while being
publicly gentle.

I read on with mounting horror.

Using trackers to know where they are,
not allowing them any privacy.

Using guilt to make them behave
differently.

Gaslighting them — making them question
their own feelings or even sanity.

Sexual violence, such as using force or
intimidation.

It was as though the glasses came off and I could for the first time see clearly.

I was in an unhealthy relationship with my husband.

'A toxic relationship' to define it properly.

I excused myself from the room, before racing to the staff toilets and shut myself in a cubicle. I could tick off almost everything on that list. My husband repeatedly belittled me, blamed my hormones for arguments, threatened to stop me working, controlled my money, tracked me with my phone and demeaned me sexually.

I knew I was going to vomit and was relieved I had left the room. I retched into the toilet, but the nausea didn't abate. How could I have been so blind to what was going on? How could I have let it deteriorate so far?

I heard a voice from outside the cubicle, 'Laura is everything okay?' It was my colleague Jasmine who had been sitting beside me at the talk.

'Yes, I'm fine, thanks, I just felt a migraine coming on.'

I flushed the toilet, wiped my mouth and went out to face her.

'You poor thing, you look awfully pale. Do you think it's the worry of coming back to work after the break?' Her concerned brown eyes observed me sympathetically.

'Possibly,' I muttered, washing my hands. It wasn't unheard of for some staff to get a bit worked up in anticipation of a stressful year ahead.

'I'm sure Mrs Gribbons would understand if you needed some quiet time in the staff room while the rest of us finish this training.' Jasmine tugged on the end of her long, black braid as she smiled at me kindly.

'That's very thoughtful. Would you mind telling her I'm going to take some painkillers and hopefully I can rejoin the training in a little while?'

'Of course.' Jasmine headed back towards the others and I skulked off into the empty staff room. The peace was soothing and I sat in solitude, contemplating everything I had learned.

Our marriage hadn't always been so difficult. In fact, until a few years ago I could honestly have said I thought it was basically perfect. I had loved James and I knew he loved me. It had been a healthy partnership and while he had liked to be in control, I was happy for him to take charge about certain things. It made me feel protected and it meant I didn't have to worry about important things. It had suited me to be ignorant about things I didn't want to think or stress about.

Insidiously though, after Robbie left home, menopause struck and James started working from home, it changed. The perfect storm. At first it had been subtle as he adjusted to the confines of the house, rather than the noisy workplace. Needing reassurance from me that I loved him as much as I loved our son. Unable or unwilling to cope with my raging hormones. Then gradually the drip, drip, drip of criticism directed at my cooking, my figure, my interests. Wanting to know who I was seeing, where I was going, why I was late. Restricting my money. And more recently, the pervasive threat of sexual violence from a man who had once held me so tenderly that I never wanted to leave his arms.

My perfect marriage had become a living nightmare and the more I struggled against his invisible shackles, the tighter his stranglehold became.

My gorgeous, charming, controlling husband had tried to rob me of my identity, my will and my independence. He frightened me now and sadly I knew that there was no coming back from the place we had found ourselves. Although he had never hit me, there is a fragile line between emotional and physical abuse, and it seemed we were drawing inexorably closer to the latter.

I sat alone on the frayed brown armchair in the silent staff room and started crying. For I was grieving the loss of the man I had once adored, the anguish I felt at breaking up our family unit and the journey I still had ahead of me to extract myself safely from this hellish situation.

And I was so ashamed of our disintegrating relationship that I couldn't confide in anyone at all. Then I felt a sliver of hope as I realised I was going to start the counselling that the GP had referred me for. I would be able to talk it through with a stranger in confidence and possibly they would help me to make an exit plan that meant I could be self-sufficient and independent.

Previously the very thought of being independent had been agonising to me, but now it was tantalisingly close and from deep within me, I felt the stirrings of an inner strength that had been long buried but not destroyed. I would survive this for I was smart, I had my family and I felt empowered as calm relief encompassed me.

I splashed my eyes with cold water from the sink to reduce some of the puffiness and felt a renewed sense of purpose. James was going on his cycling holiday next week, so it was important that I use every minute to formulate my plans. It could no longer be dismissed as 'sometime in the future', it had to be as soon as possible.

Once my eyes were presentable, I returned to the training. Jasmine told me that I could access a copy of the slides via my school email later and I mouthed my thanks back at her.

Mrs Gribbons was finishing off with her last slide.

How to exit a toxic relationship

Encourage them to ask for help, which

```
could be from friends, family or a
trained professional.
```

```
Reassure them that they don't have to
stay in the relationship while hoping the
other person might change.
```

```
Offer to help them find ways to become
more independent.
```

```
Help them make a safety plan and guide
them to resources for additional support.
```

```
Advise them to cut off all contact with
the other person.
```

Staring at the slides, I let her words wash over me as I kept my eyes focused on the second point.

```
Reassure them that they don't have to
stay in the relationship while hoping the
other person might change.
```

James would never change. I believed that now. The only person who could make the change was me.

My decision was made. I would move forward and not look back.

It was only a case of *when* now, not *if.*

There were only a couple of days now until he was leaving for Majorca. His enjoyment with forcing me to have sex at his bidding seemed to wane as he packed his case and dismantled his bike for the flight. I feigned concern about him, asking him if he needed any help with ironing the clothes he was taking, reminding him not to forget the indigestion tablets he'd been chewing like sweets recently.

The night before he left, he asked me when I was starting counselling and presented me with a list of things that I needed to 'iron out' with the counsellor before I was 'back to normal'.

'You need to ask what you can do about your temper, your irritability, your refusal to accept advice from me, your dislike of my family, your constant need to disparage and mock me in front of people, your preference for seeing your friends instead of me and your unhealthy obsession with our adult son who has flown the nest.'

Not much to fix then.

'I'm only getting six sessions, I'm not sure I can be "back to normal" in that space of time,' I replied off-handedly, thinking he was right about all those things, but I no longer saw them as faults or flaws, more like me finding myself again.

'Well, if you're not fixed with six sessions, we may be able to find the money to pay for a few sessions privately.' He came over to me and raised his hands to my face. It took a great deal of willpower not to flinch from his touch.

'It's only because I love you so much and you make me feel so sad when you prefer to spend time with other people. You must promise to never, ever lie to me again, Laura.'

I looked straight into his beautiful blue eyes and lied as I repeated 'I promise' with my fingers crossed superstitiously behind my back. Seemingly satisfied, he kissed me and I tolerated his tongue probing within my mouth as you would do a dentist's tools. It appeared I was capable of dissociating my mind from my body these days.

'Good girl.' He patted me on the bottom like an obedient dog.

For feck sake, just clear off, I thought, pretending to return his affection.

I was becoming a consummate actress.

CHAPTER THIRTY-FOUR

The Friday James left for his cycling trip dawned bright, bringing with it the hint of a sunlit future. Stretching languorously alone in bed, my thoughts briefly drifted to that morning in May, when I had woken to find the house empty after the row about the log-in details of our bank accounts. How much had changed in the four months since then, but also how much had remained the same.

On my return home from work, I made myself a light dinner of microwavable baked potato and beans, before sitting down in the living room with a pen and paper. Old-fashioned I know but it helped me to think clearly. What did I want to educate myself on this week? I made a list:

1. Bank stuff – access to online banking, savings account etc.
2. Oil/electricity providers – who, how they are paid, access to them.
3. Insurance – house & car.
4. Mortgage.

5. Car MOT/road tax - when are they due, how do you even MOT a car??

I felt deep remorse at my incompetence about our finances and utilities. I didn't even know who our mortgage was with, how much we paid monthly and when it would be paid off. Anyone would think I was a 1950s housewife who spent her days polishing the silver and scrubbing the floors on hands and knees. How and why had I let myself become so incompetent? Was it laziness or was it something more sinister? It was probably a bit of both.

James had always appeared so caring, not wanting me to concern myself about things like finances, that I had allowed him to take care of everything. It's easy to deceive yourself that you are being looked after, when in reality you're handing over control morsel by morsel. It had been so subtle, so gradual that I hadn't even twigged he had power over everything. I had practically wrapped it up in gift paper with a bow on top. Why had it taken me to my fifties to recognise this?

Upstairs, I entered what is fundamentally his domain. I rarely ventured into his study, especially since he had forced me to have sex on the desk, so I had no real idea where to start. Surveying the room with its masculine prints hung in black frames on the frigid white walls, my eyes stopped at the filing cabinet in the corner with its neatly labelled drawers. Although I was certain most of what I needed would be locked away in his online world, I presumed some of it must be on paper copies.

The top drawer was labelled 'House' and I reached for it first. But it remained stubbornly shut. I pulled harder but it still didn't budge. It took a minute, before I realised the whole cabinet was locked, and there was no sign of the key.

Irritated as hell, I sat on his swivel chair and tried to figure out where he could have hidden it. I didn't allow myself to think why he would have hidden the key. His desk had three drawers down one side and I opened each of them before rifling through them in turn. There were pens, refill pads, paper clips, all the usual detritus of a workspace but no key. It could take me a week to find the flipping key.

Annoyed with myself, our situation, but most of all my husband, I swung around so I could peruse the shelves on the wall behind me. Books, photos and a few ornaments neatly adorned them. Then I spotted an incongruous rough dish that Robbie had made in art class years ago. It was so out of place, there had to be a reason for it. Reaching inside, my fingers grazed a small key lying on the bottom. I fished it out, hope rising within me, certain it would open the filing cabinet.

My heart beating a little faster, I tried it in the lock and sure enough it was an exact fit and the lock turned. When I opened the top drawer, I saw it was full of neatly labelled files. Everything was so fastidious in this room that it made me want to wreck it, to pull the files out and throw them on the floor, to take the books and chuck them about haphazardly. The stark difference in my husband and I could be summed up in this room.

For I'm not an orderly person, I'm chaos and mess and fire and passion. And I had stamped it all out for him, to try and please him.

Swallowing down my anger, I reached for the first file labelled 'Home insurance' out of the drawer and flicked through it. It may be the digital age but my husband seemed to keep everything on paper as well. Pleased now with his meticulousness, I set it down and lifted out the next file, which was receipts for our oil supplier, next our electricity supplier then the water company. I extracted folder after folder out of the cabinet. It was all here in black and white. Thank heavens for his obsessive precision, for I could answer most of the questions on my checklist quite easily. It wasn't going to take me all week after all.

I made notes on everything I could think of until there was only the bottom drawer labelled 'Bank' left to go through. More nondescript manila folders again neatly labelled. I opened the first one titled 'Savings', which I was pretty sure would be information on our joint savings account. As expected I found paperwork relating to our joint savings account, which had £5,000 in it. But there was nothing related to a username or password. Surely there was some way for me to access this money, so it could be used for my escape. I would take this paperwork into the bank and ask for their help. Renewed frustration at my ineptitude flowed through me.

Moving on to the next folder, also labelled 'Savings', I found information on an ISA that was only in my husband's name.

That couldn't be right, he didn't have any savings of his own. Or so he had told me.

I read it again. According to the paperwork he had £15,000 in a cash ISA. Stupefied, I opened the next folder, again labelled 'Savings'. This one held details about a savings account again solely in his name. This one had £45,000 in it.

What on earth was going on? I noticed that they were both with our bank, so when any letters arrived, I wouldn't think twice about them, I'd blithely pass them over to my husband, never questioning them. Another folder, another ISA, this time a stocks and shares ISA with £14,000 in it.

He had £74,000 of savings I never knew existed.

There was a copy of our wills, but I knew what was in those so I moved quickly on.

Next, a life insurance policy – his not mine. I wasn't worth anything. He was worth £250,000 dead. And it would all come to me apparently.

On to the next folder labelled 'Savings', but in fact it was mortgage information. We had agreed to re-mortgage when we bought this house, I'm sure we did, which would have added ten years onto the mortgage. Or so I thought. Because according to this paperwork the mortgage had been paid off in full in 2018.

Bile rose in my throat at his deception and I just made it to the bathroom before I vomited in the sink.

At last my stomach was empty of food, and I sank to my knees on the hard, cold tiles, the enormity of his deceit almost overwhelming me. Apart from my secret savings account, my life savings, which amounted to less than £4,000, he had full knowledge of and control of every penny that I earned. What I earned, how I spent it, every aspect of our finances. My finances. I thought I was going to be sick again, my head was pounding, my stomach clenching in agony.

I wailed, unable to stop my primal response to this torment.

For I was married to a domineering bully who demanded nothing less than complete and utter control of my life. How could this have happened? How could the handsome, debonair father of my child have become this monster? Was it my fault? Had I been so willing to give him anything he wanted that he had become unrecognisable? It seemed that he wanted to scoop out my very core and replace it with a dependent, passive woman totally in his thrall.

I had no idea what to do. When someone drips poison into your ear it's hard not to believe it. I was worthless, I was forgetful, I was bad with money, I was unattractive, I was unstable. I cried and cried on the unforgiving floor, unable to believe the mess I had made of my life and my marriage.

For now, he demanded nothing but absolute submission.

I lay on the tiles for who knows how long, unable to think coherently, until I became stiff and frozen. At some point I moved from the floor to my bedroom and got under the covers without undressing. I lay with my eyes open for a long time, my mind in turmoil, incapable of clear thought.

Sleep must have come for me in the early hours for it was a

short blink until the alarm clock buzzed me awake. I had forgotten my plans to meet Robbie for lunch in the city centre, and then to go with Sam for a walk up Cave Hill followed by dinner. Although I felt drained after my discoveries last night, the rawness was receding and I knew it had simply reinforced how vital it was that I leave my marriage. So I dragged myself out of bed, showered and carefully put all the folders back into the filing cabinet. With one final turn of the key, I locked away all the incriminating evidence.

I made myself a coffee before I took a seat at the kitchen table a short time later. My notebook lay in front of me and I read my pathetic checklist that I thought would be the start of a new me. Who cared who supplied our electricity, or how you took a car for an MOT?

How about a checklist for a husband who likes to dominate you?

1. Makes snide comments about your weight gain and middle-aged body.
2. Calls you a nasty, underhand pet name that undermines you.
3. Lets his wife buy her clothes in charity shops while hiding a fortune.
4. Forces his wife to have sex even when she explicitly says no.

Chewing the end of my pen, I added a few more points.

5. Acts like a complete and utter prat most of the time.
6. Grows his hair and flicks it off his face like Farrah Fawcett.
7. Has a son who thinks he's a prat.

8. *Has no control whatsoever about what I think.*
9. *Is at a profound disadvantage because I'm smarter than him and I'm onto him.*

I read that last one again. It's true. I'm smarter than him but he thinks I'm a fool.

And he had completely, utterly underestimated me.

CHAPTER THIRTY-FIVE

I took another look at the RentaHome website before I left to meet Robbie. There were a couple of one-bedroom apartments to let in neighbouring towns, and if I was careful, I could probably just about afford them. A bigger place was unrealistic for now. On the spur of the moment, I rang the estate agents and made appointments to view them after work the following week. I would not be able to take any furniture with me and that left me at a great disadvantage, but there was a local charity shop with a good furniture section that I should be able to buy the basics in. Whilst I desperately wanted to pack up and leave immediately, I had to have an exit strategy in place or I would end up running back with my tail between my legs.

Carefully applied make-up disguised the fact I had hardly slept, and I was determined that I would gain control of my life again. Confident I couldn't do anything about the savings accounts that weren't in my name, I knew the mortgage had been, so it meant we jointly owned the house. There was also the joint account that I was surely entitled to half of. He couldn't prevent me from taking what was rightfully mine.

I desperately needed legal advice, therefore contacting the Citizens Advice Bureau was added to my growing list.

After the distress of the night before, I felt composed and resolute, intent on salvaging some pride and dignity from the smouldering embers of my relationship.

The bus took me into the city centre and I headed for Café Rosé behind the city hall, where Robbie and I had arranged to meet. There was a vacant table at the huge window, so I could watch the world race by as I waited for him. Saturday afternoon meant the streets were jammed with shoppers, friends out for lunch, couples in love browsing engagement rings. Glancing down at my left hand, I objectively looked at my plain gold wedding band. I would never wear my engagement ring again, but I wouldn't take this symbol of our union off until I threw it in his face as I walked out the door for the last time. In fact, I might sell my engagement ring and buy a bin for my new home with the money.

As I stared out of the window looking for my son, I noticed Vicky in the distance. With her striking height and long brunette hair she's hard to miss. Tempted to nip out and have a chat, I stood up from the chair I was perched on, but saw that she was talking to a good-looking younger man with a full black beard and wearing jeans that skimmed his sockless ankles. Then it became apparent they weren't talking, they were arguing. She held her hand out to him but he shook it off, clearly annoyed with her. Who on earth was that, and why were they arguing?

Hesitantly I stood watching them, as a crowd of people swelled forward to cross at the lights and they were lost from sight. By the time all the pedestrians had crossed the road, neither of them were visible so I heavily sat back down.

I had no time to give it any more thought for Robbie appeared through the door with a cheeky grin. As he removed his AirPods and came over to give me a kiss on the cheek, I put my concerns about Vicky to the back of my mind and instead had an enjoyable lunch with my son. Much to my surprise and pleasure, he insisted on paying.

'I'm a working man now, Mum, and it's your birthday on Monday, so please let me pay.'

'That's so kind of you, thank you,' I replied, deeply moved by his thoughtfulness. With all the recent upset, I had completely forgotten it was my birthday this week. The fact he had remembered touched the very depths of me.

Giving me a hug, he also gave me a voucher for a local beautician. 'I thought you could have a massage or one of those things old ladies have to help their aching joints. You're only fifty-three once.' He grinned cheekily as I playfully gave his arm a swipe. Then he went on, 'Did Dad leave a present for you before he swanned off on holiday again?'

'Not as far as I know.' I shrugged. Just then my phone pinged and up popped a message from the man himself.

> What are you doing today? Shopping in town?

For a short time, I had forgotten that he could track me and was probably now staring at that little blue dot and wondering who I was with.

'That's Dad, shall we take a selfie and send it to him?' I asked lightly.

Unenthusiastically, Robbie agreed and we took a photo of the two of us smiling together. *A taste of our new family unit to come,* I thought grimly as I pressed send.

After we parted, I deliberately switched my phone off, so no one could spy on me when I was with Sam. If he questioned later why my phone was off, I'd simply say it ran out of battery. You know that teeny, tiny brain of mine had forgotten to charge it before going out for the day. Maybe playing dumb was the way to go.

Before leaving the house, I'd checked the bus timetable from the city centre to Sam's street, so I walked towards the bus stop thinking about my son and how amazing it was to have him close enough to meet for lunch but far enough away that he could have his independence. It was the best of both worlds. The bus soon arrived, and I made my way to the top deck for the novelty. It gave me a bird's eye view of all the people rushing along the street who didn't know they were being observed.

As the bus was pulling away from the stop, I spotted the bearded man that Vicky had been arguing with earlier, with his arm around a brittle-looking blonde around his own age. She didn't look particularly happy and he was obviously in her bad books about something. I could have sworn I saw Vicky standing in a doorway nearby, but that was ludicrous; it looked like she was lurking in the shadows.

Disregarding it immediately, I enjoyed the short drive up towards Sam's as I left the hustle and bustle of the city centre behind as the bus slowly chugged up the hill. I wasn't completely certain which stop to get off at, but spotted Sam waiting at a bus stop with Nigel at his feet.

My breath caught slightly at the sight of him as I stood up and dismounted the bus steps. Lovely, dependable Sam who looked delighted to see me.

'Hello gorgeous,' he greeted me happily.

'Hey there,' I replied, suppressing the urge to reach out and touch him, as I knew anyone could be driving past. I'm not really cut out for deception but the sensible part of my brain was flashing a warning. The last thing I needed now was my husband to discover my friendship with another man. The fear of his reaction turned my insides liquid. Instead, I patted Nigel who was nosing my thigh as if to say hello.

Sam led me towards the end of his road, asked how my lunch with Robbie had been and what my plans for the rest of the week were.

As tempting as it was to say, 'Just going to get some legal

advice on leaving my husband, then hoping to spend the night with my friend who I'm ready to start an affair with,' I simply opted for the standard, 'Plenty of Pinot, takeaways, not doing any cleaning and seeing my friends.'

He laughed and I revelled in the sound. Every time I made him laugh or he praised or complimented me, I felt like I had scored a goal.

Not everyone thinks I'm useless and worthless and stupid. Someone thinks I'm special and witty and he chooses to be with me when he could have anyone. How I wished I could say that to my husband.

We ambled up Sam's street under the canopy of the oak trees and towards his house. Our plan was to drive up to Cave Hill Country Park, go for a walk with Nigel and then Sam was going to cook me dinner for the first time. On the way towards his house, he told me that his mum had been offered a permanent place in the nursing home.

'That's great news, isn't it?'

'Yes, it's a huge relief. She's settled in so well and Dad is adjusting to it all. He plans to visit her every other day, but he's just delighted she's being cared for so well.'

We had reached his house and as we stepped into the front porch, he wrapped his arms around my waist. Leaning forward he gave me a gentle kiss on the lips, which soon turned into something deeper as every fibre of my body responded. Nigel clearly wasn't impressed as he squeezed his way between us and we laughingly broke apart.

'Sorry, he really needs a good walk; he's been cooped up all morning.' Grabbing his car keys from the table by the front door, Sam locked up and called Nigel, who bounded over and settled on his blankets in the boot. I got into the passenger side and after Sam got in, I instinctively placed the fingers of my right hand under his thigh as the decades fell away.

Cave Hill Country Park overlooks the city and has several waymarked trails. We opted for the woodland walking route and set off with Nigel on a short lead. Conscious of all the other walkers, we roamed along close but not touching. Which was fortunate as a white-haired little lady met us on the path and exclaimed, 'Dr Brown, is that you?' She commanded her Jack Russell to sit.

I could tell Sam was having difficulty placing her, but ever the professional he responded, 'Yes that's right. How are you?'

The woman clearly hadn't deduced Sam couldn't recall her, as she sweetly offered, 'It's been hard since my Emmanuel died, but it gives me a great deal of comfort that he was so well looked after in his final days. Thanks to you and the other staff in the hospice. Pancreatic cancer is so quick, isn't it?'

'Yes, it hardly gives you time to draw breath. I'm glad you're happy with the care Mr Rafferty got from us.'

I glanced at him with admiration, for he had remembered the patient and his wife wouldn't forget that.

'Your husband does incredible work, Mrs Brown.' She nodded to us as she and her dog moved off.

I couldn't help but giggle at the mistake and Sam chortled too.

'You're very impressive remembering her husband.'

'I am indeed.' Then, 'Actually, I'm not impressive at all. I've only ever treated two patients called Emmanuel and the other one was in his thirties, so I don't think it was him. Mrs Brown.'

I lightly punched his arm and before I knew it, he had grabbed me and gently pulled me in behind the wide trunk of a nearby tree, Nigel in our wake. We kissed and hugged and I felt like a million dollars.

CHAPTER THIRTY-SIX

On our return to Sam's house, we went straight through into the kitchen, and he offered me a glass of wine, as I settled myself on a high stool at the island. A worn-out Nigel fell asleep in his bed by the radiator.

'Yes please, that would be lovely. I'm planning on getting a taxi home later if that's okay?' I was carefully avoiding Sam's eye while pretending to study a particularly interesting print of, well, who knew? I didn't care what it was of.

'Of course, just whatever you want.' He too was carefully avoiding eye contact as I studied his reflection in the glass.

He handed me a glass of white wine. 'Pinot, I presume?'

I nodded my thanks as I accepted the glass and took a sip. The chilled mouthful of Dutch courage slipped easily down.

'Do you want to listen to some music while I cook?' he then asked politely. The atmosphere had changed since we arrived at his house; it was as though we were both walking on thin ice, concerned in case we put a foot wrong. 'How about some eighties classics?'

'Good idea, though no electronic dance music please,' I requested.

'No "Tainted Love" or "You Spin Me Round"? Sacrilege,' he teased.

'Well okay then, maybe a little bit.'

He commanded Alexa to play eighties hits and Cyndi Lauper's 'Girls Just Want to Have Fun' came blasting through. Instantaneously I was transported back to school discos, frosted-pink lipstick and backcombed hair. We sang along together as he prepped the food and then Belinda Carlisle started singing 'Heaven Is a Place on Earth'.

'Gareth Weir's party when his parents went to Lanzarote!' I exclaimed. 'Denise Long and Darrell Short snogging in the kitchen – do you remember we all thought it was hilarious and called them the long and the short of it for months after?'

'Remember someone vomited cider and blackcurrant all the way down the stairs? I thought Gareth was going to explode he was so mad at them.'

'I remember us sneaking upstairs together and having a snog in his sister's bedroom after we played Spin the Bottle.'

'Funny to think the first time we kissed was in a game of Spin the Bottle right after I'd kissed that scary girl with the black eyeliner. What was her name?'

'Julie or Judith or something. I heard she ran off with a man old enough to be her father right after A-levels.'

We reminisced about people we hadn't thought about in years, making me feel both ancient and young at the same time.

'I think we took everyone by surprise when we started dating,' he said, placing two salmon fillets under the grill.

'You mean everyone was surprised the rugby star would date a nerd?'

'I think you mean an academic not a nerd.' His smile was kind.

Snorting I replied, 'Fat lot of good that did me. I was such a goody-goody then, always afraid of getting into trouble. I didn't even get a pink streak in my hair the last day of lower sixth like everyone else. I was so timid. I'll always regret that.'

'I loved that goody-goody,' he said, clearly without thinking. A faint blush coloured his cheeks as he turned back to the grill, ostensibly to check on the salmon.

Spontaneously I got up from the stool and stood behind him. Lightly touching his back, I ran my hands down his spine, eventually winding them around his stomach, which was flat and hard. Leaning slightly against me, he took my hands and held them in his.

'You know, I went to Milly's Bar in Ballyburn on Christmas Eve that first year of uni, hoping you would be there,' he said softly. 'Your friends told me you'd met someone at Queen's and were going steady. I knew then it was really over. And now I can't believe my luck in bumping into you that day, Laura.' He sounded hesitant. 'I know it's not ideal, the timing I mean, but I'll never regret this no matter what happens.'

He turned to face me, our whole bodies touching, and as he bent down the squeal of the fire alarm sounded. With a loud bark, Nigel leapt up and chased his tail around the room.

'The salmon,' Sam shouted, pulling the blackened fish out from under the grill while I flapped a tea towel at the alarm. 'That's not going to impress anyone, it's burnt!'

'If it's brown it's cooking, if it's black it's cooked,' I reassured him. 'We can drown them in whatever that sauce is you were making a while ago.'

'Red pepper and chorizo.' He was shaking his head. 'I know how you love chorizo.'

I was unbelievably moved by the thoughtfulness and planning that had gone into this evening, which was in stark contrast to my husband's condescending attitude towards his useless wife. Making a deliberate effort not to think about James anymore, I helped Sam serve up the dinner and with copious quantities of sauce, it really was rather delicious.

Sitting together in the kitchen, with our empty plates in front of us, we chatted easily. If I was going to get a taxi home, I should think about ordering it soon as they aren't easy to get in Belfast on a busy Saturday night. As I was contemplating it, he stood up and went to a drawer before pulling out a small gift bag.

He handed it to me with a flourish and said, 'Happy birthday.'

Speechless, I looked up at him. 'I didn't tell you it was my birthday.'

'I have a good memory for important dates,' he said gently.

I untied the gift bag, withdrew a small cardboard jewellery box and with some trepidation, opened it. Inside was a pair of delicate silver studs that I immediately put in my ears. We locked eyes as I made the decision that for all those months I hadn't been able to.

Reaching for his hand, I wordlessly led him upstairs.

The following morning as I woke in bed beside him, one arm slung protectively across me, I refused to dwell on the fact I'd broken my marriage vows. Rolling over to study his sleeping face, something that had been frozen within me melted. This man made me feel cherished in a way that I had forgotten was possible. There were no demands from him, no sinister intimation of mistreatment, just the warm loving embrace of someone who wanted the very best for me.

Our night together had exceeded any expectation that I might have hoped for, and those weeks of yearning for his touch had exploded into breathless ecstasy. Twice. He did not make me feel ashamed or embarrassed by my middle-age spread or my cellulite but instead made me feel beautiful and sensual. For nothing is as erotic than a partner whose desire for you leaves them moaning your name in the throes of passion.

He opened his eyes and caught me unabashedly staring at him and his face broke into wreaths of smiles as he murmured, 'So it wasn't just a dream?' and leaned over to kiss me chastely on the lips. However, it didn't remain chaste for long as we once again made up for those lost years.

Alone in the shower a little later, warm water cascading over me, I allowed my thoughts to stray to my husband. Part of me felt guilty about James, and wished that we had already split before commencing this new phase. I am not a cheat and it sat uneasily within me. As much as I wanted to be with Sam, I had unfinished business at home. I was also anxious that I would have unleashed my husband's rage by turning my phone off last night. It was like provoking a bad-tempered animal who would lash out at the slightest misdemeanour.

Towelling myself dry in the en suite, I made a bold choice.

It was time to turn off location sharing.

When I had first discovered he was tracking me, I'd been too afraid of him to remove it. But now, all these weeks later and with Sam's support, I felt strong enough to do it. I had no doubt there would be consequences, but I felt I could withstand them now.

After dressing, I quickly went downstairs and took my mobile out of my bag, which was still lying on a chair by the table. Sam was making coffee and heating croissants in the oven as I looked at the blank screen. If I turned the phone back on now, there was a chance at that very moment my husband would be staring furiously at the Find my iPhone app and would see I was somewhere on Cave Hill.

'Laura, what is it? Are you all right?' asked Sam in a concerned tone.

I raised my eyes to his. It was decision time. Should I fill him in on what a nightmare my marriage was, or would it leave him regretting getting involved with me again?

Hands trembling, I placed the mobile down on the table and simply said, 'He tracks me using an app on my phone.'

Sam didn't speak but a shadow passed over his face. Then, 'What do you mean?' he asked evenly.

'A few weeks ago, I realised he had added himself to my Find my iPhone app so he could watch where I was anytime he wanted. This was after he discovered I had changed my passcode on my phone and was angry.' I couldn't say any more, I was getting upset.

'Is that why you turned your phone off yesterday?'

Mutely I nodded, unable to look at him.

'Laura, are you afraid of him?' He came over and gently raised my chin so he was looking directly at me.

I nodded once.

'Has he hurt you?' Sam watched me intently, as the tears ran down my cheeks.

I couldn't answer but I didn't need to, for he enveloped me in a tight hug and stroked my hair. 'He's never going to hurt you again,' he whispered in my ear.

Crying openly now, his words were exactly what I needed to hear. He didn't need to know every detail about the tyranny or the toxicity in my marriage. For I understood that he would be there to help me make my escape from the nightmare that I lived with.

CHAPTER THIRTY-SEVEN

That Sunday morning as we sat together at Sam's kitchen table, I revealed a little more about my relationship.

Although I despised the man James had become, I found it hard to completely blame him. If only I'd been a better person, if I hadn't tried to reassert my independence, if I had sought help for my depression sooner, then maybe we could have remained happily married. I had to take some responsibility for our issues, I couldn't blame it all on him as tempting as it was. I'd unwittingly let him assume control for so many years, so it was no surprise that he resented my feeble attempts at taking some back.

To me the most unforgivable things were the deception about our finances and the increasing sexual violence. It simply wasn't possible for me to forget or forgive those. I recognised sadly that by pretending we had little money, he had found a way of curtailing me that was subtle but effective. And although I could not say or even think the word, forcing me to have sex when I said no, was in fact, rape.

To have admitted all of that was beyond me, as Sam sat

listening across the table from me that dull September day. He didn't probe, didn't demand that I tell him everything, but I suppose I said enough for him to surmise the bits I left out. I truly felt as though I was worthless and undeserving of someone as fundamentally decent as Sam. For I was forever sullied by the suffering at my husband's hands.

After I finished talking, we sat in silence as we both digested it all.

'What do you want to do now, Laura?' he asked softly, after I had composed myself somewhat.

'Leave him as soon as I can. I thought I could stay until I'd got everything sorted but I don't think I can even do that now.' It flew out of me, and the moment I said it, I knew it was true.

I confided, 'I'm going to view two flats this week, I've those booked already for Wednesday and Thursday evenings, and I have enough in savings to put down a deposit. I was going to speak to Citizens Advice at some point about the house, which is in both our names, but that's not going to stop me leaving.'

He replied, 'You can stay here if you can't get anywhere else, you do know that don't you?'

I nodded and said thank you, but I didn't know if that was the best thing. I really couldn't think straight. Although my marriage had been deteriorating for years, this all seemed very sudden.

'I think you need to consider telling your family as well.'

The look of fear on my face made him take my hand across the table. 'You only have to tell them as much as you want but you need the support of people who love you at the minute. I'm sure they won't judge you, if that's what you are afraid of.'

'Okay, I'll think about it,' I reluctantly agreed.

'And what about Robbie? He's going to have to hear it from you; he can't find out from James and get a distorted view on it all. Once you have finalised your plans, you need to meet him and tell him yourself.'

The thought of telling our son I was quitting our marriage

made me cry again, as I never wanted him to have to contend with divorced parents. But I knew I had to be strong because I had already stayed too long.

We sat there for an age talking it through, until it was time to turn my phone back on, to see if James had tried to contact me. Sam suggested we drive to my house first, so if he was watching the tracker, he would not be able to place me in Belfast. I had to be sure he could not locate me at this address. Agreeing this was a good idea, we got into his car and drove without speaking towards the village, my fingers tucked reassuringly under his thigh.

'Do you want me to drop you at the end of your street?' he asked as we drove over the bridge at the outskirts of the village.

'I hadn't thought about it,' I replied, then said firmly, 'No. Come up to the house because I don't care if the neighbours see you.'

'You're sure?'

'Yes,' but my words were braver than I felt. Maybe it was foolish and one of his friends would message my husband to say a gorgeous, fit bloke had dropped me off and I was wearing the same clothes I'd gone out in yesterday.

Thankfully though, no one was around as we pulled into the driveway, and I speedily went to unlock the front door.

Sam looked around the interior and wryly commented, 'You have impeccable taste.'

'It's just a house now, not my home.'

We sat together on the squashy sofa that James and I had spent weeks choosing, and nervously I switched my phone back on. It took a few minutes to boot back up to life, but once it did a series of messages sprang onto the home screen. I saw they were all from my husband and along the lines of:

Where are you? Why aren't you answering your messages or the house phone?

Thirty-two messages in total and six voicemails, which I played on speaker to Sam.

'Laura, where the hell are you? I'm going out of my mind with worry. I haven't heard anything since you sent that stupid selfie with Robbie. I even rang him and he said you were getting the bus home. Ring me back now or you'll be sorry when I get back!'

All in a similar vein.

'What a charmer,' said Sam with a wince.

'Oh, that is him being charming. Prat,' I replied and smiled at him. 'He's probably furious that my tracker was off, and he had absolutely no idea where I was or what I was doing for once. Which reminds me...' I found the Find my iPhone icon, tapped on James's name and clicked 'Stop sharing my location'.

I was seizing control and it felt good...

For all of about a minute, when alarm stirred my insides as a message appeared on the screen.

Ring me NOW

I showed it to Sam and he instantly advised, 'Don't ring him, Laura. Send him a message back to say your phone was out of charge and you missed his messages.'

'What about the landline? He said he tried it. I've no excuse, I can't think of an excuse!' I felt petrified, molten fear pumping through my veins.

'Okay, it's simple, you decided last minute to go and stay with your parents.'

'Yes, that's a good idea, I'll text him that now.' At least one of us was able to think clearly.

The two ticks turned blue as he read the message and then *typing* appeared below his name and I read,

You bitch.

I was dumbfounded as my husband thinks swearing is the

sign of low mentality. My mobile rang and with a trembling hand I hit the button and put him on loudspeaker.

'Hello?' My voice was so quiet he shouted back, 'Is that you? How dare you? Don't you know how worried I've been about you? You will pay for this when I get back. Ruining what should have been a lovely relaxing break with friends, and instead I've been going out of my mind with worry, imagining all sorts of accidents. I even considered ringing the hospitals and read the online news reports for a fatal incident.'

On and on he ranted as I set the phone on the coffee table and sat back, clutching Sam's hand in my rather clammy one. I drew strength from his calming presence.

James eventually ran out of steam with a final, 'What do you have to say for yourself?'

Taking myself by surprise, I lifted the phone and answered firmly, 'Feck you. And you'll notice I took the tracker off my phone when you next try and check up on me. See you Friday.'

I hung up and Sam gave me a proud smile. Brushing the hair back from my face with his free hand, he kissed me gently on the lips and held me tight as first the mobile and then the landline rang and rang. I could hardly contemplate the anger I would face on Friday, but I hoped that by then I would have my bags packed and somewhere else to live.

Full of bravado, I got up and abruptly tugged the landline out of the wall. This was probably foolhardy and I was backing myself into a corner.

For there was no question now that I had to leave by next weekend or the consequences would be terrifying.

We sat together in silence for a short time and then slowly discussed what exactly I needed to do this week.

Find somewhere to live, obviously, in the short term. I explored the RentaHome website and took a note of the addresses of the two flats I was to view later in the week. We would go for a drive past them tomorrow after work, and if their locations were awful, at least I could rule them out and start again.

Next was how to access money. I knew I had to open a completely new bank account that my pay could be deposited into, so that too was added to my growing list.

Our joint account had several thousand pounds in it, so I somehow had to access that. Again, I mentally kicked myself for not ensuring I knew how to. What a complete fool I had been throughout the years.

Packing was next. I really only needed clothes and my personal stuff, then I thought about all my crafting supplies, my photographs, my books, the attic full of memories and I felt deflated at the enormity of it all. How could I ever get this all sorted out in time? I didn't even have anywhere to run to.

Unable to help myself, I started to cry. Deep, intense sobs that rent me in two. I couldn't do this. There was no way I could ever leave.

But I forgot that I already had a support system in place and Sam calmed me down. Practical and methodical, he helped me to see a way through.

'You don't have to have everything planned and arranged; you just need the basics in place. If you're afraid to come and get more stuff at a later date, then I'm sure you could get Robbie or one of your brothers to come with you. Bullies are quick to back down when someone squares up to them. Keep reminding yourself, you are not alone.'

Ever practical, he suggested that I spend some time going through my things and get the important items packed this week. He would help me set up a new bank account and I could contact my employer tomorrow to inform them of the details.

Throughout all this my mobile kept buzzing as message after message appeared on the home screen. I knew instinctively that it was James, furious at me. No doubt ranting and raving and making all kinds of threats.

Somehow I ignored it completely and gradually felt more in control. We agreed that I would spend some time this afternoon on my own sorting through my stuff, and I would stay at Sam's tonight. Giving him a quick kiss as he left, I shut the door behind him and turned to face my home.

As I walked through each room, memories came flooding back. I reminisced about Robbie's excited face opening Christmas presents in the snug; dinner parties with friends in the dining room; summer barbeques in the back garden. But as I wandered upstairs those happy recollections became contaminated with more recent ones of my husband forcing me against my will in the study, the bedrooms, even the bathroom.

Vile memories that I couldn't bury no matter how hard I tried.

He would never get the chance to do that again.

Purposefully, I went into the bedroom and emptied my cupboards. I took every single striped top I owned and put them in black bin bags to be taken to the hospice charity shop. I would never wear another one again. It was the uniform of the depressed. Then I took my jeans, picked my favourites and bagged the rest.

Ruthlessly I tore through my wardrobes and drawers, craving a fresh start. I was left with a pile of clothes on the bed that I would pack into the suitcases that were neatly stored in the attic.

Next, it was my shoes, then my underwear. Taking great pleasure, petty pleasure really, I retrieved a pair of scissors from the kitchen drawer and cut up any skimpy underwear that held unpleasant memories. Wisps of lace and silk lay in a pathetic heap at my feet. Filled with immense energy, I cleared out the hot-press, taking bedding and towels and placing them on the bed.

I filled an overnight bag with essentials that I would take to

Sam's later. Joyfully smiling to myself, I packed toiletries, a change of clothes and my white noise machine. Although somehow my tinnitus had been the last thing on my mind in bed last night.

By six o'clock I was exhausted but exhilarated.

I had done enough for one day, so I went downstairs and boiled the kettle for a cup of coffee. It was a beautiful late summer evening, and I wanted to drink it out in the garden while watching the sun dip low behind the hills. Sitting at the gable end, the warmth of the sun on my face and listening to tractors chugging in the nearby fields, I was overwhelmed with nostalgia for happier times. This was the only home Robbie remembered, where he had bounced on the trampoline with his friends, had sneaked in late at night when he missed his curfew. I felt inexpressibly sad that this would be my last ever weekend here, and I would be leaving my friends and my village.

I lifted the mobile from my lap before I glanced at the screen. As expected, a plethora of messages from my husband but at the top, one from my future.

> Fancy an Indian when you get back? xx

Peace replaced sadness as I texted back:

> Sounds good, leaving soon xx.

I figured that I should at least read the ones from my husband, so I scrolled through them all. They ranged from *You will regret this* to *I only tracked you because I was worried about you, and it helped reassure me you hadn't come to any harm.*

Jekyll and Hyde.

Sighing heavily, I sent a quick *We'll talk when you're back* and then as I drained the dregs of the coffee in my cup, Vicky drove past the garden and gave me a cheerful wave.

Despondency washed over me again. Book Club. We'd never have another Book Club meeting at this house. In fact, could I ever go to my friends' houses again when we'd split up? I would have to tell them all at some point I'd left James.

But I couldn't even think about that now, I had to look forward, for I had no other choice.

CHAPTER THIRTY-EIGHT

After a night spent discovering just how high my libido could be when I was with someone I wasn't frightened of, Sam woke me with coffee and the smell of bacon wafting through the house. Holding his precious face to mine, I gave thanks for my second chance with him. Today I would open my new bank account, then have a look at the potential apartments later. If I had time, I would spend it at the house packing and sorting.

We munched on French toast with maple syrup and crispy bacon at his kitchen island, bright sunlight shining through the French doors. He asked me if I was any clearer about my plans for the coming days.

'I want to finish packing all the essentials I'll need and take a load of clothes to the charity shop. The Belfast Hospice charity shop, to support all those hard-working doctors and nurses,' I teased before my face fell. Next would be the hard bit. 'I'll have to talk to my family and friends and of course, Robbie. I can't put that off forever but somehow, I'll have to find the courage to do it.'

'Why don't you do the easier bits first and then the harder bits later?' Sam suggested, concern written all over his face.

'Good idea,' I agreed, thankful to put off the bits I really didn't want to have to do. Always the procrastinator.

We drove past the first of the apartments that afternoon, but I knew instantly there was no chance I could live there, as paramilitary slogans were daubed on the walls. Northern Ireland's violent past lingers on in some parts of the country. That left the one I had an appointment to view on Thursday evening.

It was promising, set high on a hilltop in a large town on the coast. I could see a strip of granite sea in the distance as I got out of the car and relished the tangy air. Although fifteen minutes further from Belfast, the town had a train station, meaning I could still commute easily into work. It was also where I went to yogalates at the leisure centre with my friends, so was a definite possibility.

'What do you think?' I asked Sam, as we wandered around the whitewashed apartment block with private parking. Scraggly flowers bloomed half-heartedly in a dozen chipped pots along the front wall.

'Not bad, it's a nice location,' he replied, glancing around. 'It's been a lifetime since I was in this town, I think it was to get the ferry to Scotland once.'

Down at the seafront we sat side by side on a wooden bench facing the Irish Sea, inhaling the fresh air and watching the white-crested waves chase each other. Sam brought up the subject of where I would stay after telling James I was leaving.

'I know even if I'm lucky to get that apartment, that it won't be available for me to move into straight away. So I'm not sure.'

'The offer is still open to stay with me in the interim.'

'I might need to. But it would only be short term. I need to learn how to stand on my own two feet again. I've never lived on my own, never had to do adulting properly.'

'Adulting?'

'You know, that thing where you behave in a responsible manner towards mundane tasks. Like paying bills.' As if I was the expert.

'Oh yes, that.' He laughed shortly then became serious. 'I know that's important to you, Laura. Why not think of my place as a free Airbnb for a bit.'

'Would I have to share a bed with the Airbnb owner?' I assumed my most coquettish manner.

'Oh yes, that bit is non-negotiable.' Grinning at me, he took my hand and held it tight, tucking it into the pocket of his jacket.

Everything would be all right.

We arrived at my house a short time later and sat in the kitchen as he guided me on how to open a new current account. I couldn't believe how easy it was. Feeling courageous, I suggested applying for a new credit card, as I'd never done that on my own before and it was something I wanted responsibility for. So I did. This adulting lark wasn't so bad after all.

Sam left me then, so I could continue sorting through all my belongings, giving me a chance to pack things that I would need. I found our suitcases neatly stacked in the attic and filled three of them with the clothes I wanted to take. My shapewear was lobbed into the bin. If Sam didn't care about my wobbly bits, then neither did I. I took two empty cardboard boxes from the attic and gently placed my most treasured belongings in them; my jewellery box, precious photos of Robbie growing up, my framed degree certificate. My vanity case and numerous wash bags were crammed with all my anti-wrinkle and cellulite-busting creams. My chin trimmer and eyebrow tweezers were added along with my magnifying mirror. I couldn't let Sam see me with rogue hairs just yet.

My sense of achievement left me feeling almost heady with pleasure.

Before loading the car with them, I went into the study and

opened the filing cabinet again. I wanted to find my passport, birth certificate, the copy of my will, any important document that I would have previously entrusted to my husband. Glancing again through the evidence of his betrayal, this time I spotted a single sheet of paper tucked behind some of his bank statements.

It was a list of usernames and passwords for every account. A huge grin split my face, for this meant for the first time I would be able to access my own current account and our joint savings account without having to go into the bank to beg them for help. The money would bolster my running-away-from-home account significantly.

I spent time taking photos of all the important paperwork and retrieved my own documents before replacing the folders into the filing cabinet. In a fit of pique, I mixed them all up then rearranged his shelves into glorious disarray.

I'd heard revenge stories about scorned partners taking scissors to their other halves' shirts, hiding prawns behind the radiators, subscribing to Pornhub in their name, but my own revenge was taking back control piece by piece.

After lugging the heavy cases and boxes down into the hall, I checked my phone for the first time that day.

Surprised that there was only one message from my husband, I opened it.

> You're breaking my heart. I cannot believe you would hurt me this way.

By telling him to feck off? By removing the tracker? I thought back to the training session on coercive control.

Using guilt to make them behave differently.

My heart hardened and I didn't reply. For what could I say? Sorry for finally standing up for myself? Sorry I let you control me to such an extent I thought myself worthless? Sorry for getting older and struggling with menopause?

The three suitcases were lined neatly up in the hallway and it dawned on me that there was one fundamental flaw in my plan. I drive a Mini with a boot that is little bigger than a family-sized box of Weetabix. I couldn't even take one suitcase with me today. But I could take the boxes. Thus, I loaded them in the car along with coats, gloves, hats, scarves, any small item that I could pack into bags for the back seat. I would need more work clothes, so I went back upstairs to pack them into an overnight bag.

Finally with a heavy heart, I closed my Etsy shop and looked around my brilliantly chaotic crafting room. It would take me days to sort through it all, so I had no option but to leave it for now.

I stood by the car in the driveway as day gave way to night and studied my friends' houses with an aching regret. I could never tell them exactly what had lain behind the walls of my house, the reality of my life these past few years. It would remain my guilty secret.

Unable to face any of them, I got into the car and drove off without a backwards glance. I wasn't sure I would spend even one more night in that house, for it felt almost sinister now, with echoes of my unhappiness throughout. I would return only to get my belongings and to face my husband when he got back from his trip. The very thought of his return made me quail in fear, but I told myself I didn't have to think about it now.

I'd think about it later.

CHAPTER THIRTY-NINE

The following morning, I woke to a text from Kate.

> Is everything OK? I noticed that your car hasn't been outside the house for the last couple of nights?

> Don't worry I'm just staying with Mum and Dad for a night or two. Will catch up later this week.

I hated lying, but I could hardly admit I was staying with my lover. The word took me by surprise for that is exactly what Sam was. By turns wild and passionate then soft and tender. I felt like a new person with the dark memories gradually receding.

The next couple of days sped past as I returned to work and then to Sam's each evening. He cooked me a special birthday dinner on Monday evening and I got several birthday greetings from friends and family, including a lovely one from Heather. James, however, ignored my birthday and didn't send me any more messages or voicemails. I supposed he thought he was punishing me somehow, and assumed I would be worrying about the lack of contact. Little did he know I was having the time of my life.

On Wednesday I made dinner, and Sam texted to let me know he would be home late as a complex new patient had arrived that urgently needed treatment. That left a few hours to myself, giving enough time for me to return to my house where I could empty the fridge and see what else I could pack into the Mini. I left him a note on the kitchen table.

Going to clear out more stuff, will be back later. Hope work was OK. xx

There wasn't a great deal more to sort, for I needed Sam to come and help me with the suitcases. I busied myself emptying the fridge and taking the bags for the charity shop out to the car. I'd moved the suitcases into the living room, as I kept tripping over them while squeezing past them in the hallway.

I shut the boot with a bang and took a deep breath. It was time to admit to my friends that I was leaving James. I headed first towards Kate's house.

I rang the doorbell and stared back across the street as I waited for the door to open. My house sat silently opposite, windows blank and unseeing. The secrets within would remain untold. There was no answer from Kate's, which was odd because her car was parked outside. I rang the bell again but still no one answered, so I reluctantly made my way over to Vicky's instead.

She answered the knock on the door within a couple of minutes, but looked less than pleased to see me. Her hair was scraped back in a messy bun and she was wearing a pair of dirty tracksuit bottoms that had clearly seen better days. As usual, she was carrying her mobile phone.

'Oh, hello Laura,' she said tonelessly. She didn't offer to let me in and it felt too awkward to ask.

'Hi.' I didn't know what else to say as her phone pinged with a message and she looked distractedly at the screen. She compressed her lips into a thin line and then, as if remembering I was standing there, she belatedly asked me if I wanted to come in.

Hastily, I said no, for she clearly had something on her mind and it was going to be hard enough to get the words out without her keeping one eye on her phone.

'I just wanted to see if everything was okay,' I said feebly, then continued in a rush, 'and to tell you not to worry if you don't see my car about much this week, I'm staying with my parents for a few nights.'

'Oh right. I'll see you later then,' she replied off-handedly, as she shut the door in my face.

Startled at her manner, I was so taken aback that I couldn't face trying to speak to Annie, even though I could see her car was parked in her driveway.

Dejected, I made my way towards my own house. I'd done enough sorting for today and it was time to head back and wait for Sam to come home. I couldn't remember though if I'd locked the back door or closed all the windows upstairs, so returned inside for a final check.

As I was closing the bathroom window upstairs, I heard the front door open.

'Robbie, is that you?' I called.

No answer. Feeling a little unnerved, I went to the top of the stairs and found my husband standing in the hall.

'Surprise, Teeny,' he said quietly.

I couldn't even find my voice I was so shocked and instantly afraid. He stood silently observing me for a minute and then turned his head sharply as he caught sight of the suitcases lined up in the living room.

His eyes flew towards where I stood rooted to the spot.

'What are those cases doing there?' Again the same soft tone, which was somehow more menacing than a raised voice.

'What are you doing home?' I finally squeaked. Clearing my throat, I asked again, forcing a confidence that I didn't feel. Inside, I was quaking, as he had taken me completely by surprise. I was wrong-footed and had no speech prepared. No escape route planned.

'I said, what are those cases doing there? Were you planning on surprising me and flying out to Majorca?' He slowly started to ascend the stairs. 'Or are they there for another reason?'

Saliva had filled my mouth and as I swallowed anxiously, I tried to remain strong. I had to tell him it was over. 'I'm leaving you, James,' I blurted out. No point in beating about the bush.

He simply stared at me and then he was right in front of me, blocking my only way out. Sighing theatrically, he scoffed, 'Don't be so stupid, Laura, you have nowhere to go. You have no money and no idea how to cope on your own. You're useless and always have been.'

'I found all your secret bank accounts.'

He didn't even deny it, just sneered before replying, 'So what? It's my money, not yours. It's been quite comical seeing you dress up in your charity shop finds and scraping a little bit of pocket money with your ugly jewellery. You're such a fool. Such a meek and pathetic fool that you never even questioned it.'

Abruptly his hand shot out and grabbed me by the throat. Leaning in close, he held me so tightly I feared I couldn't breathe, and said, 'You're going to take everything out of those cases and then you're going to apologise for the hurt you have caused me by washing all my clothes and making my dinner.'

Swiftly his hand moved from my throat, instead dragging me into the bedroom by my hair. My head was on fire. I was begging him to stop, to let me go, but a veil had come down over his eyes as he lost control.

He pinned me up against the bedroom wall, gripping my arms like a vice and bent in close to my face. The stale smell of his breath left me desperate to recoil but there was nowhere for me to move to.

'You're my wife, I can have sex with you anytime, anywhere, any place.' Spittle hit me on the cheek and ran down my face. 'Except no man would want sex with a dried-up old hag like you.'

He let go of my arms so quickly that I stumbled forward, but it wasn't over. Instead, he roughly seized me again and swung me around so my face slammed against the wall, my breasts in agony with the force of his weight on me. He pulled hard on my right arm as he twisted it up my back until I cried out for him to stop. He tore at my top with his other hand, exposing the delicate skin at the back of my neck. I felt excruciating pain as his teeth connected with my flesh as he bit down hard. Unexpectedly then, he released me, stepped back and strode from the room.

My legs felt weak and I was shaking from head to toe, but all I could think about was escaping. Barely able to move, I was so terrified of his return, I knew I somehow needed to get downstairs and to the car. My keys and phone were still lying on the table by the front door and I grabbed them quickly, slamming the door behind me. Blindly, I got into the car, locking the doors in case he came after me. I was in such a panic that I forgot how to start it.

I wiped tears from my eyes and snot from my nose and calmed myself a little. I had to get away. At last, the car started and I drove without thinking until I reached the edge of the village. Only then did I begin to feel safe.

I found myself on the familiar gently rising hillside, passed the oak trees and finally reached the oasis of calm. Sam's car was in the driveway and as I ran towards the front door, it opened.

He took one look at my distressed face and held his arms out to me.

I stepped into them.

CHAPTER FORTY

S am held me as I cried and slowly I was able to tell him what had happened. Letting me speak, I could tell he was finding it hard to control his emotions. In the end I showed him the bruises on my arms and teeth marks on my neck and no more words were needed. When I fell asleep, he was beside me, reassuring me everything would be all right.

That I wasn't alone.

Next morning as I stood in the shower, hot water cleansing me, I felt clear-headed for the first time in a long time. There was only one way ahead now.

When I got downstairs, Sam had made coffee and gone early to the local bakers to get me a pain au chocolat. I didn't feel remotely hungry but loved him for his thoughtfulness, so picked at it while we talked some more.

'I can't go into work today with this hanging over me. I need to go and end this properly with him today.'

'You can't go yourself, Laura. What if he's violent again?' Sam exclaimed.

I winced at the word, but knew that he was right.

'I really don't think he will be, but it needs sorted today. I can't even leave it until tomorrow.' I was getting upset again.

This had to be finished once and for all, before I lost my nerve and he toyed with my mind again.

'I can go into work this morning and leave at lunchtime. Then I'll drive you to the village and have a coffee in the café. That way I'm only a minute up the road if you need me. That bit's not up for discussion,' Sam said after a few moments. 'When you're ready you can ring me and I'll come and get you and your cases.'

Nodding, I agreed. It would make me much happier to know he was only a short distance away.

Before he left for work, I checked my phone again.

Fourteen missed calls, three abusive voicemails from last night and then one voicemail from this morning. The tone was soothing, conciliatory.

'Laura darling, I hate it when you fight with me, it leaves me upset for days. I'll see you after work and you can make it up to me. I love you.'

Sam's lip curled with disgust as I played it on loudspeaker. 'He really is unbelievable. I wish you would let me go and give him a bit of his own medicine.'

'No. I need to do this myself or he'll think he can talk me around again. He has to see I'm free of him.'

Sam nodded and gave me one final hug before getting into his car. I messaged Timothy to say I was debilitated with another migraine, but hoped to be back to work the following day. The morning was spent sitting in Sam's back garden with a blanket around me, throwing a ball for Nigel, who bounded around with delight at the attention.

It gave me a chance to think about everything rationally.

Years of being told I was no good at anything and being made to feel inept, had eroded all my self-confidence. But now I had someone who helped me realise that my opinions counted and that I had something worthwhile to say. Who believed in me.

For I had slowly discovered I wasn't useless. I wasn't a meek and pathetic fool any longer. My menopausal madness had unleashed a side of me I had kept buried for years. I was no longer the submissive wife who needed James's permission to exist.

True to his word, Sam arrived back at lunchtime and together we drove to the village. As before, he dropped me off at the end of my street and I continued alone on foot, my heart beating wildly, my mouth like sandpaper. For all my boldness, I was petrified.

I saw James's Range Rover parked in its usual space under the carport. His bike was propped against the front wall of the house, not yet washed, stroked or caressed. It took every ounce of strength I had to make my way to the front door. Oblivious to my surroundings, I had no idea if my neighbours were watching me or if I was alone.

I opened the door and compelled myself to call loudly, 'James, are you home?'

No answer. Nervously, I looked in each room downstairs. They were all empty.

I climbed the stairs and found him lying on the floor at the doorway to his bedroom. Pathetically clutching his chest, eyes closed, sweaty sheen on his face reflecting the weak sun coming through the window. His mobile phone lay on the floor a few metres away, just out of reach.

When he heard me, his eyes flickered open and he said weakly, 'Chest pain. Help me. You've done this, Laura, it's the stress of you telling me you're leaving me. This is all your fault.'

Impassively I wondered if his pain was as bad as mine had been when his teeth ripped my skin or when he had twisted my arm up my back. Or was it worse than the pain I had felt over and over as he raped me.

I looked at his long clean fingers with the precisely trimmed nails, the thick mat of hair on the back of his hands. At his hair falling forward over his teeny, tiny forehead and curling over his collar. At his padded bib shorts stretching over his distended gut.

I studied the man I had been with since I was a teenager and didn't feel pity or love or regret.

I felt detached. Hollowed out.

And then I felt the first tiny flicker of relief. I was never going to have to tell everyone I was leaving him. No one need ever know.

When I prodded him with my toe, he didn't respond, so I leaned over and said straight into his ear, 'I'm in love with another man. A man called Sam who knows you're a sadist and who thinks I'm wonderful.'

James didn't answer, didn't even open his eyes, so I was unsure if he heard me or not. But it didn't matter. I was free of his tyranny at last.

I sauntered downstairs into the kitchen, where I put the kettle on to boil and leaned against the worktop. Looking out of the window at the neatly mown grass and the bird feeder that had attracted rats, I thought again about how lovely a garden room would look in that corner. I made myself a cheap and nasty instant coffee and went through into the living room where I settled on the sofa, my feet up on the coffee table.

After I had leisurely drained my cup, I lifted my mobile and rang 999.

It was answered immediately.

'What's your emergency?'

'I think my husband is having a heart attack, you need to come quickly!'

As I waited on the ambulance, I caught sight of the Acer flaming red against the clear blue sky.

He always did love that tree.

EPILOGUE
CLAIRE

We buried my friend Laura's husband today.

It had been a terrible shock for her when she had found him lying collapsed on the floor after a bike ride. By the time the ambulance had arrived, he was gone.

It was beyond me how Laura had managed to meet and greet all the mourners at the church door before the service. Tall and willowy, she had been dry-eyed and composed in her black dress, while their son Robbie had shaken hands with everyone, his eyes red-rimmed, his face ashen. He was tall and handsome, the very image of his father.

I sobbed like a baby as the coffin was lowered into the ground, the rain falling like lead on the gathered crowd, dripping from the floral wreaths onto the sodden grass.

I had disliked James greatly. He was overbearing, full of his own self-importance and treated Laura like she was beneath him. I'm not sure exactly what went on behind closed doors, but he was so damned smooth. Thought he was God's gift to women.

After the committal, Will drove us to the hotel where I'd hosted my recent fiftieth birthday party. James's obnoxious father Donald was for once, subdued, no doubt disbelieving that his fit and healthy son's heart had just stopped after a bike ride.

After we ate the finger buffet and drank our tea, it was nearly time to go home. Looking around the function room, bare today of banners and balloons, I spotted Laura deep in conversation with a strikingly attractive man with silver hair and little round glasses. They were so comfortable in each other's company, I assumed he was a work colleague, maybe even her boss, Timothy. I went over to speak to her and the handsome man made his excuses and left. Her eyes drifted towards him as he threaded his way through the emptying tables.

'How are you holding up?' I asked her solicitously.

'I'm fine, glad today is nearly over.' She smiled tiredly at me, setting her empty cup on a nearby table. 'Thank you for coming.'

'If you need anything at all, let me know. Casseroles. Soup. Lasagne.'

Her face broke into a wide smile, no longer tired but teasing. 'I'd much rather have Book Club and several glasses of Pinot Gris if you don't mind.'

I grinned back. 'Happy to oblige. Just name the date and I'll say to the girls.'

She hugged me tight, turning to say goodbye to some other mourners, so I made my way back to our table, taking a seat beside Will. He had loosened his black tie, thrown his jacket haphazardly on the back of the chair and was scrolling through his phone. Sighing inwardly at how dishevelled he looked, I glanced around the table, where our little group sat chatting and was getting ready to leave.

These were my friends, the girls I am closest to, the ones I can tell anything to without judgement. We have no secrets.

Except I'm sleeping with one of their husbands.

THE END

ACKNOWLEDGEMENTS

Thank you so much to Betsy and the Bloodhound Books team who had faith in my book and especially to my editor Clare Law who taught me so much. Thanks also to the other Bloodhound authors from whom I have learned a great deal and who are unfailingly willing to impart their knowledge.

A special thanks to Andy, who has always been by my side and has had my back no matter what. And for being nothing like James.

Alex and Jamie, thanks for putting up with me as I locked myself away when writing.

To my sister Louise, the first person to read my book and who encouraged me to submit it for consideration. If I hadn't had your support, it may have remained unread.

And finally, this was a difficult subject and I hope I did it justice. This is for all the women who keep what is happening behind closed doors secret and the bravery they display every day.

A NOTE FROM THE PUBLISHER

Thank you for reading this book. If you enjoyed it please do consider leaving a review on Amazon to help others find it too.

We hate typos. All of our books have been rigorously edited and proofread, but sometimes mistakes do slip through. If you have spotted a typo, please do let us know and we can get it amended within hours.

info@bloodhoundbooks.com

Printed in Great Britain
by Amazon

47614351R00158